THE
CHRISTMAS
QUEST

THE CHRISTMAS QUEST

RICHARD SIDDOWAY

EAGLE
GATE

Salt Lake City, Utah

Library of Congress Cataloging-in-Publication Data

Siddoway, Richard M.
    The Christmas quest / Richard Siddoway.
        p.   cm.
    ISBN 1-57008-886-1 (hardbound : alk. paper)
    1. Real estate developers—Fiction.   2. Custody of children—Fiction.
3. Birthfathers—Fiction.   I. Title.
    PS3569.I29 C47 2002
    813'.54—dc21   2002010479

Printed in the United States of America   72076-7012
Publishers Printing, Salt Lake City, Utah

10   9   8   7   6   5   4   3   2

To the honorable
men and women
of the
Utah State Legislature
of both parties

1

• • •

I S THERE SOMEONE THERE WHO speaks English?" Will asked in frustration.

"My name is Jean Louis DuLac, and I am a speaker of English. How may I be of service?"

"Monsieur DuLac, this is Will Martin, and I'm attempting to contact one of your employees . . . Gary Carr . . . I need to speak to him about an urgent, personal matter."

"Ah, yes . . . Gary Carr. One moment, please."

Will heard strains of elevator music through the phone as he was put on hold. As the music continued, Will drummed his fingers on the desktop. Because of the difference in time, he had come into the office early to make the call to Paris, and the early rays of the sun were just beginning to shine through the windows of Martin Real Estate.

Come on! This is costing a fortune, Will thought impatiently.

Finally, DuLac came back on the line. "Monsieur Martin, I'm afraid we have no one by that name working for us. I am truly sorry."

"Are you quite sure? I mean, I know for a fact he came to Paris to work for your firm nearly four years ago."

"Monsieur Martin, I am quite sure he does not work for us now, but he may have worked for us in the past. However, that will take me a few minutes to research. Would you prefer to hold or would you like me to call you back?"

Will thought for a moment. "Perhaps I could call you. It's a personal matter, and I don't want to cause you any problems or the cost of a transatlantic phone call."

"Of course, Monsieur Martin. Perhaps half an hour?"

"That would be fine. Thank you so much for your help."

"It is my pleasure. Au revoir."

Carefully Will Martin placed the phone back in its cradle and leaned back in his chair. *Why can't it ever be simple?* he thought as he turned in his office chair and looked out the window onto the town square. The signs of spring and rebirth were everywhere. A green blush of new leaves was getting a good start on the maple trees that surrounded the square. A feeling of satisfaction washed over him. *It's hard to believe I've been home only a little less than two years and already I feel such a part of this town. An awful lot has happened in that time.*

The phone chirped on his desk, awakening him from his reverie. "Martin Real Estate, Will speaking," he said into the phone.

"Will, dear, this is your grandmother. I called you at home and Renee said you had left for the office."

"Grams," he smiled, "just trying to get a few things done. What's up?"

"Two things, dear. One of them is both good news and bad news. The other one I hope will be a welcome invitation."

"Okay," he said puzzled, "how about the good news first?"

"The good news and bad news involve the same . . . event," she said struggling for the proper word. "Lillian died early this morning." The phone fell silent for a moment, then she continued softly, "I was with her when she died."

"That must have been tough, Grams."

"As I said, it was both bad news and good. It's always a loss when someone passes on, but she'd been in the nursing home for over a quarter of a century, bedridden and speechless."

Will thought back to a year ago at Christmas when he had found Lillian at his grandmother's request; the woman who twenty-four years before had been involved in an event that forever changed their lives. "Still, it had to be hard."

"Hmm. Yes, it was." She cleared her throat, "The other thing is, I was wondering if you and your family would like to come to dinner this Sunday?"

"Sure. Any special reason?"

"It just seems as if you are so busy I never see you any more."

Will laughed, "We were there last week, Grams, but I'm sure Renee would appreciate a vacation from the kitchen. Thanks for the invitation."

"See you Sunday, dear. Good-bye."

"Good-bye, Grams." Will replaced the phone in the cradle. "Always worrying about me," he said under his breath. He heard the front door open and the measured tread of Enid Cook's feet as she climbed the stairs.

"Good morning, Mr. Martin," his office manager said with clipped tones. "You're here early this morning."

"Good morning, Miss Cook. Just trying to get some personal work out of the way."

Her eyebrows raised.

Will rubbed his chin with his thumb. "Maybe you can help."

"Oh?"

He beckoned her into his office. "Have a seat."

Enid Cook sat down primly on the edge of the chair and crossed her ankles. "How can I be of help?"

Will rested his chin on his tented fingers. "You knew Renee's first husband, Gary Carr, didn't you?"

She nodded warily, "Yes."

"I've been trying to reach him. Renee said he worked for a computer company."

"In Paris," Enid added.

He nodded, "EuroTeleCom, Renee said."

Enid nodded her head, "Yes, ETC. It's a very large firm, I believe. Mr. Carr went to work for them because of his experience in computer security."

"Miss Cook, you never cease to amaze me. For a woman

who still uses a manual typewriter, you seem pretty well informed."

The gray-haired woman smiled, "Just because I don't like computers doesn't make me deaf. I watched Gary Carr woo Renee away from this agency, and she couldn't help but brag to us about how brilliant he was." Suddenly she realized she was reminiscing about the woman who was now Will Martin's wife, and her face colored. "Just as your grandfather used to brag about you, Mr. Martin," she said, trying to cover her faux pas.

Will stared at her for a moment, "And you're sure it was ETC?"

Enid nodded her head, "Quite sure. Mr. Carr was very excited when they offered him such a lucrative contract. Renee was quite excited, too. The opportunities for Mr. Carr in this little town were fairly limited. He did some work for the bank and some for Hoggard Construction, but ETC more than tripled his salary." She looked at Will over her half-moon glasses. "But I'm rambling on, aren't I?"

"No, no. That's quite all right. I need to know all I can about Gary, and Renee is . . . well . . . a little reluctant to talk much about him."

"Well, Mr. Martin, he took the job, and that's the last any of us has seen of him. Renee waited for over a year for him to send for Justin and her and then she divorced him. I'm under the impression she hadn't heard from him during the entire time." She lowered her eyes. "He seemed like a nice enough man, but I guess you never know."

"Thank you for that information." He leaned back in his chair and rubbed the bridge of his nose.

"Mr. Martin, may I inquire as to why you're trying to reach him? He isn't behind on his child support or anything like that, is he?"

Will snorted. "There hasn't been any child support." He rubbed his chin. "Can you keep a secret?"

Enid straightened in her seat. "Mr. Martin," she said indignantly, "can you really question that?"

Will looked in amusement at the prim woman who a little over a year ago had been his chief adversary. "No, Enid, I cannot. The simple fact is, I'm trying to contact Gary about the possibility of adopting Justin."

A smile creased Enid's face. "What a splendid idea, Mr. Martin. I imagine he and his mother are delighted as well."

"I haven't told them," he replied sheepishly. "Things are pretty unsettled. I'm not sure how Renee feels, and it's really hard to read Justin. His father deserting him has had a negative effect on him."

He saw the disapproval on Enid Cook's face and tried to justify his decision.

"Justin has trouble making friends and has struggled in school. Renee even has him enrolled in summer school, so he can catch up on some of his basic skills. Besides, I'm not certain how Gary will respond."

Enid clearly wasn't buying any of it, and Will babbled on.

"It's been hard knowing which way to go. I mean, if Gary

says no, then why get their hopes up? On the other hand if Renee and Justin don't want me to adopt him, then I don't need to contact Gary. It's a real mess."

"Mr. Martin, if you don't mind me saying so, you really need to learn to trust the people you love," she sniffed.

"As usual, Enid, you're completely honest with me."

"I try to be." A tiny smile worked its way across her lips, "But, nevertheless, I think it is a splendid idea." She rose from her chair and walked slowly toward the door. "I'm sure you'll be able to find Mr. Carr at ETC." She left his office and pulled the door shut behind her. Will glanced at the clock that hung on the wall next to his grandfather's picture, then picked up the phone and pushed the redial button. He was rewarded with a very long string of beeps as the phone dialed ETC in Paris. It rang twice before a woman answered.

"Bonjour. May I help you?"

"Jean Louis DuLac, please."

In heavily accented English the woman said, "May I ask who is calling? S'il vous plaît."

"Will Martin."

"Merci, Monsieur Martin. One minute, please."

Almost immediately Jean Louis picked up the phone. "Monsieur Martin, thank you for calling back. I have had my assistant check our employee records for the past ten years. I am sorry, but no one by the name of Gary Carr has ever worked for us."

Will sat stunned at his desk and for a moment said nothing.

Completely confused, he finally responded, "Thank you, Jean Louis. You have been most kind. I'm sorry to have troubled you."

"It has been no problem, Monsieur Martin. Good luck with your search."

"Thank you," Will said again. "I don't know what to say. I was so sure he had worked for you."

"I understand. Oh, perhaps I should mention, although I don't suspect it will be of much interest or use, our search did show that we had a Gary Carr who interviewed with us nearly five years ago. It appears we were interested in hiring him, but after our initial offer, he apparently turned us down. I don't know if that information is of any help."

Will stared at the phone. "Turned you down? Any idea why he didn't accept your offer?"

"I have no idea. You realize we have over fifteen thousand employees, and it is somewhat of a miracle that we even uncovered this old application. Don't hesitate to call if I can be of help. Bonjour, Monsieur Martin."

"Yes . . . and thanks again for your help. Good-bye." Will replaced the phone, spun around in his swivel chair, and gazed out the window. *Five years ago and no follow-up on their offer. Where in the world is Gary Carr?*

2

· · ·

WILL CLOSED AND LOCKED the door of Martin Real
Estate. A swirling breeze caught the bottom of his topcoat and
flapped it against his leg. He walked briskly to where his car
was parked, climbed in, and glanced at his wristwatch. *I'd better hurry,* he thought. *Renee's last class is just ending.* The Jaguar
slid smoothly into the sparse traffic surrounding the town
square. Ten minutes later he pulled up in front of Anderson's
Shoes and climbed the stairs to the second floor to his wife's
dance studio. His stepson, Justin, was waiting just inside the
glass door and waved as Will reached the top of the stairs.

"You're late," the boy said with the hint of a smile, "but not
too late."

Will reached out and put his hand on Justin's shoulder.
"Sorry. Been waiting long?"

"Mom's talking to Andrea," he said with barely hidden disgust. "Andrea thinks the other girls don't like her." He
shrugged his shoulders. "Maybe they don't. She's a bawl baby."

"Well, she's only five years old, Justin."

"Yeah, I remember what it's like to be that little."

Will smiled at his seven-year-old stepson. "I'll bet you do." Just then Renee walked across the room toward them, holding a small, dark-haired girl's hand. Renee smiled at Will.

"Hi. I'm sure Andrea's mother will be here any minute," she said. At that moment Will heard footsteps on the stairs and the door opened. Andrea's mother, breathing heavily from her run up the stairs, burst into the studio.

"I'm sorry I'm late, cupcake," she said to the little girl.

Silently Andrea let go of Renee's hand and walked to where her mother stood. " 'Bye," she said as she waved at Justin. She tugged her mother's hand toward the door.

The woman lifted her free hand as if taking an oath. "I won't be late ever again. Promise." Quickly they started down the steps.

"Don't bet on it," Renee said quietly, as she switched off the lights to the studio. She leaned toward Will and gave him a perfunctory kiss. "Let's go home. I'm bushed."

Will led the three of them down the steps. "Tough day?"

Renee nodded, "Sometimes I have to remind myself how much I love to teach dance. Especially to hyperactive five-year-olds."

Will put his arm around her shoulders and gave her a hug. "Like herding cats?"

"Worse," she said as she nodded her head toward Justin. "I'll tell you later."

They pulled away from the curb and headed toward home. The freshening breeze splattered the first few drops of rain against the windshield. "Looks like a good night to snuggle around the fireplace," said Will.

From the backseat Justin broke in, "I've got homework. Math," he said with disgust.

Will glanced at the reflection in the rearview mirror. Justin sat in the backseat with his arms folded and a scowl on his face. "Maybe I can help you with it, Champ."

"Sure," Justin said under his breath.

The car hummed on in silence until they turned into the driveway of the compact, two-story house. Once they walked inside Justin hurried toward the bathroom, and Will turned to Renee. "Problems?"

Renee crossed her arms across her chest and looked out the front window. "Maybe. I don't know. I think Andrea's parents are splitting up . . . I'm not sure, but I sense that's what's going on. Anyway, she's really acting up."

"In what way?"

"Oh, pushing the other girls, refusing to do what I ask . . . maybe it's nothing. Maybe she's just being a five-year-old."

"How are the other girls taking it?" Will asked.

"Pushing back . . . but not the same way. Oh, Will, it's hard to explain. It's more of a feeling I have rather than anything specific." She hugged herself tighter and Will slipped his arms around her. "Then there's Justin," she said under her breath.

"Justin?"

She turned in his arms. "I guess I don't know what effect having his father leave has had on him. Not that you haven't tried your hardest to be his substitute father, but I sense he's feeling what Andrea's feeling . . . and it's . . . oh, I don't know . . ."

Will pressed her to him. "What's Justin doing?"

"He's sort of . . . I'm not sure what to call it. Brooding, I guess. He's become very quiet, not his usual lively self. Does that make sense?"

"I think so," Will said, kissing her on the top of her head. "What do you think I should do?"

"Oh, Will, I'm not suggesting you're doing something wrong, it's just that I'm worried about Justin." She nestled her head against his chest.

Justin walked quietly into the room. "Are we going to eat? I'm hungry."

Will released Renee and reached for Justin's hand. "Why don't we go out for dinner?"

Justin shrugged his shoulders.

Renee looked at Will and raised an eyebrow, then turned to Justin. "What would you like to do?"

"I don't care."

"Where would you like to go for dinner?" Will said, squeezing Justin's shoulder gently.

"Don't know. Wherever."

Renee furrowed her brow, "How about pizza at Pallermo's?"

"Okay." Listlessly he started toward the front door. Will and Renee followed him to the car, hurrying through the sputtering rain. They drove in silence to the Italian restaurant not far from their home. The aroma of cheese, garlic, basil, and oregano reached out and enveloped them and drew them through the door, and they were quickly seated at a tile-topped table. A ceiling fan rotated slowly above them. Will opened the menu.

"What do you want? Pizza?"

"I'll just have minestrone soup and a salad," Renee said. "And I'll eat a piece of your pizza . . . especially if you get Canadian bacon and pineapple."

Will laughed, "I think I'll have a Canadian bacon and pineapple pizza. What about you, Justin?"

Justin shrugged his shoulders. "Pepperoni, I guess."

At that moment their waitress arrived carrying glasses of water. "Hi, my name's Cheryl. I'll be your waitress tonight. Need another minute? Or are you ready to order?"

"We're ready," said Will. "My wife would like soup and salad . . . minestrone and ranch dressing on the side . . . Our son would like a small pepperoni pizza, and I'll have a medium Canadian bacon and pineapple pizza . . . Oh, and an order of garlic bread."

"Anything to drink?"

"Just water?" Will said, glancing at Renee.

"Water's fine," she agreed.

"Very good." She turned and walked away from their table.

"I wanted a root beer," Justin complained.

Will saw the flush rise in Renee's face, but before she could say anything he turned to Justin. "I'm sorry, Justin, I should have asked you." He signaled the waitress. "Our son would like a root beer."

They sat in silence until the waitress returned and placed a glass of root beer in front of Justin. "There you go, sweetheart. Anything else?"

Justin shook his head.

"I'll have that salad here in a minute." She turned on her heel and left.

The impending rain had made it a slow night at Pallermo's, with only one other couple in the place, sitting in a booth on the opposite side of the restaurant. Will and Renee sat quietly while Justin played with the straw in his root beer.

Finally Renee spoke quietly. "Justin, is something wrong? You've seemed awfully quiet."

Without looking up from his root beer, Justin shook his head.

Will looked at his wife and raised an eyebrow. She returned a worried look. The waitress appeared with Renee's salad and a basket of garlic bread.

Half an hour later the three of them left Pallermo's and headed for home. As they walked up the steps toward the front door, Renee said, "You'd better get going on your home-work, sweetheart."

Justin shuffled through the door. "Okay, Mom," he said despondently and continued toward his bedroom.

Renee watched him go and shook her head. "It's like a

switch flipped. He's never been this way before," she said quietly.

Will rubbed his chin. "I wonder what's happened?" They stood without speaking for a moment, then Will said, "I'm going to go talk to him . . . or at least try."

He walked down the hallway to Justin's room. The door was shut, and Will knocked softly on it. "Mind if I come in?"

"If you want."

Will pushed the door open and saw Justin sitting at his desk, with his book open. "Need help with your math?"

"I guess."

Justin sat immobile at the desk, and Will pulled a chair next to him. "What kind of problems are you doing?"

"Story problems."

"Ah. Having trouble with some of them?"

Justin pointed his finger at one of the problems. "This one."

"Let's see. 'Bob's mother sent him to the store. She told him to buy six cans of soda. Each can costs thirty-five cents. How much is the total bill?' Pretty tough?"

Justin nodded his head. "It's stupid. You just buy a six-pack of soda. You don't buy each can by itself."

Will smiled. "You're right, Champ, but they're trying to teach you how to multiply. How many cans is Bob buying?"

"Six."

"And how much does each one cost?"

"Thirty-five cents."

"So we have to multiply thirty-five by six."

Justin wrote down the numbers on the pad of paper next to his book and finally said, "Two hundred ten."

"Exactly right!" said Will emphatically. "And how many dollars would that be?"

Justin scratched his head with the end of his pencil. "Two dollars and ten cents?"

Will patted the boy's shoulders. "That's right. You're a smart boy, Justin."

"That's not what Andrea says."

"Oh, really? What does she say?"

"She says her dad's gone away and now she's just like me."

Will took a deep breath. "In what way?"

"She says we both made our dads go away. She says we must have done some pretty dumb things to make our dads so mad that they didn't want to have nothin' to do with us." Will could feel the boy's shoulders shuddering beneath his hands. "I hate Andrea." Suddenly Justin turned and threw his arms around Will's neck and began to sob.

Will stroked the boy's back and let him cry. "It's not your fault, Justin. It's not your fault."

3

. . .

WHEN WILL RETURNED to the living room after tucking Justin into bed, he found Renee sitting on the couch in the dark. He turned on the table lamp before sitting down next to her. She rested her head on his shoulder. Will could see the lamplight reflecting from the tears on her cheeks.

"It's okay, Renee, he's just reacting to something Andrea said."

"Maybe I'm just being too sensitive. I've tried to protect him ever since his father left."

Will slipped his arm around her shoulders and pressed her to him. "I know, sweetheart, and you've done a great job. He's a wonderful kid."

"So, what's the matter?"

Will shifted uncomfortably in his seat. "Well," he cleared his throat, "he thinks he's the reason Gary left." He felt Renee stiffen, and quickly added, "I think that's a fairly common reaction of kids whose parents have gone through a divorce. I talked to him before I put him into bed."

Renee stood up from the couch and began slowly pacing.

Her voice was angry. "He didn't have a thing to do with it. Gary just got too caught up in his work and didn't want the responsibilities that come with marriage and a family. He literally disappeared from our lives."

Will nodded his head. "I know that, but we're not talking about logic—we're talking about the perception of a seven-year-old who hasn't seen or heard from his real father in over four years."

"Except for the birthday cards," Renee said. "At least Gary hasn't forgotten his birthday; but it's a long time from November to November." Will could hear the bitterness in her voice.

He hesitated, then asked, "You've never talked much about what happened . . . what caused the divorce. Is that something you'd care to discuss?"

"Not really. It was a pretty discouraging time. It's hard to play second fiddle to a computer."

"I suppose that's true," Will said softly.

Suddenly she turned to him and said, "Money isn't everything, but it sure pulled Justin's father away." She sat back down next to him and looked into his face. "Don't you ever think of leaving," she said intensely.

He pulled her to him and kissed her. "I wouldn't dream of it." He brushed back a strand of her auburn hair from her face. "Never in a million years." He kissed her again and felt his wife relax against him.

Renee walked down the hall and looked into Justin's room.

He lay sleeping on his side, one arm around a stuffed dinosaur. "He looks so helpless," she said quietly.

"Maybe," said Will, "but I have the feeling he's a pretty resilient kid." He walked into their bedroom and began unbuttoning his shirt. Renee lingered behind, watching her son sleep.

The next morning they sat at the kitchen table eating breakfast. "Oh, I almost forgot. Grams wants us to come for dinner tomorrow. I hope that's okay?"

Renee smiled over her orange juice. "Of course."

Justin seemed a little brighter this morning, but he merely nodded his head.

"Well, what's on the docket for today?" Will asked.

"If my car's ready, we need to pick it up."

"Why don't we get rid of that old Chevy anyway?" Will asked. "It's costing more to repair than we'd spend on a new car."

Renee shook her head slowly. "I like it, Will. I'm familiar with it."

"If you say so, but it's ten years older than Justin."

"I know, but it's the first car I ever bought all on my own. It's almost part of the family."

Will stood up and stretched. "An older member of the family. I think it's developing arthritis," he said with a smile. "What else?"

Justin pushed his Cheerios around with his spoon and then said softly, "It's baseball sign-ups today."

"Is that something you'd like to do, Justin? Play Little League baseball?" Will asked.

The boy shrugged his shoulders. "Maybe. I'm not very good at baseball, but maybe I could learn." He looked expectantly at Will.

"I've played a little ball, Justin. We can work out together," Will said, smiling.

"I saw your trophies," Justin said.

"What do you say we go down to Christensen's and see about getting you a glove. What position do you want to play?"

"I don't know."

Will lifted Justin from his chair and held him at arms length. "You're pretty tall. Maybe first base."

A flicker of a smile crossed Justin's lips. "Yeah, maybe first base."

"And maybe when we're over at Grams's, I can show you how to hit pinecones over the fence."

"Pinecones?"

"That's how I used to practice. Of course they'll be a little soggy after being under the snow, but I'll bet there'll be a bunch of them we can rake up. You hit 'em and you don't have to chase after 'em. You'll love it!"

"What if I can't hit them?" Justin asked.

Will shrugged his shoulders, "You just keep trying. I couldn't hit them at first, either. But if you keep trying, you get better. That's what practice is all about."

Justin's face had gotten brighter, but suddenly a storm cloud shaded his eyes. "You're too busy, Will. You probably won't be able to come to my games."

"Just try to keep me away. Grandpa was always there for my games, and I'll be there for yours."

"And you won't go away? Even if I don't play too good?"

Will looked at Renee, who was still sitting at the table, then back to Justin. "No, Champ, I won't go away. Ever."

4

. . .

"YOU SEEM SOMBER, DEAR," Ruth Martin said to Renee as they looked through the kitchen window, watching Will and Justin batting pinecones in the backyard.

"I'm sorry, I didn't know it showed."

"I'm sure it's none of my business. But if you'll forgive a meddling old woman, you seem awfully quiet."

Renee smiled wanly. "Just worried a little about Justin."

"Oh?"

"Can I ask you a question?"

"Of course."

"Did you ever formally adopt Will, after his parents died?"

A gentle smile formed on Ruth's lips. "Formally? Of course." She took Renee's hand. "But then we were his closest living relatives, and I think it was merely a formality . . . a single sheet of paper that David Jobb had an associate of his draw up."

"David Jobb?"

"He was my husband Warren's attorney friend. I think he's still handling things for Will and the agency."

"I remember him."

The two women stood silently for a few minutes, watching Will show Justin how to cock his bat and stride forward as he swung. Finally, Ruth said, "Is that what's bothering you? Will and Justin?"

Renee folded her arms and sighed. "I know it's stupid, but I feel that until that happens we're not really a family."

"Have you talked to Will about it, dear?"

Renee turned, walked away from the window, and sat down on a stool at the kitchen counter. "I don't quite know how to bring it up. You know how Will hates to be pressured, and I guess I've been hoping he'd come up with the idea himself."

"Would you like me to talk to him about it?"

Renee chewed on her lip for a moment. "No," she said softly. "I think I'll just wait a while longer. After all, our first anniversary is next month. Maybe this will just take some time."

From behind, the older woman placed her hands on Renee's shoulders. "I think you need to have more faith in your husband."

"Perhaps." She swiveled on the stool and looked into Ruth's eyes. "Please don't say anything to Will."

"If that's what you want, dear."

Just then the back door swung open and Will and Justin came laughing into the kitchen. "See, I knew you could do it,"

Will said. "You ought to see this kid hit those pinecones. He's a natural."

"Aw, Will," the boy said blushing. "Just 'cause you showed me how."

"We were watching," Ruth said. "I think you're going to be an even better player than your . . . than Will."

Justin buried his face in his mitt and inhaled the aroma of newly oiled leather. "This is such a cool glove," he said.

"Dinner will be ready in a few minutes. Would you two men mind setting the table?" Ruth Martin asked.

"Just let us wash our hands and we'll get right on it. Won't we, Champ?"

"I guess," Justin said with less enthusiasm as the two of them walked together down the hallway to the bathroom.

Ruth watched as Renee's gaze followed them. "Are you sure you don't want me to talk to Will? They seem to be pretty close."

Renee smiled at the older woman. "Thank you, but I need to find the right way at the right time." She spread her hands in front of her. "Now, what can I do to help? We'd better feed these star athletes."

Ruth turned to the stove. "How about mashing the potatoes?" she said as she opened the oven door and bent to remove a roast. A cloud of fragrant steam swirled around her as she carried it to the countertop and set it on a cooling rack.

In the bathroom Justin finished washing his hands and reached for a towel. "That was so cool, Will. When can we start practicing catching? Will you throw the ball to me after dinner? Do you have a mitt so you can catch it when I throw it back? Did you remember to bring a ball?"

"We'll have to see, Champ. You never know how long Grams's dinners are going to take. We might have to wait until I get home from work tomorrow."

Justin's face fell. "You don't get home 'til after dark sometimes."

Will dried his hands, turned, and knelt down on the floor in front of the boy. "Justin, I promise you that I'll be home by five o'clock. That will give us at least an hour to practice before dark. Is that a deal?"

Justin brightened. "Promise?"

Will raised his right hand. "Promise."

Justin gave him a high-five. "It's a deal." He turned and trotted down the hallway toward the dining room.

Will watched him go. *I've got to find Gary Carr,* he thought.

5

· · ·

I'LL BE BACK IN AN HOUR or so, Miss Cook," Will said as he pulled on his sport coat.

"Very good, Mr. Martin."

"I'm headed over to David Jobb's office to have him take a look at these contracts." He waved a manila folder toward her as he headed for the stairs. Will left Martin Real Estate and jaywalked across the street into the town square. A cloudless sky stretched above and a gentle breeze wafted the aromas of spring around him. *What a beautiful day,* he thought to himself. Softly he whistled as he passed the bandstand in the middle of the square and headed toward the imposing sandstone structure that housed his attorney's office. He opened the door and stepped into the casual elegance of the offices of David Jobb, attorney-at-law. The receptionist, Patricia Ames, greeted Will.

"Mr. Martin," she said with a smile, "Mr. Jobb is expecting you. Go right on in."

"Thanks," he said as he turned toward the walnut door that led into David Jobb's office. "You're efficient as always, Patricia."

David Jobb rose as Will walked through the door, placed

the papers he had been reading in a folder, and extended his hand. "Always a pleasure," he said.

Will shook his outstretched hand, "Thanks for seeing me on such short notice. I have a couple of contracts I need you to look at." He extended the manila folder toward the attorney.

"Actually, Will, I was looking for an excuse to invite you to my office." He placed the folder on the desk and then perched on the corner of it. "Please, have a seat." He indicated an armchair upholstered in Corinthian leather.

Will sank into the butter-soft seat. "What did you want to see me about?"

David Jobb ran his hand over his bald pate, cleared his throat, and said, "How well do you know Creighton Barrow?"

Will shrugged, "I know who he is, that's about all." He looked into the older man's face. "Why?"

David folded his hands across his ample middle while he studied Will's face. "What I'm about to say can never leave this room." He walked to the door and made sure it was shut. "Okay?"

Will felt a cold chill trickle down his spine. "Of course."

"Creighton Barrow has served us in the state house of representatives for the past ten years. There are those who think he will try to become Speaker of the House during the next session." David Jobb moved another armchair in front of his desk and sat down. His knees nearly touched Will's. "I don't know how closely you've followed the legislature, Will."

"Not very closely, I'm afraid. They've just adjourned . . . I know that much . . . but I guess I've never really been caught up in politics."

"I understand—most of us don't really pay as much attention as we should. Representative Barrow has been a real stalwart in the party. He is an extremely intelligent man with a unique ability to listen to all sides of an argument, distill what is important from what isn't, then broker a compromise."

Will nodded his head. "That is unique."

"More than you know. He has been groomed to become the Speaker, but . . ." The attorney paused, "You understand this must be completely confidential?"

"Yes . . . of course," Will leaned forward.

"Creighton Barrow has been diagnosed with an inoperable and very virulent form of cancer. He's been told he has less than six months to live." David Jobb rose from his chair and moved slowly to the window that looked out on the town square. He crossed his hands behind his back and watched the activity outside the window while he composed himself, then turned to face Will. "Have you ever considered entering politics?"

"What?" Will said. "Me? You can't be serious."

Jobb returned to his chair. "I'm very serious, Will. You're young and successful. You have a spotless reputation." The lawyer leaned forward. "And your family roots go back to the founding of this community." He nodded. "I'd like you to consider it."

"I don't know what to say," Will said. "I mean, I've never

even thought about it. I wouldn't know where to begin." He sank back into the chair and feebly waved his hand.

"Don't worry. There'll be plenty of people to help. I'm not the only one who's taken note of you, seen your potential." The attorney sat down on his chair next to him. "We . . . I don't want to pressure you. Take some time to think about it . . . talk to your wife." He tented his fingers. "But there is some urgency . . . the last day to file for the office is tomorrow."

Will's brow wrinkled. "I'm not sure I even know what that means. What's the process?"

David Jobb smiled faintly. "There's a ten-day window to file to run for office. You'll have to go over to the county seat and fill out a form. There's a small filing fee."

"This is all overwhelming." He rubbed his forehead with his fingers. "Before I even consider it I need to talk to Renee."

"I understand. You probably ought to know that although everyone expects Creighton to run again, one person has already filed to run against him. I'd be pleased to act as your campaign manager." He placed the check on his desk. "But that isn't what you came to see me about, is it? What can I do for you?"

Will blinked. "What? Oh, I brought those contracts," he said, pointing to the folder on the desk. "Could you take a look and make sure everything's all right with them?"

"Of course. Anything else I can help you with?" He rose from his chair and pushed it back against the wall.

Will stood, "No, just the contracts." He shook the lawyer's

hand and started toward the door. "I'll talk to Renee and get back to you quickly."

"Wonderful. She surely will need to support you in this, as will your son."

Will stopped with his hand on the doorknob. "Maybe there is one other question you could answer."

"If I can," smiled the attorney.

"I'd appreciate it you would keep this in confidence. I'm thinking of adopting Justin. I've been trying to reach his father, Gary, and so far I've struck out. What will I have to do, if I can't find his father?"

David Jobb beamed. "What a wonderful idea. I'd imagine Renee and Justin are delighted."

"Actually, I'm trying to get Gary's approval before I talk to my wife. I'd hate to disappoint her if Gary objects."

Jobb raised an eyebrow. "I see. Well, of course I'll maintain the confidentiality. However, adoption is not my specialty, but Haven Walker does that work for our agency. Why don't I check that out for you? I can have an answer by the time you give me your decision."

"I'll talk to you later, then." Will walked out of the office and started back across the town square.

David Jobb stood at the open door and watched with his hands jammed into his pockets. *I hope he understands what I'm asking.*

6

. . .

RENEE WAS STANDING AT THE SINK, washing a head of lettuce, when Will walked in through the kitchen door. He stepped behind her, put his arms around her waist, pulled her to him, and kissed her gently on the top of the head. Renee snuggled against him.

"Tough day?" she asked as she turned in his arms and kissed him.

"Sort of," he said. "I'm just glad to be home." He walked to the kitchen table, pulled out a chair, sat down backward, and rested his chin on his hands.

"You look awfully serious," Renee said.

Will rubbed his forehead with his hand. "I visited David Jobb today," he began.

"Oh? What did you need an attorney for?"

"I needed him to look at the contracts on the Maxwell building and that strip of townhouses we're developing."

"And?" Renee prompted.

Justin exploded into the room and ran to Will. "You remembered! I've got my mitt." He waved the baseball glove.

"Let's go!" He grabbed Will by the hand and pulled him toward the kitchen door.

"Justin!" his mother said sternly. "Behave yourself."

"Just a minute, Champ," Will chuckled. "Let me go change into something more comfortable." He turned to Renee. "I guess we'll have to continue this later."

She watched as Will pushed the chair back in place and headed toward the stairs to the second story. Justin scurried out the kitchen door into the backyard and began throwing the baseball onto the garage roof and trying to catch it when it rolled back toward him. A couple of minutes later Will reappeared in his sweats with a worn baseball glove on his left hand. As he walked past her, Renee reached out and took his elbow. "What about David Jobb? You just can't leave me hanging."

He stopped. "It's a little complicated . . . and Justin really needs to be involved, too. We can talk about it over dinner." He kissed her on the tip of her nose then hurried out the door. "Hey, Justin, throw it over here," he called.

While Renee finished preparing the salad she'd been making, she watched the two of them through the window above the sink. *It involves Justin, too,* she thought. The trace of a smile crossed her lips.

Justin threw the ball in Will's general direction, and he moved quickly to catch it. "Hold your glove like this," Will said and as the boy complied, threw the ball gently back to him. After a few tries Justin was catching the ball most of the time. A half hour passed quickly.

Renee opened the kitchen door. "Are you two ready for dinner?"

"Aw, Mom, me and Will are having fun."

"Will and I," she said automatically. "Well, I hate to spoil it, but dinner's on the table, and if you two don't hurry it's going to get cold." She closed the door behind her, went to the window above the sink and watched as Will put his hand on Justin's shoulder and guided him toward the house.

"I'm telling you, this kid's a natural," Will said as he turned on the water in the sink and washed his hands.

Renee saw Justin smile before he shyly ducked his head and hurried down the hall toward the bathroom. A few moments later they sat down for dinner.

"Sweetheart, you ought to see how this kid catches a ball," Will gestured toward Justin. "Champ, you're amazing."

Justin's ears turned red from the compliment. "I'm not as good as you are."

"You will be, with a little more practice," Will said as he took a bite of salad. "We'll keep working on it." He turned to his wife. "I started to tell you about my meeting with David Jobb," he said.

"Who's that?" Justin asked.

"A lawyer, Champ." Will fidgeted a little in his chair. "He made me an interesting proposition."

Renee's forehead wrinkled. "What kind of a proposition?"

Will drew a deep breath. "He wanted to know if I've ever considered going into politics." He paused, waiting for her reaction.

"Politics? You?"

"Is it that absurd?" he asked with a chuckle.

"No, no," Renee said quickly. "It's just that I've never heard you indicate . . . I mean, it's kind of unexpected." She glanced at Justin, then back at Will. "When you said you'd gone to see Mr. Jobb, I had no idea that it was about politics."

Will stammered. "As I said, I went for a different reason, but he brought this up."

Renee folded her hands in her lap and looked into Will's eyes. "Sweetheart, I'll support you in whatever you want to do." She smiled. "The question is, do you really want to do this? Maybe we ought to think about it for a while."

"Unfortunately that's a luxury we don't have," Will said. "Tomorrow's the last day to file." He pushed a piece of lettuce across the plate with his fork. "I've got to let David know first thing in the morning."

Justin reached for his glass of milk. "What's pol'tics, Will?"

"Good question, Champ. It's a chance to serve the people who elect you." He saw the confusion in Justin's face. "It means you have to get people to vote for you."

"Like when we made Mary Jane our class president?"

"Exactly! Only this is a little larger job."

Renee cleared her throat. "Will, what does Mr. Jobb want you to run for? City council?"

"I guess I did leave that piece of information out, didn't I? Actually, he wants me to run for the state house of representatives."

A deafening silence filled the room, then Renee spoke. "You've got to be kidding." Will shook his head.

"What does that mean? I mean, I thought that was something older men did."

"I was pretty surprised myself, when he brought it up. But I've been thinking about it all afternoon."

"And?"

"Well . . . maybe it isn't so far-fetched as it seems. I mean, Patrick Henry was only thirty-nine when he gave his 'liberty or death' speech." Will pushed his chair back from the table. "How many times have we complained about something that government is doing? This might be a chance to make a difference." He looked at Renee and Justin. "So . . . what do you think?"

"Do you really want to do this?" Renee asked quietly.

"Would we still have time to play ball?" Justin interjected.

Will nodded his head. "I think I do, sweetheart. And, yes, Justin, we'd still have time to play ball."

Renee stood up and walked to the window. She placed her hands on the sill and looked out into the yard. The sun was setting and stripes of purple and orange streaked through the clouds. "As I said, I'll support you in whatever you want to do, Will. But I'm not sure that politics can't consume a person." She turned slowly. "But I will support you."

"I've never doubted that," he replied. "But there's support and then there's support, if you know what I mean." He rose from his chair and walked to where Renee stood. Gently he placed his hands on her shoulders. "I'm not going to do this, if it is going to create problems between us." He looked into her eyes. "You're much more important than any political office."

She looked away from him for a moment, then said, "If you want to do it, let's do it!" she said firmly, reaching to hug her husband. "We'll help, won't we, Justin?"

"Sure," the boy replied. "Do we get dessert?"

"How about ice cream at Lester's?" Will suggested as he and Renee released each other. "Kind of a celebration."

The dinner dishes were quickly disposed of, and the three of them climbed into Will's Jaguar. As they backed out of the driveway Renee asked, "How much time is this going to take? I'm afraid I haven't paid much attention to politics."

"Well, I have to file tomorrow, at the county courthouse, then we'll have to worry about a campaign. David Jobb offered to be my campaign manager . . . in fact he has a check . . . a contribution ready."

Renee turned in her seat. "How much is this going to cost?"

"I really don't know. I haven't dug into everything yet. This whole thing came as quite a shock, but David seemed to think that people would contribute." He gripped the steering wheel. "I guess I need to find out a whole lot of things in a hurry."

They drove in silence to the ice cream parlor and only after ordering their ice cream did Renee speak again. "I'm a little embarrassed to ask this, but just who is our current representative?"

"Creighton Barrow," Will replied, "although if you'd asked me before I met with David this afternoon, I'm not sure I could have answered you." He dug his spoon into the ice cream in front of him. "Kind of sad, isn't it, that we don't even know who we've elected?"

Renee nodded her head. "And why isn't he running again?"

"Personal reasons." Will thought of the confidence he'd been asked to keep. Quickly he scooped a spoonful of ice cream into his mouth.

"Will you be going to see him?"

"I don't know. Probably."

Renee licked whipped cream from the bottom of her spoon, while Justin continued to gobble his sundae. Another family entered the store and walked to the counter.

"Something's bothering you, isn't it?" Will said.

Renee twisted her spoon into the ice cream. "I just keep thinking of that saying that 'power corrupts.' I don't want to see you corrupted. You're too good a man."

"I'll take that as a compliment," Will said as he continued to eat his ice cream.

7

. . .

SUNLIGHT WAS STREAMING THROUGH the window and reflecting from the picture of Warren Martin, Will's grandfather, that hung on the wall of Will's office as he picked up the phone and dialed David Jobb's number. Patricia Ames answered on the first ring.

"Payne, Jobb, and Walker. How may I help you?"

"Patricia, this is Will Martin, is David Jobb available?"

"He's on the other line, Mr. Martin. Would you like to hold?"

"Please." As she put him on hold, the innocuous sounds of elevator music filled his ear. Will looked at the legal pad on the desk in front of him. He had jotted down a number of questions that he needed to have answered, and as the music played on he thought of another one that he quickly wrote down. After a few minutes of waiting, Patricia came back on the line.

"Mr. Martin, Mr. Jobb is still on the other line. Would you like to continue to hold?"

"Thanks, Patricia. Why don't I call him back in a few

minutes?" He hung up the phone and turned to the mail that was stacked on one corner of his desk. He straightened the pile of letters, then selected the top envelope, slid the letter opener under the flap, and slit it open. Before he went any further his secretary paged him.

"Mr. Martin. David Jobb is on line one."

That was fast, thought Will as he plucked the phone from its cradle. "Hello, this is Will Martin," he said.

"Will, David Jobb. I'm sorry I was on the other line when you called. Have you had time to consider my proposition?"

Will rubbed his forehead with the side of his hand. "Well, I talked it over with Renee and Justin last night, and I guess I'm ready to throw my hat in the ring. That's the expression, isn't it?"

"Wonderful, just wonderful!" the lawyer's voice boomed through the phone. "What does your day look like? We've got to get you to the county seat to file for office before five o'clock this afternoon."

"I have a meeting this morning, but I'm free after lunch, if that works for you."

Will could hear the sound of papers being rustled in the background. "How about if I pick you up at two o'clock and drive you to the courthouse? I'm sure you have a million questions, and that might give us time to talk about them."

"That would be wonderful, Mr. Jobb," Will said. He noticed that his hand was slightly shaking.

"Please call me David . . . Will. This is going to be a great experience for you." He paused for a moment. "I'll see you at two. Why don't I pick you up in front of your office?"

"That will be fine," Will exclaimed. "I'll see you then. And you're right, I do have a few questions." Carefully he replaced the phone on its cradle and turned to the stack of mail.

He slid the letter out of its envelope and tried to concentrate on the words in front of him, but he found that he couldn't keep his mind focused. He felt a mixture of fear and elation at the decision he had made. He held the piece of stationery in his trembling hand and leaned back in his chair, then glanced up at the portrait of his grandfather hanging on the wall. "Grandpa, I hope I'm doing the right thing," he said under his breath as he turned back to the stack of correspondence.

Half an hour later there was a knock on the door. "Come in," Will said.

Enid Cook's face appeared around the edge of the door. "Mr. Jenkins and Mr. Spellman are here," she said in her usual stern voice. "Would you like me to show them in?"

"Please, Miss Cook," he said as he straightened the pile of papers that had accumulated on his desk. "I think Hunter Hoggard will be along shortly."

"Very good, Mr. Martin." Her head disappeared, and a few seconds later she pushed the door open and ushered the two men into the office.

Will rose and walked around his desk with his hand

extended. "Hal, Ray. Thank you for coming," he said as he shook the two men's hands.

"My pleasure," Hal Jenkins said. "It was a slow day at the bank anyway." He smiled at Will, then turned to look at the portrait of Warren Martin on the wall. "Your grandfather was one of a kind," he said cordially.

"I agree," said Ray Spellman. "I can't count the number of times he helped me find property." He spread both hands. "And helped me get hooked up with Hal so I could get decent financing."

"How is the construction business, anyway?" the banker asked.

Spellman nodded his head. "Going well. Hard to keep ahead of the people who want to move into this little community. We're looking for another plot . . . at least 50 acres . . . to start another subdivision." He looked at Will. "Been able to find anything for me?"

"Maybe," Will said with a knowing look. "That's the reason for this meeting."

At that moment there was a tap on the door, it swung open, and Hunter Hoggard bulled his way past Enid Cook into the room. "Sorry I'm late," he said.

"No problem," Will said. He pointed to a table surrounded by four chairs in one corner of his office. "Please, have a seat."

The three men each took a chair while Will remained standing. "I have a proposition to make," he said in a controlled voice. "And I'd like to ask you to hear me through before you offer your opinions. Okay?"

"Sure," Hoggard said, "although I'm not sure Ray and I can agree on much." Ray Spellman smiled a thin smile in Will's direction.

Will cleared his throat and began. "Ray, I know you and Hunter have had your differences over the past years about developments, but maybe I have a project the two of you can work on together."

Hunter Hoggard muttered, "That'll be the day."

Will continued, "Hunter, most of your focus has been on building homes, while Ray has spent most of his time building commercial properties."

The two men nodded their heads.

"What if we could supply a two-hundred-acre parcel of land that could have a planned community built on it, and this community included single-family homes, townhouses, and a shopping center?"

Both men sat up a little straighter.

"Any interest?"

Hoggard tilted his head and looked at Will. "It's interesting, but it would cost a ton of bucks. Where you gonna come up with the cash?"

"That's why I invited Hal Jenkins," Will said with a gleam in his eye. "He's helped me find a substantial chunk of cash at a very attractive interest rate."

Hal Jenkins spoke, "Well, to be honest, Will found most of

the money. His old Wall Street contacts haven't forgotten him."

"Well, I can tell you *I'm* interested," Ray Spellman said. "We're just finishing the Clark Lane subdivision, and we're looking for a major project to keep my people busy." He scratched his chin. "Where have you found two hundred acres of undeveloped land? What about utilities and super-structure?"

"Well, I have found two hundred acres," Will said, "with a wonderful view of the mountains. And it's less than a fifteen minute drive from here." He returned to his desk, picked up a map, and unrolled it on the table. He pointed to a spot and said, "Right here."

Hoggard tilted his head to study the map, then said, "I know that piece, but I didn't think Gordon Burningham was interested in selling. How'd you pull that off?"

"Persuasion, Hunter."

For the next hour and a half the discussion went on about the planning, development, and financing of the project until, at last, the four men shook hands.

"If we're in agreement," Will said, "I'll have David Jobb draw up the contracts. It shouldn't take him too long."

Hal Jenkins started for the door. "Well, I'd better get back to the bank. Even though nothing much was happening when I left, you never know what crisis might have cropped up." He smiled at the other three men. "I think I've just witnessed something of a miracle . . . getting the two of you to agree to work together."

"Not that much of a miracle, Hal," said Will. "These are two good men who do excellent work. I suspect it will take several months to implement our plan and break ground, but the final result is going to be a community that has been thought out and meets both form and function."

"What are we going to call it?" asked Hunter Hoggard. "I mean a project like this has to have a name."

Ray Spellman looked over Will's shoulder at the picture of Warren Martin. "I think we ought to call it Martin's Glen," he said as he pointed toward the picture, "in honor of Warren."

"And Will," interjected Hal Jenkins.

Will held the door while Ray Spellman and the banker left, then turned to Hunter Hoggard. "Could I ask you a question, before you leave?"

"Shoot."

Will pointed to a couch and two easy chairs. "Please, let's have a seat. I don't think this will take long, but we might as well be comfortable."

Hoggard stepped to the couch and sank into it. Will sat opposite him. "You knew my wife's first husband, didn't you?"

"Sure. He did some computer work for me." He looked uncomfortably past Will and out the window. "Sure, I knew Gary."

"Do you know where he is now?"

"Not exactly. Paris, I think. Some big computer outfit

offered him a pile of cash, and he got out of this burg as quick as a cat."

Will nodded his head, "So I've heard. You haven't had any contact with him since he left?"

Hoggard scratched the back of his head. "How come you want to know? He in trouble?"

"Oh, no, nothing like that," Will said soothingly. "I'm just trying to locate him on a personal matter."

"I think the last time we had anything to with each other was when I sent him a check after he left for France. Gary set up our computer network and security system for us just before he left. He sent back a letter confirming that he'd received the check. 'Course we knew that, 'cause it had been cashed."

"How long ago was that?"

"Prob'ly four or five years." Hoggard was clearly uncomfortable, and he pushed himself up from the couch. "I remember Maggie was really impressed with his letter. It had that computer company logo on it and looked pretty high class, if you know what I mean."

"ETC?" asked Will.

"Beats me," Hoggard replied. "We prob'ly still have it in his file."

"Really? I'd love to have a look at it," Will said with some excitement in his voice. "Any chance I could do that?"

Hoggard shrugged his shoulders. "Sure, if we can find it. I'll have Mag look for it this afternoon. Now, I really gotta be goin'." Quickly he barreled out the door with Will following behind.

"I've got to run over to the courthouse in a few minutes. Would it be all right if I called your secretary after I return?"

"Might be a little quick. We've got a pile of work to get done. How about tomorrow mornin'?" He waved as he headed down the stairs toward the street.

"I'll call in the morning," Will called after him as Hunter Hoggard disappeared from view.

8

• • •

AT A LITTLE AFTER TWO O'CLOCK, Will was standing in front of Martin Real Estate when David Jobb pulled up in his black Lincoln Continental, leaned across the seat, and pushed open the passenger-side door. He smiled as Will got in and pulled the door shut.

"Sorry to keep you waiting," David said as he pulled away from the curb.

"No problem. It's sure a beautiful day," Will replied.

"In more ways than one, I suspect." He guided the Lincoln around the square and onto the main road leading out of town. "You're going to enjoy this, Will."

"I hope so. Right now all I feel is nervous."

The lawyer chuckled. "I think I understand. Now, what questions do you have?"

Will looked at the legal pad on his lap. "Well, first, I'm guessing it is going to cost quite a bit of money to run a campaign. Any ballpark figure?"

"Well, it depends. Right now there's only one other candidate who has filed, and he's from the other party, so you probably won't have a primary race." He ran his hand over the few strands of hair that crossed his bald head. "But there's no guarantee that someone else won't file today. I'm sorry, that doesn't really answer your question, does it? If there's no primary, you'll probably need to spend around ten thousand dollars for the race."

"Ten thousand dollars!"

"Oh, but don't worry. I'll be able to easily raise that much for you from contributors. It really won't cost you anything."

"What kinds of contributors?" Will asked.

"Well, the party itself will contribute and then there are a lot of people and businesses who just want to make sure good people are elected to office. You'll be surprised who will give you a couple of hundred dollars." He guided the car onto the freeway entrance. "Don't worry about it. I'll take care of raising the money for you." He reached into the inside pocket of his suit coat. "In fact, here's your first contribution." Jobb withdrew a check and handed it across the seat to Will.

Will took the check and examined it. "A thousand dollars!" he exclaimed. "I can't believe this. Why?"

"Let's just say I want to make sure that an honest, thinking person is representing me."

Will lay the check down on the seat between them. He could feel a trickle of sweat running down his back as he sat silently staring at the thousand-dollar contribution.

"Next question?"

"What? Oh." Will shifted his gaze from the check to the

pad of paper. "Time. How much time will this take . . . what's the commitment?"

"The legislature begins in January and runs for forty-five calendar days. During that time you'll be at the capitol all day. I won't sugarcoat it, they will be long days, some of them very frustrating. You will be appointed to committees, and you'll spend a lot of time in committee meetings." He glanced at Will. "But why don't we worry about those things after we get you elected. Just know that you'll have those forty-five days to worry about and one interim day per month."

"It seems overwhelming," Will said under his breath.

"Will, I want you to realize that everyone there had a freshman year. You won't have to know everything at once . . . no one will expect that of you. You'll be fine."

"I hope so."

"It sounds as if you're having second thoughts. That's natural. This is a big step. You know, there aren't that many people who are willing to stick their necks out and run for public office. But think of the good you can do." They were approaching the off-ramp that led to the county courthouse. "You're a good man, Will Martin, and we need more good men in the legislature."

David Jobb pulled into a parking place and stopped the car. "Now let's go get you filed and ready to run."

The two men walked into the courthouse. It was clear that David Jobb knew his way around. He led Will to the clerk's office and greeted the elections clerk as they walked through the door.

"Marti, do you know Will Martin?"

"I don't believe I've had the pleasure," the short, dark-haired woman said as she extended her hand over the countertop. "I'm Marti Martinez."

Will shook it as David Jobb said, "Will's here to file for Creighton Barrow's house seat." He smiled broadly. "Anyone else showing any interest in it?"

"Well, let's see." She slid open a drawer in the counter and withdrew a bound book. She flipped quickly through the pages until she found the one she was looking for. "Looks like just one other man, a Milton Phillips." She looked at David and her forehead wrinkled. "I suppose Representative Barrow will be here before five?"

"Perhaps," David Jobb said with a wave of his hand. "Regardless, Will needs to file."

"Of course," she said with a smile. "Just fill this out and pay your fee." She slid a sheet of paper across the counter to Will. "Make sure you read the whole thing before you sign it."

Ten minutes later Will and David Jobb walked out of the courthouse together. "Well, you're an official candidate. How does it feel?"

"Sort of unreal."

Jobb clapped him on the shoulder as they reached the car. "You're going to be a great representative, Will."

They were pulling out of the parking lot when Will asked, "What do you know about Milton Phillips?"

David Jobb smiled. "Good! You're starting to think like a politician already." He ran his hand across his head again. "He's supported by a group called the Coalition for Constitutional Government. They'll help him run a very aggressive race."

"Meaning?"

"Meaning you'll have your work cut out for you. The CCG is well organized and very influential. If they think Milton Phillips can beat you, they'll put a lot of money into his campaign. But don't worry, Will. You're going to be just fine."

They drove on in silence for a time and then David Jobb spoke again. "Incidentally, I looked into that adoption matter for you. Haven Walker says you need to make an honest effort to contact the boy's father, but if that fails then all it requires is that we put two notices in the newspaper of your intent to adopt." He smiled briefly at Will. "It seems as if you've made the effort to contact him. Would you like me to put a notice in the paper?"

Will thought for a minute. "No, not yet. I've actually stumbled on another clue that might help me find Gary Carr and if you put a notice in the paper, Renee is sure to see it." He turned in his seat. "Can you imagine the disappointment if Renee sees that and then Gary disagrees with the adoption?"

"Whatever you say, Will."

"I've just got to work this out my own way. I've got to get Gary Carr's permission before I talk to Renee and Justin."

"It seems to me . . ." the lawyer began.

"What?"

"Never mind."

"No, tell me," Will persisted.

David Jobb gripped the wheel firmly. "I was going to say, if he hasn't had anything to do with his son in over four years, I don't think you're going to get an objection."

Will pondered that for a moment. "You're probably right, but I've got to be sure. I just don't want to hurt Justin. Do you understand?"

"I understand, but I don't agree."

9

. . .

JUSTIN HAD ACCUMULATED A large pile of pinecones near the garage and was throwing the ball onto the roof when Will pulled into the driveway.

"Will! You're home."

"How you doing, Champ?" Will said with a grin. "Looks like you're ready for a little more practice. Give me a few minutes, and I'll be back out."

"Hurry," the boy said as the ball bounced past him.

"Where's your mom?"

Justin threw the ball onto the roof again. "Over at the dance studio." He caught the ball as it rolled off the roof. "She's giving Andrea a private lesson." He drew out the word *Andrea* like bitter molasses.

"Oh, I see. And who's keeping an eye on you?"

"Gramma Martin," Justin said, "but I'm old enough to take care of myself."

Will smiled and climbed the back steps. "I'll be out in a minute."

Justin continued his routine of throwing the ball onto the roof.

Ruth Martin sat reading in the living room and when Will walked through the door she closed the book. "It's good to see you, Will. Renee had to run over to her studio for a few minutes and asked if I'd mind tending Justin."

Will kissed his grandmother on her cheek. "I appreciate you doing it, although I don't think Justin wants to be 'tended.'"

Ruth smiled. "I understand. He really is a remarkable boy . . . much like you." She stood up from the couch. "Renee tells me you're thinking of dabbling in politics. You really are following in your grandfather's footsteps, aren't you?"

"I am?" Will said, bewildered.

"Of course. He served on the city council when your father was only a couple of years old." She pursed her lips. "He quit because he thought it took too much time away from the family." She looked at Will over the top of her half-moon glasses.

"I didn't know that part of his life. I guess there are still a lot of things I don't know about him. Anyway, I filed to run for the House of Representatives this afternoon."

Ruth raised her eyebrows. "Well, that's a big step, but I'm sure you'll be a very effective legislator."

"I still have to win the election, Grams."

"Yes, there is that," she conceded, then, changing the subject, she said, "May I ask you something?"

"Of course."

"Have you ever given any thought to adopting Justin?"

Will stared at his grandmother. "Whatever gave you that idea?"

"I guess I've just watched the two of you, and you seem so close."

Will stammered, "Actually, I've been trying to reach Gary Carr . . . you know, Renee's first husband . . . to see if he objects."

"And have you asked Renee for her help?"

"Grams, I'm nervous about talking to her about it until I locate Gary and get his permission."

"I'm an old woman, Will, and I hate to meddle, but I think you ought to talk to your wife."

"I will, Grams, but I don't want to raise any false hopes, and I've got to be sure that Gary won't oppose the adoption. Of course that assumes that Renee and Justin will want to go along with it."

"Will, you really need to have more faith in your wife." She picked up a canvas tote bag, stuck the book into it, and said, "Well, since you're home, I'm sure you can take care of Justin."

"Would you like me to drive you home?"

"Oh, Will, I'm not that old. It's only a two-block walk." She opened the back door and called out to Justin, "See you later, Justin." The two of them waved to each other and then she turned and walked briskly down the side of the house toward the front sidewalk.

Will closed the door after her and a few minutes later re-appeared dressed in his sweats. Justin smiled, grabbed the ball from his mitt, and threw it to Will, who caught it easily.

"Good throw, Champ," he said. "How about a little batting practice?"

"Okay," the boy said and walked to the pile of pinecones.

"What if we start with the ball, instead of the pinecones?" Will bounced the ball in his hand. "But we're not trying for home runs. Just hit the ball back to me easy."

Justin picked up the bat and walked to a spot near the corner of the garage while Will approached him and adjusted his stance. "Keep your eye on the ball, Justin. Okay?"

The boy nodded his head and gripped the bat tightly. Will lobbed a slow pitch toward him, Justin closed his eyes and swung with all his might, missing the ball by several inches. It passed him and bounced off the wall of the garage. Justin retrieved the ball, threw it back to Will, and dug his feet into the dirt again.

"Don't try to kill it. Just keep your eye on it and hit it softly back to me. Okay?"

Again the boy nodded his head. Will pitched the ball and Justin missed again. While the boy went after the ball Will walked to the makeshift home plate. Patiently he said, "See that willow tree? We're going to try for accuracy, not power. I want you to hit the ball softly enough that it just makes it to the roots of that tree. Think you can do that?"

"I'll try."

"Good." Will walked several paces away. "Ready?"

Justin nodded his head and Will lobbed another pitch toward him. This time Justin swung more slowly and dribbled the ball across the lawn toward the willow tree.

"Fantastic!" Will said. "I can't believe you did that. You put that ball right where I told you to."

Justin beamed at him. "I hit it, didn't I?"

Renee's car pulled into the driveway and parked next to Will's. She stepped out of it and slung her gym bag over her shoulder. She was wearing a pale green workout suit that complemented her dark, auburn-colored hair. She walked to Will and gave him a kiss. "What are you two sluggers up to?"

"Will's teaching me to hit the ball. I just hit one right where he told me. This is so cool."

Renee smiled. "I saw your grandmother walking down the sidewalk. I sure appreciate her dropping everything and keeping an eye on Justin."

"I think she likes to do it," replied Will. "With Grandpa gone she doesn't have a lot to occupy her time."

"Do you two guys want to go get Chinese tonight for dinner?" Renee said.

"Sounds good to me—how about you, Justin?"

"Can't we play ball a little more?"

"Sure, while your mom gets ready." Will said as he picked up the ball.

"Give me a few minutes to shower and I'll be ready to go," she said.

Renee disappeared into the house and Will and Justin continued working on hitting the ball. Half an hour later Renee reappeared. "Do you two want to wash your hands before we go eat?"

"Let's go, Justin," said Will. "The Golden Dragon awaits."

"Let me hit just one more," Justin pleaded. "Watch this, Mom!"

Will tossed a soft pitch to Justin, who put his bat on it perfectly and lined a shot right back at Will. The ball made a pop as it smacked into his glove.

"What did I tell you?" Will shouted. "You da man, Justin!"

Justin glanced at his mother, trying not to grin, but was unable to contain his pride. He shouldered his bat and headed for the back door.

A few minutes later the three of them climbed into Will's Jaguar and headed for the Golden Dragon. The road was fairly busy for a Tuesday night as they threaded their way through town and to the restaurant.

"Must be spring," Renee said. "Look at all the traffic." She settled back into the leather seat. "So, did you go file today?"

Will nodded his head. "Yup. I'm your newest candidate for office."

"Scared?"

"A little. David Jobb is going to call later tonight and help me get a handle on what we have to do to run an election."

"You'll be wonderful, sweetheart. I can't think of a better person for the job."

Will blushed slightly. "I'm not sure Grams was that excited about it."

"To be honest, I'm not sure I'm that excited, either. So many people are negative about politics . . . you know." She smiled. "But if that's what you want to do, I'll support you all the way."

"Thanks for your vote. Now if we can convince the rest of the people . . ."

10

. . .

THE PHONE WAS RINGING as Will unlocked the door and let Renee and Justin into the house, and he groped in the dark for the receiver. "Hello?"

"Will, this is David Jobb," the voice said. "Is this a good time to talk?"

"Sure. We just walked in from dinner. Do you want to talk on the phone or would you like me to come over?"

"What if I come to your home? I think we ought to include your wife in what we need to do. Would that be all right? I'm still at the office, so I could be there in about ten minutes."

"That would be fine." Will noticed that his hand was trembling slightly. "We'll be watching for you." He walked into the living room and turned on the porch light, then turned to Justin. "Have any homework tonight?"

Justin shrugged his shoulders. "Just math."

"Well, if you need help we'd better get right on it. Mr. Jobb is coming over in a few minutes."

"That's okay. I can do it myself." He shuffled down the hallway toward his room.

"Are you sure?" Will asked as Justin's door closed behind him.

Renee reached down and picked up the newspaper from the floor. "I'd better straighten up this room if we're having company." She ran her hand over the tablecloth, straightening a wrinkle.

Absently Will picked up Justin's coat from the back of a dining room chair and hung it in the closet. He anxiously peered out the front window as he passed.

"Nervous?" his wife asked.

"I suppose," he replied with a gentle laugh. "I know so little about politics. I'm barely beginning to understand the real estate business . . . now this."

Renee put her arms around his neck and kissed him. "That's what will make you so valuable. You'll be teachable."

"I guess," he said, kissing her back. "I'll take that as a compliment."

They stood in companionable silence watching the dusk deepen until David Jobb's black Lincoln pulled up in front of their home. Will opened the front door as the lawyer made his way toward the front steps. "Thanks for agreeing to see me," he said, extending his hand.

"My pleasure," Will replied.

"Mrs. Martin," David Jobb said with a slight bow, "I'm not sure if you remember me?"

"Of course I remember you, and please call me Renee," she

replied. "Won't you sit down?" She extended her hand toward the couch.

"Thank you. I'll try to make this brief, but I do think we need to decide a couple of things." He sat down heavily.

Will and Renee sat down opposite him. "Let me grab some paper," Will said. "I probably ought to be taking notes."

Jobb waved his hand back and forth. "No, no, that won't be necessary. We just need to make a couple of decisions. First, you ought to know that no one else filed for office, so you won't have to worry about a primary election fight. That's good news, believe me. You can spend a lot of money on a race against someone in your own party, and when you're finished, all you've done is coat each other with dirt that you have to scrape off before the final election. I believe that's one reason why people think politicians are disingenuous—the way they throw their support behind someone they've just lost to in an election."

"I suppose," Will said thoughtfully. "But when we were at the courthouse they indicated someone else had filed, a Milton Phillips."

David Jobb's face darkened. "Well, you'll face him in the final election. That will be an interesting race." He rubbed his chin. "Yes, very interesting."

Renee saw the sudden change in his face and said, " 'Interesting' covers a lot of sins, Mr. Jobb."

"Yes, it does, doesn't it," he said without elaborating. "And please, Renee, call me David."

"What decisions do we need to make?" asked Will.

The lawyer opened his briefcase. "First, we need to decide how much exposure you need to get your name in front of the people. You're pretty well known locally, but your district covers parts of three other communities. You're probably not as well known there. So, should we get some lawn signs printed and distributed before the county convention, even though you don't have a race there?"

"What do you think?"

"It's sixes. We can spend money now to get you some name recognition, but it is a long way until the final election in November, and most people's memories are pretty short. We might be smarter to just put an announcement in the paper and wait until October to get the lawn signs out."

Will interrupted. "David, you offered to be my campaign manager, for which I'm grateful. I'm really a novice at this whole thing. Can I leave these decisions in your hands?"

"If you wish, but I'll feel more comfortable if we discuss them."

"I understand, but you're much more experienced than I. We'll just need to rely heavily on you to do what's needed." Will sank back on the couch.

Renee put her hand on Will's knee. "Mr. Jobb . . . David . . . If the challenge is to get Will's name better known, should we mail something to every home? Should we start knocking on doors? Or do we try to set up town meetings? Is that a good idea?"

Jobb smiled. "Probably all of them are good ideas. The question is when do we do what? Timing is everything."

"And," she continued, "I suppose all of this costs money. How much will we need to spend?"

David Jobb smiled at her. "I've already told Will I'd take care of fund raising for him. I think it will take at least ten thousand dollars."

Renee drummed her fingers on the arm of the couch. "I had no idea it would cost that much."

"Don't worry. I'm sure there won't be any trouble raising the money." He stood and paced across the living room. "There're nearly seven months until the election. We just need to pace ourselves so that Will wins the race in November." He returned to his briefcase, reached in, and removed a sheet of paper. "This is a press release I've prepared for the newspapers. I'd like you to go over it and make sure you feel all right about it."

Will took the paper and he and Renee read what David had written.

Will Martin announces his candidacy for the House of Representatives in District 85. He is currently the president of a family business, Martin Real Estate, which was founded by his grandfather, Warren Martin. Will was a junior vice-president with the New York investment firm of French, Cawley, and Partridge before returning home to take over Martin Real Estate following the untimely death of his grandfather. He is married to the former Renee Watkins Carr.

Will is committed to serving the people of District 85 and pledges to them that he will maintain an open-door policy toward his constituency. He sees growth as the major issue facing the state in the coming decade. Unchecked and unplanned growth will impact the roads, the schools, and the available water resources. He pledges to work aggressively to solve these problems.

"I couldn't have said it better myself," Will said as he handed the sheet of paper back to David.

The attorney returned the paper to his briefcase, snapped it shut, and started toward the door. "I've kept you people long enough. Think over what Renee suggested, and let's put a plan of action together. I'll get this press release sent to the papers and get moving on the fund raising. You're going to be a wonderful candidate, Will."

"Thanks," Will said, rising from the couch and walking to the door. "I suspect I might have two votes," he said with a smile.

11

• • •

CLOUDS DARKENED THE HORIZON the next morning as Will climbed the stairs to his office. He and Renee had talked late into the night about the impending campaign. Finally they had gone to bed but had continued to talk until early in the morning. Consequently, he was later than usual getting to the office. Enid Cook greeted him as he threaded his way through the half-dozen desks that occupied the main part of the firm.

"Good morning, Mr. Martin."

"Good morning, Enid. It looks like rain," he said wearily.

"We could use the moisture." She followed him into his office. "Margaret Fowler, Hunter Hoggard's secretary, brought this by a few minutes ago." She handed Will a manila envelope.

Will reached for a letter opener on his desk and slit open the envelope. He removed the single sheet of paper and looked at it carefully. Enid Cook turned to go, but Will stopped her. "Enid, take a look at this." He extended the paper toward her.

She took the page and examined it. "Why, it's a letter from

Gary Carr!" she exclaimed. "Just as I thought, he went to work for ETC. It's on their letterhead." She returned the sheet to Will.

"Then why don't they have any record of him working for them?" he asked. "I've talked to their CEO, and he says they've never heard of him."

"You can't be serious." Enid pointed at the sheet of paper in Will's hand. "But this proves he works for them, doesn't it? Why would they deny it?" She sat down slowly. "Unless he was working on some secret project. I know computer companies often have those kinds of things going on."

Will shook his head. "I don't know, Enid, but I'm going to find out."

"Have you asked your wife if she knows where Gary is?"

"No, I haven't," he said quietly. "He doesn't seem to be one of her favorite topics. And I'm afraid she'll want to know why I'm trying to reach him."

Enid Cook folded her arms and glared at Will. "Mr. Martin, if you don't mind me saying so, you need to start treating the people you love with a little more trust."

"You're probably right, Miss Cook."

"I usually am," she sniffed as she turned and marched out of Will's office.

Will watched her go, sighed, and looked again at the letter from Gary Carr. It was neatly typed on an ETC letterhead, dated five years earlier, and instructed Hoggard Construction to deposit his check directly in a local bank. The signature was cramped and difficult to read. Will searched inside the manila envelope to see if there was anything else in it. There was not, nor was there any other indication of a return address. He slipped the paper back into the envelope and dropped it on the credenza behind his desk.

Maybe Enid's right, he thought. *Maybe I ought to ask Renee if she knows where Gary is. But then she'll ask why I want to contact him. And what if Gary won't give permission for me to adopt Justin? What if Renee doesn't want me to adopt him?* He placed his face in his hands and rubbed his temples. Just then the phone rang.

"Will, this is Hal Jenkins at the bank. Do you have a minute?"

"Sure, Hal."

"Good. I just thought I'd bring you up to date on the Martin's Glen project. Your old contacts really are good. I received a fax from Fairbourne and Sinclair in New York, and they are willing to do the financing if we can have an acceptable proposal to them by October 15. They want to see the plat plan and will need the planning commission's approval in writing. I don't think this is going to be a problem as long as we can keep Ray Spellman and Hunter Hoggard talking to each other. Do you have an architect in mind? Or, do you want me to arrange for one?"

"Hal, that gives us barely six months to get this whole thing designed. I guess it's going faster than I anticipated." Will looked at the portrait of his grandfather. "I should have had more of this planned before I brought Hunter and Ray into this."

"That may be, Will, but I think we can do it if we really put our shoulders to the wheel, so to speak. Charles Merrill has done some good work for us in the past. He designed the buildings for the Colonial Springs development. He works well with the county planner, as well. I can call him, if you'd like. He's a good architect, and he has a large enough stable of people that I think he'd be able to complete the project."

"Wonderful! Please approach him, Hal. If you need me to go with you . . . I mean I don't want to drop the whole thing in your lap."

"Let me give him a call," the banker said. "What does your afternoon look like?"

"Nothing I can't rearrange."

"Good. I'll get back to you as soon as I give Charles a call."

"Thanks, Hal."

"You're welcome. I'll talk to you later."

Will looked again at the picture of his grandfather and thought, *Grandpa, you handled projects like this and didn't even seem to work up a sweat. I wonder if I'm up to this kind of pressure?* He stood up and walked to the window that looked out over the town square. Several people were strolling through the square, an elderly couple sat on a bench by the bandstand, and a woman was pushing a baby stroller. *They look so peaceful. Why can't my life be like that? Why do I always have so many unanswered questions?* He turned back to the portrait. "How did you do it, Grandpa?" he said under his breath. "How did you organize your life to accomplish so many things?"

Enid Cook knocked softly on his door and stuck her head into the room. "There's a gentleman here from the *Examiner*. He'd like ten minutes of your time, if that's possible."

Will walked to the door and pulled it open. "Of course, Miss Cook." A short man in an ill-fitting, wrinkled suit stood beside Enid Cook's desk. His ample stomach strained a belt that was cinched around his waist, and he held a reporter's notebook in his left hand. As soon as Will walked out of his office, the heavy man squeezed past Enid's desk and threaded his way through the several agents at their desks, his meaty right hand extended.

"Mr. Martin. I'm Lloyd Randell from the *Examiner*. Thank you for seeing me. Do you have ten minutes?"

Will took the outstretched hand. "Of course. Please," he said, indicating his office.

"Nice place," Randell said as his eyes darted around the room. "I see your grandfather's picture is still on the wall. He was a good man."

Will nodded. "Please have a seat."

The couch wheezed as Lloyd Randell settled into it. "I won't waste your time," he grunted and flipped open the cover of his notebook. "I see that you've filed for the House of Representatives. Why?" He waited expectantly with his pencil poised above the pad of paper.

Will sat down, placed his elbows on the desktop, tented his

fingers, and rested his chin on them. "That's an excellent question," he said, trying to think of an answer. "To serve the people," he finally said.

"Oh, come on. That's no answer." The reporter shifted his weight on the couch and it whooshed a muted groan in protest. "What's your real motivation?"

Will pushed down the lump of annoyance that rose in his throat. "I'm not sure what you want. That is the answer. I just want to serve the people. I have no personal agenda, Mr. Randell."

"Humph, well then, perhaps you can answer this question: Why isn't Creighton Barrow running for re-election? He was a shoo-in for Speaker of the House, and heaven knows he's ambitious enough. Why?"

Unable to mask his growing irritation, Will said, "I'm afraid you'll have to ask him."

Randell's eyebrows shot up. "Look, Martin, I'm not your enemy. I'm just trying to get a story for the paper." The pencil scribbled on the paper. "What's your view on abortion?" Lloyd Randell looked up from his writing.

Will took a deep breath and tried to refocus his thoughts. "I've never had one," Will said without smiling. "And I don't expect to have one in the future."

The reporter's eyes hardened. "Cute answer, Martin, but it's going to take more than a glib tongue to win this election." He flipped over the page in his notebook. "What about your view on gun laws? Where do you stand on that?"

Will stood and walked around his desk until he was looking down on the reporter. "Mr. Randell, if you've come here to try to get material that you can sensationalize in the newspaper, you're going to find that I'm not a very sensational person. I'm just a guy trying to earn a living, who's been persuaded to run for public office."

"By whom?" Randell said, moistening the tip of the pencil with his tongue.

Will walked to the door and opened it. "Some very good people," Will replied. "Now, if you don't mind, I really do have a very busy morning." Lloyd Randell struggled to get to his feet. He fastened his eyes on Will's face.

"Martin, I'm not your enemy, but I'll tell you one thing: if there's any dirt you've swept under the carpet, I'm going to find it." He wedged his way between the desks and headed toward the stairway. He stopped at the top of the stairs and turned back to where Will stood in the doorway of his office. "One more thing. If you think you're going to win this battle, you'd better find out who your friends are, Mr. Martin." He dragged the "Mister" out like the sound of fingernails on a blackboard. Then he lumbered down the stairs and out onto the street.

The office had been completely silent during the brief exchange, but it now came back to life. "What was all that about?" Enid Cook exclaimed.

Will stood next to her desk. "Friends, I'd better tell you what I've done before you read about it in the newspapers."

12

. . .

I THINK THAT WENT WELL, don't you?" Hal Jenkins said as he and Will pulled away from Charles Merrill's office building. "Charles seems to feel that they can deliver all of the needed plans in plenty of time."

Will shifted in his seat. "If we can get Ray Spellman and Hunter Hoggard to agree on what goes where."

The banker glanced at Will. "Maybe that is your call, Will. You've got to be the genius behind the project and let them work for you."

"Hal, they're both so much older and experienced than I am. Don't you think they'll feel uncomfortable letting me take such a . . ." He struggled for the right word.

"Dominant role?" Jenkins finished. "No, I don't. In fact, if we leave it up to them I suspect they'll still be debating what to do five years from now." The sun was sinking low in the west, and he reached up to pull down the car visor. "Will, your grandfather would have jumped at this chance, and I think you're every bit as talented as he was."

Will squinted into the sun as they drove on in silence for

several minutes until the banker stopped in front of Martin Real Estate. "I just hope I'm up to the challenge," Will said as he opened the door of the car.

Hal Jenkins reached across the seat and rested his hand on Will's arm. "I'm sure you are. But if you're not going to go ahead with this I need to know soon. I don't want to spend a lot of energy getting the financing arranged for a project that isn't going to happen. Understand? I don't think you'll have any problem with the residential construction, but finding anchor tenants for commercial property sometimes isn't easy. You've started putting together a pretty good team with Spellman and Hoggard, but you might need to add more people. I can see this taking the majority of your time for the next half year."

Will nodded his head. "Let me think about it tonight and I'll get back to you first thing in the morning." He got out, closed the door, and watched the car slide away from the curb. Will glanced at his watch, then across the street toward the town square. The late afternoon had turned colder, and clouds were building over the mountains to the east, promising rain. No one was sitting on the benches in the park. Will stuffed his hands in his pockets, walked across the street, and seated himself on one of the benches near the bandstand. *It's all coming so fast. I don't know if I know enough to pull this project off. The risk is pretty big, and if it crashes I could take down Martin Real Estate with it. There are a lot of people who rely on the company . . . no, on me . . . for a livelihood.*

He rested his elbows on his knees and his chin on his hands. *Not the best time, either, what with the political campaign. I wonder how much time that's going to take? How is that going to impact the business and our family?* He leaned back on the bench and closed his eyes, and the first drops of rain spattered his face. *My family . . .*

The rain began in earnest, and he hurried back across the road to where his car was parked, fumbled in his pocket for the keys, unlocked the door, and climbed into the front seat. He sat there for a time, listening to the rain drumming on the roof of the Jaguar. Even though it was not quite six o'clock, darkness had begun to descend, and the street lights were starting to flicker on. Will started the car, turned on the windshield wipers, and pulled away from the curb, headed for home.

He thought about Renee and Justin. He truly loved Renee, and he wanted to provide Justin a safe environment—give the boy the stability that would help him overcome his insecurities. In spite of his moodiness, Justin was a neat kid, and Will felt a genuine affection for the boy. He felt they were coming together as a family. He hoped adopting Justin would be the answer. *But where is Gary Carr? And how will he react to the idea of my asking to adopt his only son?*

Renee had turned on the porch light and was waiting for Will when he walked wearily into the kitchen. She dusted the flour from her hands. "Tough day?" she asked, kissing him.

"You might say that," he replied. "Where's Justin?"

"In his room doing homework. I think he gave up on the baseball lesson."

Will felt a stab of guilt. "I'm sorry."

"It's not your fault, sweetheart. I think the game was called on account of rain." She hugged him and felt the tension in his body. "What's the matter?"

"Nothing. Just some decisions I have to make."

"Can I help?" she offered.

Will shook his head. "Renee, my grandfather was able to walk through the doorway into his home and leave all of the business problems behind. I'm trying to do the same thing. You deserve more from me than just rehashing the events of the day."

Renee drew back. "Will, I like to know what's going on. I worked for your grandfather, and I know the people at Martin Real Estate. You don't have to try to protect me." There was a slight edge in her voice.

Will's shoulders slumped. "It's something I've got to work out by myself." He turned and climbed the stairs to their bedroom.

Renee turned back to the counter and continued kneading the mound of dough. She punched it vigorously and felt the beginning of tears and wiped her nose with the back of her hand, leaving a streak of flour on her lip. *I won't let this happen,* she thought. *Gary started doing the same thing, so I never knew what was going on in his life. And look where that led.* She brushed a tear from her cheek, leaving another streak of flour, then punched the dough even harder. *Why does he have to be so independent? I thought we married for better or worse.*

Will changed his clothes and sat on the edge of the bed. *How in the world can I run a campaign, superintend a project like Martin's Glen, and still give enough time to Renee and Justin? I'm not going to be like Gary and never spend any time with my family. Why can't life ever be simple?*

He looked up to see Justin standing in the doorway.

"You said we could play catch."

"I'm sorry, Champ. I got held up at work, and then it started to rain. We'll have to do it tomorrow."

Justin looked as though he might cry.

"Can you help me with my homework?"

"Sure. What are you working on?"

Just then, a bolt of lightning slashed across the sky, and a second later a clap of thunder exploded, seemingly right over the house. Justin's eyes flew open wide, and he ran to where Will sat on the edge of the bed, threw himself into his arms, and buried his face in Will's chest.

"Whoa, that was a big one, wasn't it?" Will said, holding Justin and gently stroking the boy's thin back.

Trembling, the boy clutched Will tightly.

"Don't worry. I've got you. Everything's going to be all right."

13

. . .

WILL LAY ON HIS BACK STARING at the dancing flecks of light cast on the living room ceiling by the headlights of a passing car. The rain continued to spit against the windows and occasional flickers of lightning sent their stroboscopic flashes through the drizzle. Dinner had been a singularly silent event with little conversation. While Renee cleaned up, he had helped Justin with his homework and then put him to bed. By then, the house was quiet. Renee had gone to bed. Feeling too agitated to sleep and not wanting to disturb her, he'd turned on the television set in the living room to watch the late news, but couldn't focus on any of the stories. Instead, his mind raced over the events of the day. He felt smothered by the demands being placed on him and his family.

After the news, he had flicked the TV off and lay down on the couch, his thoughts racing in the dark. Things had been so much simpler when he was single, living in New York, working for someone else, having to worry only about himself.

In the bedroom, Renee shifted on the bed, rolled over onto

her side, and sighed deeply. She wondered what Will was doing and listened to the far-off rumble of retreating thunder. She closed her eyes and tried to sleep, but found herself wrestling with a sense of growing despair. Will hadn't said a word during dinner, and Justin seemed so withdrawn. What was happening to their family? Why wouldn't Will share what was going on in his life? She knew about the campaign, of course, and she was willing to help, but even that hadn't been discussed tonight. In fact, nothing had been discussed, and when she'd gone to bed, hoping Will would follow, he'd stayed in the living room and ignored her. A tear trickled down her cheek onto the pillow.

Why can't I ever get things in the right order? Will thought. *I found the land for this project and then I thought I needed to see if Ray Spellman and Hunter Hoggard were interested before I spent a lot of time and money getting the actual plan in place. Then I thought I needed to make sure the financing was there before we went any further, and it turns out I needed to have all the plans in place before I did any of those other things. But what if I'd gotten all of the planning done and then I couldn't find the contractors to build it? It's just like trying to reach Gary Carr before I talk to Renee and Justin. But what if I get Gary's permission and then Renee doesn't want me to adopt Justin? She doesn't seem to want anything to do with me right now. And why in the world did I agree to this political thing? I didn't handle that interview very well, and I suppose I need to maintain a good relationship with the media. But I wouldn't even have to worry about that if I hadn't let David talk me into running. That's going to take time, and I need all the time I can get to work on this project because I didn't get everything in place before I began.*

At two o'clock, he tiptoed into the bedroom, undressed in the dark, and slipped quietly into his side of the bed. If Renee was awake, she didn't say anything. His mind continued to argue in circles until he finally dropped off into a troubled sleep.

Early the next morning Will struggled out of bed, showered, and dressed. Renee was still asleep when he kissed her gently on the cheek and headed downtown. He climbed the steps to his office, sat down in his swivel chair, and stared through the window at the town square. The storm had blown itself out, and the community was beginning to come to life. He watched from his vantage point as Mr. Taylor unlocked the door to his jewelry store and walked inside. A young woman in a jogging outfit pushed her baby in a stroller as she circled the park. *None of them even knows I'm watching,* Will thought. *I wonder if that's the way God feels? He watches us run from place to place without our really seeing the big picture. Sometimes I think we're so busy doing things we think are important that we don't do the really essential ones.*

He heard the sound of Enid Cook's feet on the stairs.

"Good morning, Mr. Martin," she said, sticking her head through his open office door.

"Good morning, Miss Cook," he replied.

She nodded her head slightly before looking at Will more

closely. "If you don't mind me saying so, Mr. Martin, you look like death warmed over."

"I'd be offended, but that's kind of the way I feel, too."

"Anything I can help with, Mr. Martin?"

"Just some things I need to work out," he said.

"What kinds of things?" she asked.

Will sighed. "Miss Cook, I'm not sure I'm cut out for this job."

"Whatever makes you say that, Mr. Martin?" She sat down demurely in the chair in front of his desk.

"I'm trying to develop two hundred acres of land," he began.

"I'm aware of that, Mr. Martin."

"Well, it seems I jumped the gun. I've got two contractors onboard and the financing seems to be coming together, but I've neglected to actually get the project planned out. I don't have any of the plat plans, building designs, or really anything down on paper." He tapped the side of his head. "It's all just sort of up here."

She smiled. "Seems like a good place to have it."

"You might think so, but the bank wants documentation, and it's a little hard to run my head through the Xerox machine. I don't even know where to turn for help. I might still have my contacts in New York, but that was the financial end of things, and I don't have a clue who might be able to pull this whole thing together."

"It seems to me you've started putting a pretty good team

together, Mr. Martin. Ray Spellman and Hunter Hoggard are both very respected developers. And, if I'm not mistaken, you've been to see Charles Merrill. There's no one better at designing any kind of project."

Will nodded his head slightly. "You may be right, Miss Cook, but what about getting tenants for the stores? I don't have any idea how you go about that." He sank lower in his chair. "I'm just not sure if I know enough to carry this off."

Enid rose from her chair and walked to the window. "Do you remember the bird nest on the ledge?" She pointed out the window toward the corner of the building.

Will turned in his chair. "Sort of. I was pretty young when that happened."

"I'm guessing you were only seven or eight. Your grand-father watched the birds build that nest, and he brought you here to see it. There wasn't much to anchor it to, and it wasn't a very hospitable place. The janitor wanted to stick his broom out the window and push the nest away, but your grandfather stopped him." She turned to look at Will. "You used to come here every afternoon and watch the birds. They laid eggs that hatched into little naked creatures that finally grew feathers and one day flew off the ledge and down into the square."

"I think I remember."

"When they flew away you were quite excited. Your grand-father pointed out that it didn't matter how difficult it was for the parent birds to build the nest, they had completed the task and now they were reaping the rewards."

Will smiled. "Subtlety has never been your strong suit, Enid. You think I ought to go ahead with the project, don't you?"

"That's entirely your decision, Mr. Martin. But I have learned in this life that there are workers and there are watchers. The watchers like to sit on the sidelines and throw out discouraging and disparaging remarks, but the workers just keep working."

"Thank you, Enid."

"You're quite welcome, Mr. Martin." She started for the door, turned, and said, "That was quite a bombshell you dropped on us yesterday. I had no idea . . . nor did anyone else in the office, I warrant . . . that you were interested in politics."

"That's another part of the problem. I don't have any idea how much time the political race will take. I don't know how much time this project will take, and I don't want to neglect my family. Renee seems as if she's already upset with me, and I don't want to do anything that will cause real problems."

"I understand," Enid said.

"The biggest problem is that I don't even know what I did wrong. It's as if she doesn't trust me."

Enid's eyebrow raised. "Is there any reason she shouldn't?"

"No!" Will said sharply.

"Mr. Martin, I'm going to be pretty blunt. Do you trust her?"

"Of course!"

"Oh, really? Then why don't you try sharing some of these problems with your wife instead of with an old woman who's close to retiring?" Her face flushed slightly. "I really shouldn't have said that, Mr. Martin. Please forgive me."

Will rubbed his forehead. "No, Enid, you have nothing to be forgiven for. I guess it's just that I've always tried to work things out myself. I've trusted some people in the past who have let me down."

"At the risk of being rude, may I say that you'll find life much easier to live if you trust people and have a few of them betray you, than to distrust everyone and take glee in the occasional person who fulfills your expectation."

"You're probably right, Enid."

She answered smugly, "Yes, I think I probably am." She was standing in the doorway of Will's office. "Have a nice day, Mr. Martin. Oh, by the way, have you had any success locating Gary Carr?"

Will shook his head. "I haven't really had much time to work on it."

"And have you talked to your wife about your plans?"

"Not yet."

"I see," she said primly. "Well, do have a nice day." She stepped out of the office and closed the door behind her.

Will stared after her a moment, then swiveled in his chair and looked out the window. His mind swirling with decisions that had to be made, he closed his eyes and leaned back in his chair. Five minutes later the phone rang.

"Martin Real Estate, Will speaking," he said into the receiver.

"Will, this is Hal Jenkins at the bank. Have you made a decision yet? I'm not trying to pressure you, but I do need to get back to Fairbourne if we're going ahead with the project."

Will took a deep breath. "We're going ahead," he said, looking at the empty ledge outside the window. "I'll be assembling a team to work out the details as quickly as possible."

"Good, good! I'm glad to hear you've reached that decision. I'll let Fairbourne know we'll get them the necessary documents. It's going to be a great development, Will."

"Thanks for your vote of confidence, Hal. I'm going to turn the financing over to you completely. Just keep me apprised of any problems."

"Let me know when your design team is in place. I'd like to be part of it, if you don't mind."

"I'm counting on you," Will said. "Thanks again for your support." He hung up the phone and felt a weight lift from his shoulders. The first decision of the day had been made.

14

• • •

HUNTER HOGGARD TOOK another bite of his cheese-burger and spoke with his mouth full. "So, you want me to go over to Charles Merrill's place and give them an idea on the kinds of houses we want to build?"

"That's right," Will said. "I've given Charles a general idea of what we need built, but you're much more experienced than I am when it comes to building homes. I think you have the vision of what ought to be built. I trust you to get it done and done right."

Hoggard wiped his mouth with a paper napkin. "What about Spellman? How's he going to feel about this?" He took a sip from his cup of coffee. "Me and him don't always see eye to eye, if you know what I mean."

"I'm meeting with him later today. I'm going to ask him to help design and build the commercial buildings. It will be a little hard because we don't know exactly who our tenants are going to be. But I think he has a pretty good idea of what is needed for a kind of generic building."

"Me and him have to get together to agree on things?"

Will took a sip of lemonade. "Occasionally we'll have planning meetings with all of the design team. Other than that, you're on your own. Are you okay with that?"

Hoggard shrugged his shoulders. "Sure. As long as me and Ray don't have to duke things out." He slid out of the booth pulling his jacket from the seat beside him. "Thanks for lunch."

"You're welcome." Will extended his hand to the older man. "You're a good builder, Hunter. I know you won't let me down."

"I'll try not to, Will. This'll be my last project before I retire. I'd like it to kinda be my legacy." The corners of his mouth turned up slightly in the bulldog jowls of his face. "Incidentally, did you get that letter I sent over . . . Gary Carr's?"

"Yes. I appreciate that, Hunter. Although I must admit it only confused the issue."

"Sorry about that. Anything else I can do to help, let me know."

Will watched Hunter Hoggard walk out of the café. He sat alone at the booth until the waitress brought their check. *I hope I'm doing the right thing.*

Two hours later he was sitting in Ray Spellman's office. "Ray, if I just turn the whole commercial project over to you, will you be able to handle it?"

Spellman sat behind his hand-rubbed oak desk. His fingers were tented together in front of him. "What do you mean, 'turn it over'? How will we make sure that what I'm doing is what you want done?"

Will leaned forward in his chair. "You know the general plan, Ray. We'll have periodic meetings to go over the whole plan, but you know a lot better than I how to build a building. We've got Charles Merrill designing the store fronts and giving us an idea for the whole concept of Martin's Glen, but most of that seems to be window dressing. I'm sure you can design fairly generic building spaces, can't you?"

"It depends. If what we're building is a restaurant, it has a very different layout from, say, a retail store."

Will smiled. "I see what you mean. I'm trying to find a firm to help locate tenants. Whoever they are, I'd like you to work with them as you design the buildings."

Spellman nodded his head. "It sounds as if you've thought this through pretty well. Of course, I'd be happy to work on the project. I told you that the other day when we first met, but there is one small problem we might run into."

"Oh, what's that?"

"Candidly, it's Hunter Hoggard. The two of us have never seen eye to eye. He's never had a good word to say about me, although I've tried to be a little more circumspect about him. I'm not sure if the two of us can work together."

"I understand," Will said quietly, "but I don't think it will be much of a problem. Although you're both working on the same project, he's building houses and you're building offices. Except for our team meetings, I suspect you'll never have to work with each other."

"If you say so."

"Ray, you're the best commercial builder in the state. I trust you to get this job done."

"I won't betray your trust. You can count on me."

"I knew I could," Will replied. "Now, I should mention that we're on a pretty tight schedule. Hal Jenkins needs to have plat plans and the design of the buildings, both yours and Hunter's, by October."

"You're kidding."

"I wish I were, but that's what the money people say."

Spellman stood and clasped his hands behind his back. "Ordinarily I'd say it can't be done, but after working with Martin Real Estate all of these years, I'm sure we'll be able to pull it off." He clasped Will's hand and led him to the door of his office.

Half an hour later Will pulled into his parking place at Martin Real Estate and climbed the stairs to his office.

"David Jobb's been trying to reach you," his secretary said, handing him a note.

"Thanks, Janice. Did he say what it was about?"

She shook her head. "Not really. He just said to have you call him as soon as you came in."

Will nodded his head. "Okay." He went into his office and sat down at the phone and a minute later was talking to David Jobb.

"Will, have you seen this morning's *Examiner*?"

"No, I haven't. I left home before it was delivered. Why?"

"If you have a few minutes, why don't you come over to my office."

"I'll be right there," Will replied. He left his office and said to his secretary, "I'll be over at David Jobb's if you need me." He made his way quickly across the town square and walked into his lawyer's office. David Jobb stood in the front office, waiting for him, newspaper in hand.

"What did you say to that reporter?" David asked nervously.

"Not much. He started asking questions, and I realized I wasn't sure where I stood on a number of issues. I just tried to be noncommittal. Why?"

Jobb spread the newspaper on his desk. "Well, they printed your press release, pretty much the way we wrote it. That's the good news. The bad news is this article on the opposite page." David pointed at the headline, "Martin Noncommittal on Abortion."

"What!" Quickly he read the article.

"What did you say, Will?"

"Nothing! He asked me about abortion, and I told him I'd never had one. I was just trying to be a little funny."

"Oh, great. Well, Lloyd Randell's reputation isn't that great as an investigative reporter, but he's one of the forces we'll have to reckon with. I'll try to take care of this." He pointed to the article again. "But I ought to give you some advice, if you want it."

Will sat down heavily in a leather chair. "Fire away."

"Let me screen your interviews. I know who's a friend and who isn't. Okay?"

Will nodded his head. "Okay."

"Next, now that you've announced your candidacy you'll start getting a lot of questionnaires from various groups. My advice to you is to throw them away. The only ones you might want to answer are the ones from the newspaper, but avoid the others."

"Why? Shouldn't the voters know how I stand?"

"Of course, but most of these questionnaires have questions like 'Have you stopped beating your wife?' Either way you answer it you're in trouble. Understand?"

"You're kidding me."

"I wish I were, Will." David opened the drawer of his file cabinet and removed a folder. "This is a collection that I kept from Creighton Barrow's last election." He opened the folder and handed Will the top sheet of paper. "Take a look at that first question and tell me how you'd answer it."

Will looked at the question. "'Do you believe in censorship?'" He looked at David Jobb. "I guess it depends. There ought to be freedom of the press, but we ought to screen materials that are likely to fall into the hands of children."

"That isn't one of the choices, Will. You have to answer either 'yes' or 'no,' and there's no room for an explanation. Answer it 'yes' and you'll have the ACLU going after you. Answer it 'no' and you'll have the children's advocacy groups on your case. That's the problem with these questionnaires." He handed him another sheet. "How about that one?"

Will read the question. " 'Seventy-three percent of all children wounded by an accidental gunshots die. Do you support restricting guns in homes?' Is that accurate?"

David answered, "I have no idea. The problem is the way the question is asked, it almost forces you to answer the way the group who sent you the questionnaire wants you to answer, or you sound like a complete idiot."

"I'm starting to understand. Maybe I am a complete idiot."

"I doubt that, Will. If you feel you need to answer one, please let me talk it through with you. I used to do that with Creighton all the time."

"Anything else?"

David shook his head. "That will do for now. But I do feel some urgency in getting together with you and your wife to decide on our strategy for the election. When would be a good time?"

Will thought for a moment. "I'd better talk to Renee and get back to you."

"That will be fine. Oh, incidentally, Creighton would like to meet with you when you have a few minutes."

"I'd like that," Will said.

"I'll set it up then. Is there some time that would be better for you?"

"I can slip away for a few minutes almost anytime during the day."

"Good. I'll make the arrangements. Now, Will, is there anything I can do for you?"

"David, I think you're doing more than I could hope for. Thank you for being a good friend."

The attorney smiled. "You're welcome. Please understand, Will, I'm not trying to tell you how to run your campaign. I just want to be of help."

"And you are. More help than you know. I just wish I had someone to help me with this building project we're doing."

David ran his hand over his head. "I didn't know you were contemplating a major project, Will. Tell me about it."

Will described the two hundred acres he had located on the outskirts of town and how he had brought Hunter Hoggard and Ray Spellman together to do the construction.

"You have those two working together? You must be a miracle worker."

Will went on to describe the funding package that Hal Jenkins was putting together and the design team with Charles Merrill.

"It sounds as if you have it pretty well in hand. What is it that you're missing?"

Will scratched his head. "I don't know anyone who can locate tenants to occupy the buildings. I guess I just thought that we'd build it and people would be clamoring to get in."

" 'Build it and they will come?' " Jobb said with a smile. "You know, that might be another reason for you to meet with Creighton. He's been involved in bringing quite a few companies into the state. He might be able to help you."

"I'm even more excited to meet him," Will said as he walked out of David's office.

15

• • •

THE JAGUAR PURRED INTO THE driveway and Will saw Justin in the backyard, throwing the baseball onto the roof of the garage. The boy waved and trotted toward the car.

"Can we practice baseball?" he asked.

Will glanced at his watch, "Just give me a minute to change clothes." He hurried into the house. His grandmother was sitting in the rocking chair in the living room, dozing. Will tiptoed up the stairs to his bedroom and changed into his grubbies.

Ten minutes later the two of them were playing catch. Will tossed some ground balls across the lawn, and Justin struggled to pick them up with the mitt. Patiently Will showed him how to back up the mitt with the fingers of his other hand. Soon Justin was fielding most of the balls Will threw his way.

"Where's your mom?" Will asked.

"Over at her studio."

"How come? I didn't think she had lessons this late."

"Andrea," he said, barely disguising his disgust.

"Problems?"

Justin shrugged his shoulders and threw the ball to Will. "Her mom and dad are getting a divorce." Will grounded the ball back to Justin. "Just like my mom and dad," the boy said quietly.

Will walked over to Justin, took his hand, and led him to the garden swing. The two of them sat quietly swinging for several minutes. Finally Justin said, "Why did my mom and dad get divorced?"

Will thought carefully about what to say. "I'm not sure, Justin. Sometimes people who were once in love kind of fall out of love. Does that make sense?"

Justin pulled his feet up onto the swing and stared at his toes. "What did I do to make them fall out of love?"

Will reached over and pulled Justin next to him. With his arm around his shoulders he said, "You didn't do anything, Justin. Sometimes adults get so tied up with things other than their families that they just drift apart. I'm not sure why your dad went away, but I think it was because he wanted to earn more money to take better care of you and your mom."

"I'd rather have a dad than money," Justin said simply. He snuggled against Will. "When are you going to go away, Will?"

Will stiffened. "I'm not going away, Justin. Like it or not, I'm here to stay."

Just then Renee's old Chevrolet pulled into the driveway, and she got out. She shaded her eyes with her hand until she saw Will and Justin in the swing. She crossed the lawn to where they sat.

"What are you two up to?" she asked.

"Taking a little break," Will answered. "We've been playing catch."

"Hi, sweetheart," she said to Justin.

"Hi, Mom." He slipped out from under Will's arm and hugged his mother.

"I sure appreciate your grandmother . . . ," she looked at Justin, " . . . dropping by," she said.

"She's still in the house, sleeping," Will said. "I didn't have the heart to wake her. Why don't we see if she'd like to join us for dinner."

The three of them walked into the house. Ruth Martin was still sleeping in the rocking chair but awoke when Will put his hand on her shoulder.

"Oh, hello, dear," she said to Will. "I was just resting my eyes for a minute."

"Grams, how would you like to go to dinner with us?" Will asked.

"It depends," Ruth answered.

"Depends on what?" asked Justin.

"On where we're going to go. And whether they let old ladies in," she said with a smile. "Of course, I'd love to go with you."

After Renee had changed her clothes, the four of them walked to Will's car. "Why don't you ride in the front seat, Mrs. Martin," said Renee. "It's easier for me to get into the backseat."

"How thoughtful, Renee. But the name is Ruth, remember?"

"I know, but it's hard. When I worked for your husband, I got in the habit, and it's been hard to break."

"Many habits are, dear."

An hour later they left the restaurant and drove Ruth to her home. Will opened the car door for his grandmother and walked with her up to the house. She searched in her purse for a key, finally located it, and opened the front door.

"Thank you, dear, for such a lovely dinner."

"You're welcome, Grams."

"Well, hurry back to your family." She started to close the door, then stopped and said, "Will, it would be such a blessing if you'd adopt that wonderful little boy."

"I know, Grams. I'm working on it."

Will chauffeured Renee and Justin home in silence. Once inside, Justin hurried to get ready for bed. After brushing his teeth, he ran back to the living room and gave Will a hug before scurrying off to his bedroom. Renee loaded a batch of clothes into the washing machine while Will went to the living room and opened the newspaper. He turned to the article by Lloyd Randell and reread it. He was still thinking about it when Renee walked into the room and sat down next to him on the couch.

"Did you see this?" he asked, handing her the newspaper.

She nodded her head.

"What do you think?"

"I'm not sure what to think. I don't think the article says much, but the headline . . ."

"Yeah, I know what you mean. I talked to David Jobb today, and he gave me some good advice. I've got a pretty steep learning curve on politics, I think."

"I suppose."

"He wanted to know when the three of us could get together to outline a campaign strategy. He wants to do it soon."

Renee chewed on her bottom lip. "Are you sure you want my input on this, Will? You and David seem to be doing pretty well all by yourselves." *And you don't seem to want to let me in on what's going on in your life,* she thought.

"If that's what you want. I know you said you didn't want to be involved . . . but I . . . oh, never mind." *At least you could show some interest in the campaign.*

"I'm tired, I think I'll go to bed," Renee said. *You could come, too, Will, and we could talk. What's wrong with us? With me? Why don't we talk anymore? This is just what happened with Gary . . . he kept everything inside.*

"I'll be there soon," he said. He kissed her on the cheek. *I'd sure like to talk, the way we used to. What's wrong with us? I'm just being selfish, she needs to get her rest.* She got up and went out of the room. Will flipped on the television set and sank back into the couch. He dozed off and awakened to the sound of the news.

"Mystery surrounds the decision of longtime legislator, Creighton Barrow, not to run for reelection. Having served for the past four years as majority leader, it was assumed he would seek the seat of Speaker of the House, now that the present speaker, Lyle Warburton, has decided to run for the Senate.

Representative Barrow refuses to comment on his decision, other than to say it is for 'personal reasons.'

"Well-known political activist, Milton Phillips, and a new face on the political scene, Will Martin, have filed for the seat.

"Now, in late breaking news, a traffic rollover on the Interstate has taken the life of one man and another, critically injured, has been life-flighted to . . ."

Will pushed the remote control and turned off the set, then brushed his teeth and prepared for bed. Renee had left the lamp on his side of the bed on. She was lying on her side with her back to him when he slipped wearily between the sheets, reached over, and extinguished the light. He rolled onto his back and stared again at the ceiling. His mind raced over the events of the day. The Martin's Glen project seemed to be getting under way. He was excited about meeting with Creighton Barrow and possibly solving another of the Martin's Glen problems. He was excited, too, to draw on the rich political experience of the seasoned politician. *I wish Renee were more excited about this election. I really do value her ideas, but she seems so withdrawn.*

He thought of Justin sleeping in the room next to theirs. The little boy had seemed so frightened, so worried that Will would leave as Gary had. Justin was so vulnerable, and Will's heart ached for the little guy, who by now had become such a big part of his life. *I wonder how he'd respond if I asked if he'd like me to adopt him? Tomorrow I've got to spend some time trying to locate Gary Carr.*

16

• • •

"CREIGHTON HAS AGREED TO see us at three o'clock," David Jobb said over the phone. "Does that work for you?"

Will checked his planner. "That will be fine. I have a one o'clock appointment, but I'm sure we'll be through well before three. Would you like me to pick you up?"

"No, no. Is your appointment at your office?"

"Actually I'm meeting with Gordon Burningham and his lawyer to finalize the purchase of that two hundred acres I mentioned. We're going to meet at the site so they can point out the property lines. I don't suppose you know where that property is?"

"I'm quite familiar with it," replied the lawyer. "Your grandfather tried to purchase that parcel about twenty years ago, but the Burninghams weren't willing to sell."

"Well, things change, I guess, although they want a pretty penny for the land. Anyway, that's where I'll be, but it's only fifteen minutes back to the office."

"Do you need me to go with you? Will you need legal counsel?"

"Eventually I'll need your help, but this time I'm just taking a look at the property and picking up some papers."

"I'll meet you about two-thirty, then, in front of your office. See you this afternoon."

Will hung up the phone, slid open the lower drawer of his desk, and removed an empty manila folder. He wrote the name 'Gary Carr' on the tab, then inserted the ETC letterhead he'd received from Hunter Hoggard into it. He searched through a stack of notes on the corner of his desk until he found the information from Jean Louis DuLac in Paris, and dropped that into the folder as well. Will closed the file and drummed his fingers on top of it. *Where do I go for more information?*

There was a rap on the door, and Enid Cook opened it. "Mr. Martin, will you be here this afternoon to go over the first quarter report?"

"Actually, Miss Cook, I have a one o'clock appointment with Gordon Burningham, then I'm going to see Creighton Barrow with David Jobb. I don't know if I'll be back at all after lunch. Maybe tomorrow?"

"Very well, Mr. Martin." She started to close the door.

"Miss Cook, would you come in for a minute? I need to ask you something."

"Of course, Mr. Martin." She closed the door behind her and seated herself stiffly on the chair across from his desk. "How may I help you?"

"You know I'm looking for Gary Carr. Do you have any idea who might know where he is?"

Enid Cook pushed her reading glasses up to the bridge of her nose. "Well, he's not from around here . . . but I suppose you know that. He moved to town probably less than two years before he and Renee married. I'm trying to remember where he came from . . . Arizona, I think . . . or maybe New Mexico. I'm afraid I'm not much help."

"You attended the wedding, didn't you?"

"Oh, the whole office did. Your grandfather closed up for the day, and we all went to the wedding." Enid smiled slightly. "It was a lovely affair." Enid looked at Will Martin and her eyebrows raised. "Of course I'm sure it wasn't nearly as lovely as your wedding, Mr. Martin."

"Please, Miss Cook, don't worry about offending me. I'm just trying to gather some information on Gary. Were his parents at the wedding?"

Thoughtfully she tapped her finger against her chin. "I'm trying to remember." Her forehead furrowed and she pursed her lips. "No, I don't think so. I think it was just Gary and Renee and the maid of honor and the best man." She closed her eyes and thought before answering. "Yes, it was just the four of them. I remember thinking how tragic it was that neither the bride nor the groom had parents there beside them."

"Well, Renee lost her parents at a comparatively early age. Of course she likes to say she was the child of their old age. Still, sixty is pretty young to go," Will mused.

"Yes, it is," Enid replied, "especially when you're my age. Sixty seems very young. Cancer is a terrible thing."

Will nodded his head. "Yes, it can be. Do you remember who the best man was?"

Enid touched her upper lip. "I'm sorry, but I really can't remember who it was. I don't think he was from here in town . . . probably an old college friend."

"Could it have been his brother?" Will persisted.

Enid closed her eyes and rubbed the bridge of her nose. "No, I don't think so. There wasn't much resemblance between the two. I think he was just a college friend."

"You don't happen to know which college he attended, do you?"

"I'm afraid I don't. Mr. Martin, if you don't mind me saying so, you ought to ask your wife. She'd know all of these details, and she probably knows where to reach Gary Carr."

"I can't, Enid, I just can't."

"Why not, Mr. Martin?"

"She'll want to know why, and until I get Gary's permission for the adoption, I don't want to answer that question. She and Justin have been disappointed before, and I don't want to hurt them anymore."

Enid rose from the chair and stood to her full height. "Mr. Martin, do you have so little faith in your wife?" She strode to the door. "With all due respect, Mr. Martin, you're a slow learner." She pulled the door firmly shut behind her.

Will stared at the closed door, digesting what Enid Cook

had said, then turned around in his chair and looked out the window toward the square. A week before the maples had barely been covered with a green velvet, but now they were in full leaf. It was warm enough that people were strolling through the park without coats, others were going in and out of the storefronts that bordered the square. Half an hour passed as he thought about avenues that might help him find the missing Gary Carr. *There's got to be a clue somewhere. There's something I'm missing.*

He glanced at his watch and realized that he needed to quickly gather his documents and head to the Burningham property. Will pulled the manila job folder from the desk drawer and dropped it on top of his desk, then put on his blazer before picking up the folder, along with the one beneath it, and walked through the front office.

"I'm headed out to the Burningham property," he said to his secretary. "I'll have my cell phone if you need me. I probably won't be back for the rest of the afternoon."

"Very good, Mr. Martin," Janice Harr said.

Will threw the folders onto the passenger seat of the Jaguar, removed his blazer, and laid it on top of them before getting into the driver's seat. Fifteen minutes later he turned onto the lane that formed the south border of the property he was trying to acquire. An old truck and a new Toyota were already there and four men stood near the front of the bright red Celica. Will parked behind them, retrieved his blazer and the files, and walked to where the four men were standing.

"Will Martin, right on time, I see," said Gordon Burningham. He ran his hand through his sparse white hair. "Let me introduce you. This is my lawyer, Stephen Chipman; my neighbor, Wendell Sweeten; and our computer man, Les Jardine." Will shook hands with each of them, then said, "It's a pleasure, gentlemen. I think this is going to be a wonderful project."

Wendell Sweeten cleared his throat. "I hope so. I'm not so sure I want to have all that development so close to my home."

Will sensed the man's apprehension. "Where is your home, Mr. Sweeten?"

The old man pointed to the west. "Over there, about four miles. You can't quite see it from here, but if you drive down to where the road makes a turn, it's right ahead of you."

Gordon Burningham interrupted, "That's why it took me so long to agree to sell, Wendell. I didn't want a whole lot of folks livin' so close. But after my heart attack, I realized the farm was more than I could handle by myself and neither of my two boys show any interest. One of them's a civil engineer down in Phoenix, and the other one's a teacher in Boise." He gazed across the land. "Once my wife died, I knew I couldn't farm this whole piece." He pulled a handkerchief from his back pocket and blew his nose loudly. "Thought I might as well sell and give the kids their inheritance."

Stephen Chipman clapped the old man on his shoulder. "Oh, I think you're doing the right thing, Gordon. This land has sat unused for nearly six years now. I've dealt with Will's family and with Martin Real Estate for nearly a quarter of a century. They're honest and fair." He snapped open his briefcase and placed it on the sloping hood of the Celica. "I've drawn up the bill of sale and attached the description of the land and all of the other necessary documents. I'm sure you'll want your attorney to look at them before you sign." He smiled at Will, then turned to Gordon Burningham. "If we were dealing with Will's grandfather, we'd probably just shake hands and worry about the details later." He chuckled. "But in today's world I suppose we need to have all the paperwork finished."

"I suppose," said Will. He looked at the weed-covered property in front of him. "Now, part of the reason for coming to the site was so that someone could show me where the actual property lines run."

The lawyer spoke, "That's why I've brought Les. He's put the whole thing into his computer."

The young man pulled a rolled up set of papers from inside a cardboard tube and spread them out on the top of the car. The map showed the legal description of the property, but Jardine had drawn recognizable landmarks on the paper. A line of cottonwoods that could be seen across the field was drawn in. Similarly, an irrigation ditch that ran in front of them had been noted on the plan. The young man ran his finger along the map. "This is that ditch," he said, pointing toward the ground. "If you want, we can walk the property lines. I've been out here and checked them against the county description with my GPS. I'm pretty familiar with the whole piece of ground."

"GPS?" Will said.

"Global Positioning Satellite," Jardine replied. It tells where you are within a half an inch. But we can walk the property if you'd like."

"Ain't no need for that," Gordon Burningham said. "See that old dead cottonwood?" He pointed to the northwest, and Will nodded his head. "That's about where that corner is . . . maybe forty feet further north. Then, if you follow this ditch to the east, you'll see where there's a head gate and another irrigation ditch running due north. That's the east side of the property."

Jardine touched Will's arm. "That's a pretty good description," he said to Gordon Burningham, then whispered to Will, "Maybe we could come back another time and I'll show you where they really are."

Will nodded his head. "I appreciate all of you coming. This gives me a much better picture of what needs to be done. I'll take these papers back to my attorney—in fact, I'm meeting with him later this afternoon. Then we'll get our design to the city planner so we can get approval for the project."

"You ain't in the city, Mr. Martin," Gordon Burningham said. "You're in the county. The city line's back there about four roads." He pointed back down the road toward the city.

The attorney interjected, "That's probably in your favor,

Will. I don't think they're nearly as picky as the city is over little details."

"Good to know," Will said with a smile. He took the documents, opened the manila folder he'd brought and placed them inside. He tapped the bottom of the folder on the hood of the Celica and the second folder beneath it, the one with Gary Carr's name on it, slipped out of his fingers and skittered down the hood. Les Jardine's hand shot out and he caught it before it hit the ground. The ETC letterhead slid out of the folder.

Les Jardine picked up the piece of paper. "EuroTeleCom," he said. "One of the big boys." He handed the folder to Will, then, as he started to hand him the letterhead he stopped, pulled it back, and inspected it closely. "Pretty good forgery," he said, handing the paper to Will.

"What? What's a forgery?"

"That ETC letterhead. Looks like somebody scanned their letterhead so they could write letters on it. They did a pretty good job, but if you look at the logo you can see some dithering around the edges. Still, pretty good work."

Will stared at the paper.

"Is something wrong?" Stephen Chipman asked.

Will slipped the letterhead back into the manila folder. "Maybe. I don't know, really."

"Well, if I can be of any further help . . ." Chipman shook Will's hand.

"Thank you. All of you." Will shook the two old farmers'

hands. Then he held onto Les Jardine's hand as he walked him around the car. "I'd like to take you up on your offer to come back here. Would you give me a call?" Will let go of the young man's hand, slipped one of his business cards out of his pocket, and handed it to him. "Maybe tomorrow?"

"Sure," Jardine said. "I'll call you tomorrow as soon as I get up, around ten or eleven."

Will walked back to the Jaguar, waved to the other men, slid into the front seat, and headed back to his meeting with David Jobb.

17

· · ·

THE ATTORNEY WAS WAITING in his Lincoln as Will pulled up in front of Martin Real Estate. Will parked the Jaguar and walked over to where David Jobb sat idling at the curb. "Sorry to be late."

"Actually, you're a few minutes early. I just finished an appointment and it seemed fruitless to go back to the office. I've just been listening to the news. Milton Phillips has started his campaign."

Will sat down in the passenger seat. "What has he done?"

"Oh, not much," David looked over his shoulder and pulled out of the parking place. "He's just held a press conference and explained that he's experienced and his opponent is a young, untutored, ambitious, political novice." He glanced quickly at Will. "I think those are all the adjectives he used."

Will smiled. "Probably pretty accurate . . . except for the ambitious part." He settled into the seat. "Does it worry you, David?"

"Not really, at least not yet. It's still nearly seven months until the election, and we'll hear a lot more from Milton. I'm just surprised he's starting so early. He must be worried."

"Do we need to respond?" Will asked as they made their way through town.

David Jobb shook his head. "No, I don't think so. But we do need to get together and decide exactly what your campaign strategy is going to be. And I suspect we'd better do that soon. Did you have a chance to talk to your wife about the campaign?"

Will nodded. "I did, but I don't think she's very interested in helping with it." He sighed. "But you're right. We need to figure out what we're going to do."

David turned a corner and eased the Lincoln down the street. "Perhaps after we talk with Creighton we'll have some better ideas."

"I hope so." Will looked out the side window of the car at the mansions they were passing. "This is a pretty swanky part of town," he commented.

"I suppose it is," the attorney replied. "Yet, I think you'll find Creighton Barrow to be a very down-to-earth, ordinary man." He pulled up into an expansive circular driveway in front of one of the impressive homes and stopped the car. "Perhaps I ought to warn you, Will. Creighton has gone downhill quickly since his last public appearance. He's often quite jaundiced, and he's sensitive about it. I guess what I'm trying to say is that you shouldn't be surprised at the way he looks."

"I understand," Will said as David Jobb reached out and rang the doorbell. A few moments later the door was opened by a petite, white-haired woman, wearing a flowered skirt and cream-colored blouse. She smiled when she saw David Jobb.

"David, how good to see you," she said, presenting her cheek for a kiss.

"Louise, what a pleasure," he said, pecking her on the cheek. "This is my good friend and our newest candidate, Will Martin."

Louise Barrow extended her hand. Will noticed the almost transparent skin and prominent liver spots as he took the hand gently in his. "You're the grandson of Warren Martin, aren't you? He was such a gentleman and such a wealth of information to Creighton. We thought the world of him." She smiled at Will.

"Thank you," Will said. "I thought the world of him, too."

"Well, please come in." She turned back into the house. "Creigh is waiting for you. He's in his study." She led them across the foyer. Will noticed the Persian rug spread over the oak hardwood floor and the wall hangings from around the world. Louise opened the door to a small, elegantly decorated room. "I'll leave you boys alone," she said with a smile.

David Jobb led Will into the room. Creighton Barrow sat in an upholstered chair in one corner of the room. The walls behind him were lined with bookshelves from floor to ceiling. The single window in the room was draped with forest green velvet drapes fringed in gold. A table lamp on an end table next to Barrow's chair provided the only light in the room.

"David, my old friend," Creighton Barrow said in a mellifluous voice.

David Jobb walked quickly to where the man sat and extended his hand. Will followed close behind. "Creighton, this is Will Martin, the young man I've told you so much about."

"Warren Martin's boy. Yes, I can see the resemblance."

"Actually, I'm his grandson," Will said as he took the older man's hand.

"Of course, of course, your father was Samuel." He waved toward a couch across from his chair. "Please, have a seat."

Will could not help but notice the yellow tint to the man's skin and that Creighton Barrow had not stood up from his chair. *I wonder just how sick he is?*

"Now, what can I do for you?"

David Jobb leaned forward. "Creighton, I worked on your campaigns with you for years, and I've come to respect your political acumen. You had a background in city politics before you ran for the House, but Will lacks all of that. I'm not quite sure how to help him with his campaign." He stopped for a moment. "I'm just pleased you agreed to spend some time with him and perhaps give him the benefit of your counsel."

Barrow laughed. "You sound like a lawyer, David." He turned his attention to Will. "Why are you running for this office?" he asked.

Will stammered, "I guess because David talked me into it."

"Wrong answer," Creighton said forcefully. "First, you don't guess. Second, you need a better answer for why you're running." He thumped his hand on the armrest of the chair. "Understand?"

"I guess—I mean, yes sir." Will felt like a schoolboy being lectured by the principal.

"Good. Now, why are you running for office? We'd better figure that out. Do you have an ax to grind?"

Will shook his head. "No, sir." He felt uncomfortable under the unflinching stare of Creighton Barrow.

"What about any particular problem you see with society that you'd like to change?"

Again Will shook his head. "I just want to serve the people."

The old man barked a laugh. "In what way?" He coughed into a handkerchief in his left hand. "How are you going to serve them?"

David Jobb interjected, "In my conversation with Will, he's expressed a concern about growth."

"Growth? If we don't have any growth, we can't sustain the economy. What's your point?"

Will shifted uncomfortably on the couch, "With more people, you've got to have more roads and more schools," he offered.

"Now you're starting to sound as if you know something," the old man said. "Don't be put off by my questioning. I'm just trying to get you to understand that you have to have some reason for being there. Unless, of course, you're doing it for the glory." He laughed again. "Because, son, there isn't a lot of glory in this job." He coughed into the handkerchief. "Mr. Martin, you're going to be all right. But we've got to develop a reason for you to be elected or that weasel, Milton Phillips, is going to slither right into office."

"He's started his attack," David Jobb said quietly. "He held a press conference today and—"

"And started to tell the world why he's so great and Will, here, is a nobody. Right?"

"I think you know him pretty well," David said.

A slight grimace crossed Barrow's face. "Will, my boy, you've got to get some name recognition, especially in the outlying areas of the district. So, you either buy some newspaper ads, which cost quite a bit, or you put up some lawn signs, or you hold press conferences. Milton Phillips will hold press conferences on a regular basis, I suspect, and he'll rarely mention you by name, because that would give you some name recognition. You'll become 'my esteemed opponent,' or 'my challenger,' but never 'Will Martin' unless he's forced into it." He rubbed his chin with his hand, "The problem is that it is so long until the election that you've got to pace yourself so that the people know who you are just before they go to the polls."

"Seven months from now," Jobb interrupted.

"Yes, seven months from now." The old man rubbed his

chin again, "You know, I wouldn't be too worried about doing anything for at least five months. Oh, you can gather some campaign funds, and get your handouts printed, and so forth, but I don't think you need to do much else."

"Is that really wise?" Jobb asked.

"People have very short memories, David, and I think we ought to focus on the last sixty days before the election." He chuckled. "Besides, it will drive Phillips nuts because we're not responding to his barbs. That's how he works, you know—he tries to get you to lose your composure and attack him and then he comes off looking like a martyr and makes you look like a mudslinger. Don't get into that kind of a fight with him, or you'll lose."

Will nodded his head. "I'm not much of a mudslinger."

"David, would you get that folder for me, please?" Barrow pointed toward a thick folder that lay on top of the desk.

"Of course." David stood up from the couch, picked up the folder, and handed it to the silver-haired politician.

Barrow flipped open the file. "You asked me about my advice on flyers and such." He withdrew a brochure from the folder. "This is one I used eight years ago. If you put Will's picture on the back instead of mine, you can just have it duplicated. It deals with the issue of growth." David Jobb took the brochure from Barrow, walked across the room, and handed it to Will. He sat back down on the couch and went through the brochure with Will.

"Good stuff, Creighton," the attorney said. "I think you're right. The issues haven't changed and this is well thought out."

"Thank you, feel free to use it." He lifted the folder toward the two men on the couch. "There's more stuff in here that I've used over the years. There are designs for posters, lawn signs, newspaper ads . . . you name it. It's yours."

David Jobb walked back across the room and took the folder. "Thank you, Creighton."

"You're welcome. Now is there anything else I can do for you?"

Will cleared his throat. "There is one thing that doesn't have a thing to do with politics. I'm developing a mixed-use project on the Burningham property, and I'm looking for an outfit to help me entice some businesses to locate there. David thought you might have some ideas or contacts."

"Gordon Burningham's place? How much of it?"

"Two hundred acres," Will replied.

"Not big enough for much of a commercial development. You're probably looking for a food store and some small businesses for a strip mall." He closed his eyes and covered them with his right hand. "Have you got utilities on that property?"

"Water, sewer, gas all run up the road on the south side," Will replied.

"What about the road? You can't put very many cars on those back country lanes. You're going to have to get one of those roads widened to handle the traffic, and that is politics."

He uncovered his eyes and looked at Will. "That's in the county, isn't it?"

Will nodded his head. "Yes. I guess I hadn't worried about the road."

Creighton Barrow sank back into his chair. "I've worked with the LaPoint Group in the past. They do a good job of matching businesses to market. I could make an appointment for you."

"I'd appreciate that," Will said.

"No problem," Barrow chuffed. "Have you got a scale model of the project?"

"Not yet," Will replied.

"Plat plan? Building design?"

"We're working on it," Will said uncomfortably.

"What do you have?" the old man asked.

"I met with Mr. Burningham and his lawyer today to finalize the purchase of the land."

"Sounds as if you have a whole bunch to do before you're ready to meet with the LaPoint Group."

"Probably," Will said, "but I'm kind of the new kid on the block, and I'm not sure what to do next . . . or even what order to do them in."

"Well, let me give LaPoint a call. Maybe they can act as an advisor to you while you try to put all of this together." He coughed again.

"I'd appreciate that," Will replied. "Would you like me to call you, or—"

"No, no. I'll have someone from LaPoint call you. You're at Martin Real Estate, I presume." He laid his head back against the chair and closed his eyes. "You'll be hearing from them."

David Jobb took Will's elbow. "Well, Creighton, we've taken too much of your time. Thank you for this," he waved the folder, "and for the advice."

"Nonsense, no problem at all."

"We can let ourselves out," David said.

Creighton Barrow opened his eyes and stared at Will. "If there's anything I can do to help you with your campaign, you call. We can't let this seat go to Milton Phillips. There are too many zealots in the House right now." He closed his eyes again.

David Jobb led Will out of the library. Louise Barrow heard them and came out of the living room. "Leaving so soon?" she said with a smile.

"Yes," David said, "I think we've worn Creighton out."

Her face became serious. "Unfortunately, that doesn't take much anymore." She turned to Will. "It has been a pleasure to meet you, young man. Best of luck in your campaign. We need more good men in office." She opened the front door to let them out.

"How sick is he, Louise?" David asked.

Tears came unbidden to her eyes. "He doesn't want anyone to know, David. But if you're going to ask him for help, I'd do it soon." She struggled to smile. "I blame myself, you know. I should have taken better care of him."

David patted her hand. "Now, Louise, I've known Creighton for a lot of years, and I don't think he let anyone make decisions for him. He was always in charge."

"Superman," she said. "I'm going to miss him." She blinked at the tears that began to run down her cheeks. "Excuse me, I'm being a silly old woman."

David hugged her briefly and then he and Will walked to the Lincoln. Louise Barrow waved from the front porch as they pulled away.

18

• • •

RENEE WAS SITTING ON THE COUCH in the living room watching the evening news when Will came through the door. He walked to her side and kissed her on the cheek. She patted the couch beside her. "Have a seat." He sank wearily down beside her. "How was your day?" she asked as she began rubbing his neck.

Will closed his eyes and moaned softly as she kneaded the muscles of his shoulders. "A busy one, that's for sure." He turned on the couch so that Renee could work more easily on his neck. "I met with Gordon Burningham and got the final papers to purchase his land. I hope I'm doing the right thing. There seems to be an awful lot of work left undone on that project." He paused while she massaged his shoulders. "Then David Jobb and I met with Creighton Barrow. He gave me some good advice on my campaign."

"Oh? Like what?"

"He had a lot of material from his past campaigns that he shared with us."

"And are you going to use it?" she asked.

"I thought you weren't interested in this campaign stuff," he said with a smile.

Renee finished kneading his neck. "I said I'd support you, didn't I?"

Will stretched his arms. "Yes, you did. But I got the distinct impression that you didn't want to get involved."

"I suppose whether I want to or not, I will be," she said with a shrug.

Will shut his eyes and leaned back against the couch. "I'm not sure I'm cut out for politics. And strangely enough, after visiting Creighton Barrow, I'm not sure I'm cut out to develop the Martin's Glen project." He rubbed his forehead. "Maybe I just feel overwhelmed."

Down the hallway a door opened and Justin bolted into the living room. "You're home, Will," he shouted. "Can we practice? Huh?"

"Will's really tired right now, sweetheart," Renee answered.

"Oh," Justin said. His disappointment was evident as he turned back toward his room. "I'm pretty busy doing homework anyway," he said dejectedly.

Will stirred on the sofa. "Just give me a minute to change clothes, Champ."

"You really don't have to," Renee said as she placed a restraining hand on Will's shoulder.

"Yeah, I really think I do," he replied. "I really do." He went to their bedroom and changed into his sweats. When he walked through the kitchen toward the backyard, carrying his ball glove, Renee was fixing dinner. He walked to her side, put his arms around her, and said softly, "I love you, sweetheart."

She kissed him. "And I love you. Just don't forget that."

"You can count on it," he said as he hurried out the back door. "Hey, Champ, throw it over here!"

Renee watched out the kitchen window as Will and Justin played catch. In less than a week, Justin had overcome his fear of the ball and become fairly proficient at catching and throwing it. She finished peeling the potatoes and put them on the stove to boil, then started toward the living room to turn off the television set that droned in the background. As she reached for the remote control the news anchor's voice caught her attention.

"In breaking news, State House majority leader, Creighton Barrow, was taken to the hospital this afternoon with an undisclosed illness." The picture on the screen showed a file photo of an ambulance pulling up in front of the hospital emergency room. "We go now to reporter Allisa Skowren at the scene." Renee watched as the slim, blonde reporter touched the earphone in her right ear and looked into the camera. She held a microphone with the familiar Channel 8 logo clipped onto it.

"Chuck, Representative Barrow was brought here by ambulance less than half an hour ago. The nature of his illness is unknown and hospital personnel have not yet disclosed any information. We have tried repeatedly, since the session ended, to interview the House Majority Leader on the environmental impact of the Clawson Reservoir project he succeeded in pushing through the legislature in the final moments of the session, but have not been able to reach him for comment. There have been rumors of health problems, which may be confirmed by the events of today. We'll have more information on the news at ten. This is Allisa Skowren for Channel 8 news, and back to you Chuck."

Renee clicked the remote control, turned off the set, and returned to the kitchen. She looked out the window at the two baseball players on the back lawn. "I guess I'd better interrupt the game," she said sadly and softly as the phone rang. She lifted the receiver to her ear. "Hello?"

"Mrs. Martin? This is David Jobb."

"Yes, David."

"Is your husband there?"

She glanced out the window. "He's involved in another project at the moment. Can I give him a message?"

"As soon as he's available, please have him call me. I'm still at the office. If I leave, he can get me on my car phone at 555–0704."

"I'll give him the message," she said.

"Thank you. It's imperative that I talk to him as soon as possible."

"I understand, Mr. Jobb. I'll give him the message as soon as he's free." She put the phone back in its cradle and returned to fixing dinner. Half an hour later she opened the back door and called Will and Justin to the table. Reluctantly the two of them finished their game of catch and headed into the house.

"David Jobb called a few minutes ago. He wants you to call him," she said as Will and Justin headed to the bathroom to wash their hands.

"I'll call him after dinner," Will called over his shoulder.

"He said it was important," she said quietly as she heard the bathroom door close.

During dinner Justin and Will carried on an animated conversation about baseball. Renee sat quietly watching them. The phone rang again.

"I'll get it," Will said as he headed for the kitchen. "Hello?" He listened for a moment. "You're kidding me. When did this happen?" He retrieved a pad of paper and pen from a wicker basket that sat beside the phone. "Which room is he in?" He scratched a number on the pad. "All right. I'll be there as soon as I can." He hung up the phone and returned to the table. He leaned on the back of his chair with both hands. "Creighton Barrow is in the hospital. David Jobb said he wants to see me."

Renee chewed on her lower lip. "Would you like me to go with you?"

Will smiled at her. "Yes, I would. Do you think we could drop Justin off at Grams's on the way?"

Justin straightened up in his chair. "I can stay here by myself."

"We might be a little while, Champ. Why don't I see if

Grams can come over?" Despite Justin's protests, Will quickly dialed his grandmother.

Justin turned to his mother. "Mom, I'm old enough that I don't need a baby-sitter," he said.

She tousled his hair, "I'm sure you're right, Justin, but I think Grams likes to come over here to see you every once in a while."

Will returned. "I explained the situation, and she'll be ready for me to pick her up. I'm going to put on something more presentable and then I'll run over and get her." He started up the stairs toward the bedroom.

"Why don't I run and get her while you change your clothes?" Quickly Renee hurried out the back door and backed her car out of the driveway. Justin began clearing the dishes from the table and putting them in the sink.

Will appeared a few minutes later in a white shirt and tie. He watched Justin rinse off the dishes before putting them in the dishwasher. *He really is awfully mature for a seven-year-old,* he thought. He heard Renee's car pull into the driveway. Almost immediately the back door opened, and his wife and grandmother entered the kitchen.

"Well, I'm here. Now, you two had better hurry. Justin and I will take good care of things. Won't we?"

Justin nodded his head and finished putting the last glass in the dishwasher.

"Thanks, Grams, we'll be back as soon as we can." The two

of them raced out of the kitchen, climbed into Will's Jaguar, and sped away.

"I wonder why he wants to see me," Will said.

In the growing darkness Renee shook her head. "I don't know. David seemed awfully grim when he called." She fought a rising feeling of guilt. *I wonder if I should have interrupted their game?* A spear of ice slid down her spine. *Sometimes it's hard to know the right thing to do.*

19

. . .

"THANK YOU FOR COMING SO QUICKLY," David Jobb said as he glanced at Renee. They stood outside the hospital room door waiting for a nurse to emerge. "Apparently just after we left him he had some severe abdominal pain, and Louise had him brought here to the hospital. They've checked him out and given him something to relax him and kill the pain." The lawyer ran his hand over his head. "I'm afraid things are deteriorating more quickly than we had known." He blinked back tears. "He is such a good, honorable man."

The door opened and a pair of nurses exited the room. "You can see him now," one of them said, "but please be brief. He's been given a sedative that will be taking effect very soon."

Creighton Barrow turned his eyes toward them as the three of them entered the room. His silver hair lay against the whiteness of the sheets and the yellow tint to his skin was even more pronounced than it had been in the lamplight of his study. His wife sat on the other side of the bed, gently stroking Creighton's arm. Will was amazed at how much he seemed to have aged in the few hours since they had last seen him.

"Thank you for coming," he whispered.

"Our pleasure, Creighton." Jobb nodded his head. "Good evening, Louise."

"They've given me something to put me to sleep, and I'm afraid it's working," he said with a trace of a smile. "So let me be brief." His eyelids fluttered closed and he struggled to open them. "They tell me I'll be here a day or two before I go home. I need you to send a stenographer here in the morning, David, so I can endorse this young man." He smiled wanly at Will and as if for the first time saw Renee standing slightly behind him. "This must be your lovely wife," he said in a whisper. "You're a lucky man." His eyes tried to focus on David Jobb. "And I need to wrap up some loose ends . . . some legal . . ." His eyes drooped shut.

David Jobb patted the old politician on his shoulder. "I'll be here first thing in the morning," he said. "Now I think we'd better go and let you get some sleep." Will could see David's glistening eyes as Jobb turned to Louise Barrow. "Our prayers are with the two of you, Louise. Is there anything we can do for you? Do you need a ride home?"

"Thank you, David. I think I'll stay here for a while."

"Of course. The three of us probably ought to be on our way." He glanced back over his shoulder at Creighton as he turned toward the door and led Will and Renee back into the corridor. They stood there for a few moments while David composed himself.

"Why did he want me here?" Will asked.

David reached out and took hold of his arm. "So that you'd know that he is going to endorse you, I guess. I don't think he's ever endorsed anyone else for office. He must feel very strongly about this." Jobb smiled at Renee. "Your husband is pretty impressive to have won this old workhorse over so quickly. I just wish we'd have been here a little earlier, before he fell asleep. I think there was more he wanted to say."

Renee smiled guiltily at him. "I hope we have that opportunity tomorrow."

"So do I." He let go of Will's arm. "I'll be here early, Will. I'll give you a call and let you know what is happening."

"I'd appreciate that," Will said. "You're a good friend, David." Will and Renee walked slowly down the hallway toward the elevator.

They punched the button, and waited in silence until the doors opened. Renee spoke haltingly while they rode to the first floor. "Will, I need to tell you something. David called while you and Justin were playing ball, and I didn't want to interrupt you." She leaned against the back of the elevator. "We could have gotten here sooner if I'd just let you know." The elevator door opened and Will stuck his hand against the door to keep it from closing while Renee walked past him into the lobby.

"You couldn't have known," he said. "I guess we'll just have to see what happens." He took her hand and they walked out of the hospital and to the car.

The next morning Will sat in his office going over the

tentative plans for the Martin's Glen project when the phone rang. "Martin Real Estate, Will speaking," he said.

"Will, this is David. I'm at the hospital, and Creighton seems to have rallied this morning. They may be releasing him in an hour or so, about noon. He'd like to see you if you have a few minutes."

"Of course, how soon?" Will replied.

"As soon as you can get here."

"I'm on my way." Will rolled up the plans he had been working on and slipped them into a cardboard tube, then reached for his sports coat and headed out the door. "Miss Cook, I'm going over to the hospital," he said.

"Oh? Who's sick?"

"Creighton Barrow."

"I heard that on the news," she said.

"I'll be back soon. I'm sure you can handle any problems." Will started toward the stairs.

"That will be fine, Mr. Martin. Oh, by the way, you had a call from a Les Jardine while you were on the phone with Mr. Jobb. He said you wanted him to call you." She raised one eyebrow. "Should I refer him to one of our agents?"

Will paused at the top of the stairs. "No, I need to talk to him personally. I assume he left a number?"

Enid nodded her head.

"I'll call him as soon as I return."

"Very good," she said as he hurried down the stairs and

drove quickly to the hospital. David Jobb was waiting for him as the elevator doors slid open.

"Thank you for coming so quickly," he said, taking Will by the arm. "He's feeling much better." They walked briskly down the corridor to Barrow's hospital room and entered.

"Will Martin," the old man said with a smile. "I hope I didn't make too much of a fool of myself last evening." He had adjusted the hospital bed so that he was nearly sitting up.

"Not at all, sir."

"I just wanted you to know that I've written a letter of endorsement this morning. I'll have it sent as a press release to the local papers at the proper time, but feel free to use all or any part of it in your campaign literature."

"Thank you, sir."

"Nonsense, you're the right candidate for the job, and I want to give you all the support I can."

"I appreciate that, sir," Will said, "I hope I don't disappoint you."

"Oh, I don't think you'll do that, although we may not agree on a few issues." He chuckled a low, wheezy chuckle. "You'll be just fine. I can tell you're a quick study. You'll learn the ropes very easily." He reached for the cup of water that rested on the table across his bed, and took a sip through a straw. He cleared his throat. "But it's time to talk about some serious matters."

Will reached into the inside pocket of his sports coat and withdrew a small pad of paper. "I'd be pleased," he said.

"I hope you are when we finish," the old man said before

coughing into a wad of tissues he held in his left hand. "To be blunt, Milton Phillips is a formidable opponent. He has the backing of the CCG, the Coalition for Constitutional Government. They're not a very large group, but they're very well funded and very well organized. You can be sure that at this very moment some of them are sniffing through everything you've ever done in life to see if they can pin some unsavory scrap on your lapel. Do you understand?"

"I think so, sir," Will replied quietly.

"There's an old joke that goes something like this, 'I didn't have any money to do genealogical research, so I ran for office.' There's some truth in it. So, uncomfortable though this might be, I want to know, Will, is there anything in your background that they can use against you?"

"I don't think so," Will stammered.

"No arrests?"

"No, sir, nothing at all."

"Good! Ever use drugs? Even recreationally?"

"No, sir."

"What about an affair? A jilted lover? A married woman?"

"Not really. I mean, I dated a number of women when I lived in New York . . . even when I returned here, but nothing serious and certainly no infidelity."

The old man looked at David Jobb. "You may be right, David, this kid is squeaky clean."

Jobb nodded his head. "I told you he'd be a great candidate."

Will took a spot beside the lawyer. "What do you think

they'll do?" He noticed that David and Creighton caught each other's eye.

"Almost anything. They are so convinced that they have the only corner on truth and righteousness that they'll lie, cheat, and steal to achieve their ends. We just need to be very careful in how we deal with them."

Will felt a cold chill slither down his spine. "You seem quite experienced, Representative Barrow."

"Please, please call me Creigh; but in answer to your question, yes, I'm well acquainted with Milton Phillips and his organization." Will saw the old man's jaw harden. "If I didn't know better, I'd say they're the ones who gave me cancer." He coughed again into the wad of tissues.

David turned to Will. "Please don't underestimate what your opponent is likely to do." Will nodded his head.

Creighton interjected, "At David's request I've put together a timeline and a campaign strategy that I think will work well for you. It's one that I used for the last several elections." He waved his hand toward the two of them. "David, give the boy the envelope I gave you this morning."

Jobb withdrew the envelope from his coat pocket and handed it to Will. Inside were two sheets of paper written in a small, crabbed script. There was a list of things to do and a date when they should be done. Included were references to the design of campaign fliers, lawn signs, and newspaper articles that Creighton Barrow had given them the night before. Will read through them with a mixed feeling of gratitude and dread.

"There seems to be an awful lot to get done," he said.

"That's why I've put together your whole strategy. You can go to the printer and have him print all of your flyers at the same time . . . saves a little money, but more importantly it means that all of them are ready when you decide to distribute them. At the same time, you can get signs printed . . . I've included the name of the man who has done mine for me . . . and I called him earlier this morning and told him you'd be contacting him." He sipped again from the straw. "And I've included references to the material I gave you yesterday. There are some fully written newspaper press releases you can use, when you need to. Besides, this lets you figure out how much it's going to cost you, right up front, so you don't get caught by any surprises."

Will continued to read the list in front of him. "Thank you, sir. This seems very complete."

David Jobb read over Will's shoulder. "I told Will I'd raise funds for him. He already has a thousand dollars."

"Good! Good!" Barrow said. "Another nine or ten thousand should be enough for your campaign. I'll call a few friends when I get home."

Will folded the sheets of paper, replaced them in the envelope, and slid it into the inside pocket of his sports coat. "I can't thank you enough."

"Nonsense!" He sipped some more water. "Now on your building project. I called the LaPoint Group just before you arrived. They've agreed to meet with you and discuss your project. Give me the envelope."

Will fished it out of his pocket and handed it Creighton Barrow, who retrieved a pen from the drawer in the hospital table and wrote a number on the envelope. "There, call them and tell them I told you to call." He handed the envelope back to Will. "Now, why hasn't someone come to release me?" he said, staring at the clock on the wall behind Will.

As if on cue, a doctor and nurse appeared at the door. David Jobb shook the old man's hand and led Will to the door. "Do you need a ride home, Creigh?"

"No, no. Louise is on her way. I just sent her home a little while ago to bring back some clothes for me. She ought to be here any minute. You two go on and I'll talk to you tomorrow." He grabbed the clipboard from the nurse and began scribbling his name on the bottom of the release form.

The elevator took the two men to the ground floor and as they walked toward the parking lot David Jobb said, "It looks to me as if you have about two months to get your Martin's Glen project organized before you're going to have to spend a lot of time campaigning. I'll get busy raising you some money so that when July rolls around you're ready to go. And if you want some help designing brochures and signs, I'm sure we can get some help there." They'd reached Will's car.

"Thank you, David, for all your help. Would you consider designing the signs, or having someone do it for me? You are such a godsend."

"Oh, I haven't done anything yet," David said with a smile. "But I have a feeling this is going to be a very interesting few months."

20

. . .

ON THE JOURNEY BACK TO his office, Will pondered the months ahead. Mentally he tried to construct a time line of the things that needed to get done . . . Martin's Glen, finding Gary Carr, then Justin's adoption, and finally the campaign. By the time he arrived at his office, his head was swimming and he couldn't decide what he needed to do first. He slid out of the seat of his car, slung his coat over his shoulder, and climbed the flight to his office. Enid Cook was sitting at her desk as he crested the top of the stairs.

"How is he, Mr. Martin?"

"He seems to have rallied from when I saw him last night," Will said wearily.

"You saw him last night?"

"It's a long story, Miss Cook."

"Mr. Jardine called again. He seems quite anxious to talk with you." She handed Will the small square of pink paper with Les Jardine's phone number on it.

"I'll call him right now," he said as he entered his office and closed the door behind him. He hung his coat on the coatrack, loosened his tie, and dropped heavily into the chair behind his desk. Will took a deep breath and exhaled slowly, trying to calm himself, then reached for the phone and dialed Les Jardine's number.

The telephone rang once and an automatic answering machine began to play a perfect imitation of Ronald Reagan. "Well, Nancy and I are down at the store buying jelly beans. We'll be back shortly, before you can say, 'There you go again.' Leave your name and number and one of us will get back to you." Beep.

"Les, this is Will Martin returning your call. I should be in the rest of—"

Someone picked up the phone at the other end. "Will, this is Les. Just wondering if you're serious about going back out to the Burningham spread and having me show you where the property lines really are?"

"I'd like to do that, Les. When are you available?"

"Almost anytime, Will," the young computer whiz answered. "Make it easy on yourself."

"What if I picked you up in an hour?"

"Sounds great. You know where my place is?"

Will reached for a pad of paper. "Just give me an address, and I'll find you." He wrote the address on the pad, ripped off the sheet, folded it, and stuck it in his pocket. "I'll be there before one, okay?"

"See ya then."

Will hung up the phone and unrolled the plans for the

Martin's Glen project on his desk. He weighted the corners down with the telephone, a desk lamp, and a paperweight. Carefully he followed the lines and tried to match them with the written description Gordon Burningham's lawyer had supplied. He was still studying the plans when Enid Cook knocked on his door and entered the office.

"I don't wish to intrude, Mr. Martin," she said, "but I just wanted to make sure that this check request is accurate."

Will looked up from the plans. "The one for Gordon Burningham?"

"Yes, Mr. Martin. For two million dollars? That will require us to either cash in some certificates or borrow."

Will began to roll up the plans on his desk. "Actually, Hal Jenkins at the bank has arranged for a line of credit that will permit us to borrow whatever we need. Will you please call him and arrange to have the money transferred into our account?"

She closed the door behind her and leaned against it. "Are you sure, Mr. Martin? If we get into trouble with this project, it could bring this whole agency down."

Will inserted the plans into their cardboard tube. "I wish I were more sure, Enid, and I wish more of the planning was already done, but something in my gut tells me this is going to work. I guess I'm just going to have to ask you to trust me on this one."

"You're the boss," she said curtly.

Will nodded his head, picked up the Martin's Glen folder and the tube of plans and, as an afterthought, picked up the

Gary Carr folder as well. Enid Cook stood guarding the door. "Enid, if the agency goes down, so do I. Please get the check ready for Gordon Burningham. I'll need to deliver it in the morning."

Reluctantly she stepped aside and let Will pass her. She was still shaking her head as he plunged down the stairs, hurried to his car, and drove away. She returned to her desk, removed the checkbook from its locked drawer and cautiously filled out the check for two million dollars. "I think I'm glad I'm close to retiring," she said under her breath.

Will guided the Jaguar down a winding street on the outskirts of town until he found Les Jardine's home. The young man was sitting on the front steps of the modest two-story house. He jumped to his feet as Will pulled into the driveway and walked quickly to the passenger's side.

"Cool car," he said as he slid into the seat beside Will. "Must have cost you a pile of bucks."

"Actually, it was part of the package where I used to work."

"Man, this is a pretty rad perk."

Will backed out of the driveway and started toward the Burningham property. "Les, you seem to have done your homework on this piece of ground. What do you think—is it a good place for a development?"

Jardine shrugged his shoulders, "Okay, I guess. It seems like it's kinda out of the way right now, but a year or two down the road I guess people will be moving out that far." He ran his hand over the dashboard. "Man, this is one bad machine."

Ten minutes later Will stopped on the shoulder of the road and the two men walked to where the two irrigation ditches intersected. Les jumped easily across the ditch and walked to a small clump of orchard grass. He dug the back of his heel into the grass until he had worked it loose, then pulled it up and threw it into the ditch. He continued to work until he uncovered a concrete circle that had been covered with dirt. In the center of the circle was a brass stud about the size of a quarter and somewhat domed. "Government corner," Les said pointing at the marker.

"How in the world did you find that?" Will asked in amazement.

"Had my GPS receiver to help me locate the spot, then I used a metal detector. The description of the land indicated it was here. I just never dug it up till now." He reached for the file that Will had carried from the car. "See," he said, pointing to the description of the property, "it says that this piece of property begins at this point."

Will looked back at the irrigation ditch that was nearly fifty feet behind him. "So the property line isn't the ditch, is that what you're saying?"

Les nodded his head. "Yup. It's right here." He straddled the marker and pointed straight north. "And if you look real close you can see a fence post down there with a rusted metal can shoved down on top of it."

Will followed the direction Jardine was pointing and saw the post. "Are you telling me that's another corner?"

"Yup, that one's kinda tricky, 'cause it's just a single post stuck out in the middle of the field. Do you want to walk down there and take a look at it?" He looked at Will's carefully polished loafers. "It's kinda dusty."

"That's okay," Will replied. "I think I need to make sure where this property is. Let's go."

Jardine began walking at a brisk pace through the orchard grass toward the distant fence post. When they finally reached it, he knelt down and cleared away the grass near the bottom of the post. A short length of rusted pipe with a shut-off valve appeared. Les gave the handle of the valve a tug but it refused to move.

"Corroded big time," he said. "I guess we shoulda brought a wrench. 'Course I don't know where the pipe goes to. Might have watered stock down here years ago. Anyway, this post is the northeast corner of the property."

"Well, next time I come, I'll bring a wrench or a hammer," Will said with a smile.

Les straightened up. "Now the next corner's the real tricky one, 'cause it's hidden behind the cottonwood trees. I heard Mr. Burningham try to tell you the trees made up the line, but they don't. The line's a good seventy-five feet on the other side of the cottonwoods. Maybe we just need to walk down there, 'cause I'm not sure I can point out the marker from here."

The two men walked as quickly as the weeds and undergrowth would permit until they passed through the shade of the cottonwood trees and came to a two-foot-long piece of splintered two-by-four that Les had driven into the ground. Nearby an ant hill crawled with half-inch-long red ants.

"I made the mistake of standing over there," Les indicated, "when I first came out here and those little fellows can bite." Les scratched absently at the back of his leg. "Anyway, then we go back to the road. I had to measure from the government corner up the road to the last spot. I just marked it with three rocks in a stack." He began walking toward the road, and Will hurried to keep up. The pile of rocks was still where Jardine had placed it. "That give you a better idea?"

Will nodded his head. "Thanks, this has been a big help. Did you find any surprises when you walked the property originally?"

"Not really. There is a real hard patch of ground near the northeast corner where nothing is growing, but that's about it."

They walked back to the car, and Will unrolled the plan and spread it on the roof of the Jaguar. "We're standing right here," he said pointing at a spot on the plan."

Les nodded. "Yup." He jabbed a finger at the plan. "And here's the spot with the rusty pipe." He trailed his finger across the plan. "Here's where the wooden stake is . . . and here's the other corner on the road."

Will rolled up the plan and stuck it in the backseat of the car. "Anything else you need to show me before I run you back home?"

Les shook his head. "Nope, I think that about does it." He

dusted off his hands and climbed back into the car. Will surveyed the plot one last time before sliding in behind the wheel and pointing the car toward town.

"Would you do one more thing for me?" Will asked as they stopped in the Jardine's driveway.

"Sure, as long as it's technically legal," the young man grinned.

Will reached into the backseat of the car and picked up the Gary Carr folder. "The other day you indicated that this was a forgery," he said, removing the ETC letterhead from the folder. "Would you explain that to me one more time?"

Les took the piece of paper from Will. "Maybe we ought to get out of the car," he said. "It's easier to see in brighter light." He pushed open the door, walked to the driver's side of the car, and held the document where Will could see it clearly through his open window. "If you look closely at this dark green circle," he pointed with his finger at the upper left-hand corner of the page, "you can see that the edges aren't really smooth." Will nodded his head. "Well, that's called dithering. I'm guessing someone scanned in a real ETC letterhead and then used it to generate computer copies."

Will looked more closely at the logo. "Why would someone do that?"

Jardine said, "Are you kidding? So you'd think the letter came from ETC." He scanned down the letter. "Probably left the signature, too. Want me to show you how it's done?"

Suddenly he pulled the letter closer to his face. "Hey, this is from Gary Carr."

Will felt the hairs on the back of his neck stand up. "Yes, it is. Do you know him?"

"Sure. I used to work for him when I was first getting started. He hired me right out of school to help with some networking problems."

"Do you know where he is now?" Will asked.

Jardine shook his head. "Nope. I haven't heard from him since he closed up shop and headed to Europe. Maybe four or five years ago." He thought for a long moment. "Yeah, about five years ago. Why? He owe you money?"

"No, nothing like that," Will said. "I'm trying to locate him for a personal reason. Is there anything else you can tell me that would help me find him?"

"Well, let me think for a minute." He handed the letter back to Will. "You want me to show you how you copy this stuff? It's real easy, man."

"Sure. It sounds interesting."

Les started toward the house. "Don't mind the mess. I haven't gotten around to cleaning up this morning." He opened the front door and the odor of pizza sauce wafted out. An open box sat on the coffee-table, displaying a half uneaten pizza. Clothing was strewn around the room. "Wouldn't make my mother proud," Jardine said. They stepped over piles of clothing and headed down a hall to a closed door. A flat, slightly luminescent panel was attached to the wall next to the door. Jardine placed his left hand on the panel and the locks to the door released. "Biometric," the computer whiz said.

In contrast to the living room, the computer room was spotless. Counters ran around the walls and a half-dozen monitors flashed different images. Jardine pulled a chair in front of one of the computers. "Have a seat," he said to Will, then he reached for a folder that sat on top of a file cabinet in one corner. Les selected a sheet of paper, then sat down next to Will.

"The easiest way to explain is to show you," he said. "Here's a letter from Atlas Computer Supplies." He handed it to Will. "Now suppose I want to write a letter to you and make it appear that it is from Atlas." He took the page back and placed it on a flatbed scanner, then turned to a computer and clicked on an icon on the screen. Almost immediately the scanner began to hum and whir. Less than half a minute later a small image of the document appeared on Jardine's monitor. He clicked on the screen and the scanner whirred again.

"See, I've got an electronic copy of the letter that they sent to me. Now the fun begins." The letter appeared on the screen and Jardine began electronically erasing the type until only the logo appeared at the top of the sheet and the signature remained at the bottom. "Now I'm going to save this blank sheet as a file," he said with a click or two of his mouse. "And I can open it in any word processor and type anything I want." He clicked on another icon, and in a few seconds the blank letterhead appeared on the screen. Jardine began pecking away at the keyboard and Will watched as words appeared on the monitor.

"I highly recommend Les Jardine to your firm. He has been a top-notch employee with Atlas Computers for the past twenty-seven years. There is no computer problem he can't fix. I consider him to be the best in his field. You should hire him and give him at least a million dollars a year."

Jardine grinned. "I may have inflated my resume a little bit." He clicked his mouse again, and a printer across the room hummed into action. Les rolled his chair to the printer, picked up the piece of paper, and rolled back to where Will sat facing the screen. "*Voilá*! An authentic-looking reference." He handed Will the sheet.

Will looked closely at the paper in front of him. The logo was there, the phony reference was there, and the signature of the president of Atlas Computer Supplies was there. "I can't believe this," he said, handing the sheet back to Jardine.

"Well, you shouldn't believe it, I made it up," Les said with a grin. "Notice mine doesn't have any dithering. I have a better scanner than whoever did the ETC one."

"I'm sure you do," Will said. He stood up. "Well, thanks for the demonstration. If you think of anything that would help me find Gary Carr, I'd sure like to know."

Jardine erased the image from the screen. "Like I said, I went to work for him because he had too much to do for one person, then he got this offer." He clicked on the screen a couple of times. "I guess it was from ETC. Anyway he left for a few days . . . went back to Boston or New York, I think, for an interview. Then he came back and a couple of weeks later he told me he was going to France."

"I don't suppose you know who he interviewed with?" Will asked.

"Nope. I know he had to spend an extra day there 'cause he needed to get a physical. You'd think he was going to work for the NBA or something, but I don't think he ever told me who he interviewed with. Sorry. Wish I could be of more help."

One of the monitors began to flash and a dull chime sounded. Jardine spun around in his chair and rolled to the console in front of the screen. "Oh-oh. Looks like somebody's trying to hack into Walker's." He began pecking furiously at the keyboard. "Ha! Thought you could outsmart old Les, did you?" He laughed. "Let's see what happens when this little bomb reaches your hard drive, dude." His fingers fairly flew across the keyboard.

"Looks like you're busy," Will said. "I'll let myself out."

Jardine glanced quickly over his shoulder. "Thanks, man. This is gonna be fun." He returned to the keyboard while Will walked down the hall and stepped over the piles of clothing on his way to the front door.

21

• • •

T HE CHECK IS READY FOR YOUR signature," Enid Cook said sourly. She extended the check as if it were a dead fish that had lain in the sun for a week.

"Thanks, Miss Cook," Will said, taking the check from her. He walked into his office, shut the door behind him, and placed the check on his desk. *Two million dollars!* He sat in his chair, turned slowly around, and gazed out the window at the people in the town square. In the late afternoon sun the shadow of the bandstand stretched nearly to the east side of the park, veiling much of the square in shadow. *Life's like that,* he thought. *If we could only see clearly what lies ahead, maybe we'd make different decisions. But we see through the glass, darkly.* Slowly he turned back to his desk and picked up the check with both hands. *Two million dollars!* Will looked through the pebbled glass of his office door at the shadowy images beyond. *What are their lives worth?* He looked at the check again, then reached for the phone. He punched in the number for Hal Jenkins at the bank, and Hal picked it up after the second ring.

"Good afternoon. Hal Jenkins. How can I help you?"

"Hal, this is Will Martin. I have the check ready. When would be a good time for me to bring it over?"

"We've closed for the day, but I'm still here if you want to put it in a safe place overnight. I'll deposit it in Gordon Burningham's account in the morning and notify him."

"I'll be right over," Will said.

"Just knock on the side door when you get here. I'll wait for you."

Will unscrewed the cap from his fountain pen and signed the check, then placed it in an envelope, stuck it in the inside pocket of his blazer, and hurried out of his office. "I'm going to run this check over to the bank," he said to Enid Cook. "I'll see you in the morning."

"Whatever you say, Mr. Martin," she said icily.

Will crossed the street and sped through the town square to the bank. He knocked on the door and Hal Jenkins opened it. "Come in, Will," he said pleasantly. "How are things going?"

"I'm a bit frazzled, right now, but things are going well." He reached into his pocket and removed the envelope. "Here's the check. I appreciate you waiting for me."

"No problem." He took the check and walked to the open vault of the bank, where he opened a steel drawer and inserted the check. "I'll take care of it in the morning." Jenkins closed the heavy vault door and spun the handle on it. "That'll keep it safe and secure. It's a lot of money, but I'm guessing you're going to see a lot more from your investment. I think you hit a home run on this one."

"I hope you're right. And speaking of home runs, I'd better get home. I'm helping Justin get ready for Little League."

"He seems like a wonderful boy," Jenkins said as he led Will to the side door of the bank. "And the two of you seem to get along well. That doesn't always happen."

"He's a great kid," Will said. "Thanks again, Hal. I guess we're in it now for better or worse."

"I'm sure it will be for the better," the banker said as he closed the door.

Will returned to the Martin Real Estate parking lot, unlocked the door to his car, and headed for home. The sun had dropped below the rim of the western hills by the time he pulled into the driveway. Renee's car was gone, and there were no lights showing in the windows of the house. He climbed the steps to the kitchen door and found that it was locked. He unlocked the door and found the house completely silent. Puzzled, Will walked through the kitchen into the living room. There was no one there. He returned to the kitchen, where he saw a yellow stick-it note on the cabinet next to the phone.

Coach Morris called. We're at Simpson Park for practice. Love, Renee

Will sat down on the couch in the living room and rubbed his eyes with the fingers of his hand. *How could I have missed that?* He leaned his head back and stared at the ceiling. *I've got to get my life in order. I've got to prioritize.* He heard a car pulling into the driveway and rose quickly and walked into the kitchen just as Renee and Justin came through the back door.

"I'm sorry," he said.

Renee looked at him quizzically. "For what?"

"For missing Justin's practice."

"You couldn't have known," she replied. "Coach Morris called this afternoon and asked if I could get Justin up to Simpson Park for practice. He wanted to meet his team." She put her purse on the kitchen counter. "There are only three kids returning from last year, so Justin fits right in." She tousled Justin's hair. "Don't you, sweetheart?"

Will turned to Justin, who had a big grin on his face.

"How'd it go, Champ?"

"I can hit better than most of the new kids. And I can catch the ball better, too."

"That's great, Justin." Will put his hand on the boy's shoulder. "I'm sorry I wasn't there."

Just then the phone rang and Renee answered it. "Hello?" She listened for a moment, then said, "I see. Well, we're just going to have some dinner." She paused again. "I suppose that would be all right. Do you need to speak to Will?" She raised her eyebrow. "We'll see you about eight o'clock, then. Goodbye." She stared at the receiver before hanging it up. "That was David Jobb. He's put together a proposal for your campaign and he'd like to talk to you . . . to us . . . about it. He's coming at eight o'clock."

Justin chattered about the tryouts all through dinner, then somewhat reluctantly went to his bedroom to do his homework when David Jobb arrived. The lawyer sat down in the living room and opened his briefcase, from which he removed a mock-up of a campaign sign. "I've taken a close look at Creighton Barrow's campaign materials and tried to put together a campaign strategy." He turned the face of the sign toward Will and Renee. " 'Vote for Will Martin for responsible government.' It has a nice ring to it, don't you think?"

Renee looked at the red, white, and blue sign. "Perhaps we could change it to say, 'Will Martin, a vote for responsible government.' It doesn't change it much, but it seems to flow better, and it puts Will's name first."

Jobb considered the suggestion, then said, "I think you're right, Mrs. Martin." He made a note on the sign, then removed a folder from his briefcase and opened it. "I thought we'd have about 300 of these printed for lawn signs and then have about 20 large ones made . . . for some really prominent locations. What do you think?"

Will started to answer when Renee said, "That ought to do, Mr. Jobb. When are we going to put them up? I've been thinking that a good strategy might be to put some of them up fairly early . . . Will needs the name recognition, as you said last time you were here . . . then continue to put a few more up each day up to election day. How does that sound?"

David Jobb smiled, "It's clear you've given this some thought. I think that's a fine idea. There's a county ordinance against putting political signs out until six weeks before the election, so, if we get them all ready, we could put out the first ones the last week of September."

Will turned to Renee. "I thought you didn't want to get involved in this," he said with a smirk.

"Will, I always said I'd support you." She turned back to David. "Now, how about flyers and door hangers? I've been wondering about starting to place some small ads in the newspaper . . . you know, something to get Will's name out in front of the people."

The old lawyer smiled, "I brought all of Creighton Barrow's campaign flyers." He tapped the folder in his hand. "It won't take much to get them reprinted with Will's picture . . . oh, by the way, do you have a picture we can use? I need one of you, one of you and your wife, and one of you, your wife, and your son."

"We'll have to have some pictures taken," Renee said. "We can get that done next week." She reached out toward Jobb. "May I see those, please?" He handed her the folder, and Renee began perusing the campaign materials. "How soon do we need to get this kind of stuff to the printer?" she asked.

"I'm sure we can get anything printed within a week, and I agree with Creighton, I don't think we'll need to start delivering materials until the first of September. As he said, people have short memories. But I do think your idea of putting an ad in the paper, especially one with Will's picture, is a great idea. I'll find out how much that will cost and get back to you. That reminds me, I really do need to get started on some fund-raising for you, Will."

Will shifted uneasily on the couch. "You said this might take ten thousand dollars, David. Are people really willing to donate that much money to a campaign?"

Jobb nodded his head. "I don't think we'll have any trouble raising that money." He smiled at Renee. "It appears to me that I'd better leave that campaign material with you, Mrs. Martin. If you and Will can make some final decisions in the next week or so, we'll start getting the flyers printed." He stood up and snapped his briefcase shut. "Now, I'd better get out of here and let you two have some time together. This next few months will be interesting." Will stood up and walked with the lawyer to the door.

"Thank you, David, you're a good friend and an invaluable resource."

"My pleasure," David said as he started down the steps toward his car. Will waited until he drove away before he walked back into the house. Renee had moved into the dining room and was spreading the materials over the tabletop.

"Some of these look pretty dated, sweetheart," she said. "I think we can do better than this."

22

• • •

ENID COOK WINCED AS SHE climbed the stairs of Martin
Real Estate. "At least the air-conditioning is on," she said
softly as she reached the top of the steps and looked around
the office. The bright morning summer sun flooded the building. "I've had forty good years here," she said pensively. "But I
think it's time for me to go." She shook her head sadly and
examined the office as if she were seeing it for the first time.
She walked to her desk, opened the bottom drawer, placed her
purse in it, and slid it shut.

"You're here early," Will said from the doorway of his
office.

Enid's hands flew up to her face. "Oh, Mr. Martin, you
startled me."

"I'm sorry, Miss Cook. I thought you knew I was here."

She fanned her face with one hand as she sat down at her
desk. "No. I didn't know anyone was here."

Will walked to her desk. "I'm going to miss you, Enid," he
said with feeling. "You've been my right-hand man . . . or

woman, I guess would be more precise. I'm not sure things will go as smoothly with you retiring after all these years."

"Mr. Martin, I've tried to be of help to you, but there is a time and a place for everything. I'm getting old, and I'm not very good at making changes."

Will sat down on the corner of Enid's desk. "Are you worried about the Martin's Glen project?"

Enid folded her hands in her lap and looked down at them. When she looked up at Will, there were the hints of tears in her eyes. "Yes. Yes, I am. If I might say so, I don't think your grandfather would have put the whole agency in jeopardy without consulting with the rest of us. Yes, Mr. Martin, I'm worried. I'm not seeing much progress with the project and with the downturn in the economy, I'm not sure this is the time or the place to be spending two million dollars on some ill-conceived idea." She looked down at her hands again. "Oh, Mr. Martin, I've spoken out of turn, haven't I? I had no right to say what I just did."

Will stood up. "You're wrong, Miss Cook. You had every right to say what you just said. Frankly, I'm worried, too. I'd expected a lot more to happen in the past two months than has, but I guess we'll just have to have faith that it will all work out." He rubbed his temples with his fingers. "At least the architectural drawings are nearly finished, and next Saturday we're going to have an announcement of the project at the site. I hope that gets things moving a little faster."

"I hope so, too, Mr. Martin." She straightened a small stack of papers on the edge of her desk. "Would it be too presumptuous of me to ask if you've found any businesses interested in locating at Martin's Glen?"

Will sighed. "Not yet. I've met with the LaPoint Group, and they're trying to line up tenants, but it's a little premature, I think, when we don't even have the plat plan finalized." He leaned heavily against a filing cabinet. "Enid, my whole life is tied up in these circles. How do you attract a business without having a building? And how do you build the building to meet the needs of a business without knowing what the business is?" He slumped down into a chair across the desk from Enid Cook. "Do you see what I mean? I'm not sure if I've put the cart before the horse, or even if there is a cart . . . or a horse." He shook his head wearily.

"Well, I suppose it will all work out. But maybe not as quickly as you'd like," she said. "You're a very capable young man, if you don't mind me saying so."

A sad smile crossed Will's lips. "Besides that, Enid, I can't find Gary Carr, and that's kind of stalled me on the adoption issue. I've been looking for over two months, and I just can't find him."

Enid pursed her lips. "Have you spoken to your wife about it?"

Will shook his head. "It's another one of those circles, Enid, where I need to contact Gary before I talk to Renee, but maybe . . ."

"Mr. Martin, I think you make things too difficult for

yourself. What possible reason could your wife have for not wanting you to adopt that sweet little boy?"

Will looked into Enid's eyes. "You're probably right, Enid."

She nodded her head. "I usually am," she replied.

"But I've got to be sure."

She sighed. "If you say so, Mr. Martin. After all, you're the boss."

Will heaved himself to his feet. "There are days when I wish I weren't." He started to walk toward his office when he heard the front door of Martin Real Estate open. David Jobb hurried up the stairs.

"I hope you don't mind me coming to your office," he panted. "But I thought you ought to know. Creighton's been taken to the hospital again." He noticed Enid Cook sitting at her desk. "Oh, I didn't know anyone else was here."

"It's all right, David, Miss Cook is a trusted employee . . . and friend. She can be counted on to keep a confidence."

Jobb ran his hand over his head and straightened the few strands of remaining hair. "I think this may be the end." His voice was uncharacteristically husky. "Sorry," he said, "it's tough to lose an old friend." He struggled to compose himself. "I'm going over to the hospital in an hour or so. Would you like to come along?"

"Of course," Will said. "Would you like me to pick you up?"

David nodded his head. "I'd appreciate that," he said as he turned toward the staircase.

When she heard the door close, Enid said, "He must be very close to Mr. Barrow."

"They've been friends for a long time, and I think David's going to take this loss very hard." Will sat back down on the chair across from Enid. "I've only known him for the past two months, but I think this community's losing a real leader." He rubbed his eyes with his fingers. "And I'll lose a political mentor. Everything that Renee and David have put together for campaign materials, Creighton Barrow has reviewed. If I end up winning this race, I think it will be due to his guiding hand. And you know what, Enid? I think the only reason he's doing this is because of Grandpa. The two of them were very close." They sat quietly for a few moments, then Will stood up. "I'd better call Renee. I think she'll want to go to the hospital with David and me."

Enid Cook watched him walk into his office and close the door. *You're a good man, Will Martin,* she thought. *If only you weren't so darn stubborn.*

An hour later Will stopped the Jaguar in front of David's office and waited for the attorney. He had the radio tuned to a news station and was surprised he hadn't heard any mention of Creighton Barrow. David Jobb opened the door and sat down heavily in the passenger seat. "Thank you for the ride," he said. His eyes were red-rimmed and it was obvious that he had been crying.

"My wife would like to come along, if that's all right."

"Of course. I think it's about time the two of them spent

more time together." Jobb blew his nose into his handkerchief. "They've both taken such an interest in your campaign and yet we've never gotten the two of them together for any length of time. Of course, Creighton hasn't let many people see him during the past several months." He lapsed into a contemplative silence.

After picking up Renee and driving to the hospital, the three of them took the elevator to the fifth floor. The door to Creighton Barrow's room was closed when they arrived. David Jobb knocked softly and then pushed the door open. The silver-haired politician lay with his eyes closed. The three visitors stood quietly looking at him. It had been less than two months since Will had seen Creighton Barrow, but the old man was shockingly thinner, and his skin was a sickly yellow color. Creighton Barrow's eyelids fluttered open, and a smile creased his lips. He struggled to extend his hand toward David Jobb.

"My old friend," the dying man wheezed. "How kind of you to come."

The door opened again, and Louise Barrow slipped silently into the room. She nodded at Will and Renee, then took David's hand. "Thank you for coming," she said in a choked voice.

David patted her on the arm and led her to her chair near Creighton's head. She reached out her hand and smoothed her husband's hair.

Barrow's eyes fluttered open again and he struggled to focus on Will. "It's up to you, my young friend. Just make your grandfather proud," he whispered. "This old workhorse is about to cross the finish line." He blinked his eyes a few times. "And your lovely wife." David Jobb took Renee's elbow and guided her to the bed. "Take good care of this young fellow," Barrow said with a trace of a smile. "He's a very good man."

"I know that, Mr. Barrow," she said.

Barrow's eyes closed and his breathing became regular. David Jobb led Will and Renee from the room, and Louise followed them into the hall. "I'm going to miss him," she choked out. "We've had nearly fifty wonderful years together." She dabbed at her eyes with a tissue before turning to Jobb. "I'm afraid, David. Creigh took care of me all these years, and I'm afraid to be alone."

The lawyer put his arm around her shoulders and hugged her. "You'll be fine, Louise. You're as strong as he is. It will be tough at first, but you'll muddle through."

"I suppose you know that, as well as anyone." She burst into tears, and Jobb held her against him while she sobbed, as Will and Renee stood awkwardly nearby. After a few moments Louise composed herself, dabbed at her eyes again, and said, "At least they've been able to control the pain." She wiped her nose. "And it hasn't dragged on. He's been so worried about being a burden to me." She began crying again while Jobb tried to console her. Finally, he led her, followed by Will and Renee, down the hallway to a small chapel that was located near the elevators and helped her to a seat.

He turned to Will and Renee. "I think I'll stay for a while."

"Of course," Renee said.

"Call me, if you need a ride," Will said, shaking the lawyer's hand. Jobb nodded his head and turned back to where Louise Barrow sat. Carefully he lowered himself to the seat next to her.

Renee looked back over her shoulder as she and Will walked to the elevators. "I have some empathy for her," she said as the chime sounded and the doors slid open. "I know what it's like to be left alone." The two of them entered the elevator and looked back at the grieving pair until the door slid shut and they descended to the lobby of the hospital.

"Do they have children who need to be notified?" Renee asked as they approached the Jaguar.

Will shook his head. "I suppose that's part of the sadness. They never had any children, and Creighton is an only child. Louise really will be alone."

"We need to make sure she isn't forgotten," Renee said.

Will nodded his head. "Sweetheart, if I ever get that sick, I don't want any heroic measures taken to keep me alive." He glanced at his wife. "Does that seem selfish?"

Renee shook her head. "I don't even want to think about it." They rode on in silence for several blocks. "I guess I understand your feelings," she said. "A prolonged illness can be devastating to everyone concerned."

"I suppose that's true," Will replied. "You sound as if you have had some experience."

Renee nodded her head. "I've never talked much about Justin's father."

"No, you haven't."

"One of the reasons Gary moved here was because of the death of his parents. His father was in a coma for months, and the wear and tear on his mother was tremendous. I guess she tried to take care of him at home, and it wore her down to where she actually died before he did."

"I didn't know that," Will said, glancing at his wife.

Renee stared straight ahead through the windshield of the car. "Gary ended up putting his father in the hospital and taking care of his mother's funeral. Then a week later his father died. By the time he settled all of their expenses he'd had to sell the family home." She turned to Will. "I'm not sure he ever fully recovered, but he moved here to try to start over. He made me promise the same thing you just asked . . . no heroic measures."

They approached the driveway to their home. Will pulled in and stopped the car. Renee sat immobile in her seat. "I suppose that's why money became so important to Gary." She opened the door of the car, then turned to Will. "I think that's why I'm so worried about your campaign. I'm afraid that politics will become too important in your life." She slipped out of the seat. "I don't want to be alone again."

23

. . .

CREIGHTON BARROW'S CONDITION remained fairly stable through the rest of the week, and Will immersed himself in the plans for the Saturday announcement of the Martin's Glen project. Late Friday afternoon he called Charles Merrill's architectural firm to confirm that the renderings were complete, then drove across town to pick them up. The drawings were mounted on a light-weight, foam board and were too big to fit in the trunk of the Jaguar.

"Why don't I deliver them to the site in the morning?" Charles Merrill suggested. "I have some tripods that we can use, and they'll all fit in our van. Just tell me what time you need everything set up."

"I'd appreciate that, Mr. Merrill," Will said wearily. "The announcement is scheduled for eleven o'clock."

Merrill nodded his head, "No problem. We'll have everything ready half an hour before." He watched while Will inspected the drawings. "What do you think? Are they all right?"

Will smiled. "You're amazing. I can see the whole project

coming to life. I'm just going to leave all of this in your hands."

"One question though," Charles said, "do you want these covered until the announcement? Or do you want the media to be able to look at them beforehand?"

Will thought for a moment. "Why don't you cover them? Then we can have an unveiling at the proper moment. Is that all right?"

"Whatever you'd like, Mr. Martin. You're the boss."

"So I'm learning," Will said under his breath. "Well, we'll see you in the morning." He drove home and parked in the driveway. Justin was in the backyard throwing the ball onto the roof of the garage. He ran to the car as Will opened the door.

"How ya doing, Champ?"

"Okay. Kinda worried about my first game."

Will reached out and took the ball from Justin's mitt. "Here, let me throw you a few."

"Don't you want to change clothes first?"

"Oh, I don't think I'll get too dirty." He pulled his necktie off and laid it on top of his blazer on the front seat of the car. "But go easy when you throw back. I don't have my mitt."

Will threw the ball to Justin, who caught it fairly easily and threw it back. "You're getting pretty good, Champ." Justin beamed and caught the ball again.

Renee watched the two of them through the window above the sink and smiled to herself. A few minutes later she walked outside. "Would you start the barbecue? I thought we'd have hamburgers tonight."

Will kissed his wife. "What a great idea." He lighted the grill, threw the ball one last time to Justin, and said, "Hey, Champ, we'd better go wash up." The two of them followed Renee into the house. Will patted Justin on the shoulder. "You're going to be great."

A few minutes later they sat on lawn chairs in the backyard while hamburgers flared on the grill. Will leaned back on the chaise lounge and closed his eyes.

"Tough day?" Renee asked.

"I just hope we have everything ready for tomorrow's announcement."

"I'm sure everything will be fine. What time have you decided on?"

"I've got to be there about ten-thirty. Everyone's coming at eleven." He pushed himself up, walked to where the hamburgers sizzled on the grill, and flipped them over. "Are you going to come?"

Renee sucked in her lower lip. "I guess that depends on how long it's going to take. Justin's game starts at noon, and he needs to be there a few minutes early to warm up."

Will pushed the burgers around with the spatula. "Then I guess we'll have to make it short, won't we?" he said.

Renee walked to his side and slid her arm around his waist. "I can take Justin to the game, if you'd like. I know this is a big moment for you, and there will be other games."

Will swatted a mosquito that landed on his arm. "If you don't mind. I'll come to the game as soon as we've completed the announcement."

"Of course," Renee said with a sad smile. "That will probably work out." She handed Will a plate and he shoveled the hamburgers onto it.

The next morning Will drove early to Martin's Glen. He hadn't slept well and decided he'd take another look at the land before the media arrived. The sun had just topped the mountains to the east and was sending shimmering beams across the field. Will walked to the government marker where a bright orange flag now marked the southeast corner of the property. He looked north half a mile to where he could barely see another flag waving in the morning breeze. Bright flashes of sunlight reflected back to him from near the base of the flag. Puzzled, he jumped over the irrigation ditch and walked toward the marker. As he neared it he could see that someone had opened a valve on the rusted pipe and created a puddle about ten feet in diameter and an inch deep that was draining into the irrigation ditch. Water continued to bubble from the top of the pipe and fill the depression around it. Will considered removing his shoes and wading through the mud to try to turn off the valve, but decided against it. From his vantage point he looked west, trying in vain to see the next flag marker a half mile away. He walked toward where he knew that marker should be and when he reached the spot found that someone had removed the flag and driven the post into the middle of the anthill. The staff and flag were covered with red ants, and Will quickly decided not to try to move the flag back to the spot where it belonged. Instead he walked the half mile back to the road. As he arrived back at his car he saw two more cars approaching, raising a cloud of dust.

Will glanced at his watch . . . just after ten o'clock. The first car, an older model Ford van pulled up behind his Jaguar and immediately the back door opened and ten people emerged. The driver jumped out and walked toward Will. He stood well over six feet, was dressed in coveralls and a plaid shirt, and sported a uncombed full beard.

"Are you Will Martin?" the man demanded, shaking his shoulder-length hair.

Involuntarily, Will took a step backward. "Yes."

The unkempt man walked up to Will until he was barely a foot away from him. "You're the guy creating this sprawl, aren't you?" He pointed toward the empty field.

"I suppose," Will took another step backward. "We're developing this project."

"Well, we're here to protest it," the man said, spitting on the ground next to Will's foot. "You're destroying wetlands and contributing to the smog problems."

"What? There aren't any wetlands on this property, and we don't have any smog problem." Will stared dumbfounded at the man.

"There's a wetland back there," the man said jabbing his finger toward the northeast corner of the property. "I seen it with my own eyes." Abruptly he turned and walked back to the van. The men and women who had emerged from the back of the van were removing protest signs and assembling themselves on the side of the road. The driver of the van began chanting, "No more sprawl. No more sprawl," and the others joined in.

Will was so absorbed in what was going on that he failed to notice the newspaper reporter, Lloyd Randell, step out of the car that had pulled in behind the van. Randell had a photographer with him, who immediately began taking pictures of the cluster of protesters. Will glanced at his watch . . . there were still fifteen minutes until Charles Merrill was due to arrive with the drawings of the project. He was at a loss what to do. Lloyd Randell separated himself from the protesters and made his way to where Will stood watching the demonstration.

He was wearing a tweed coat that was too small to button across his ample middle and as he approached Will, he removed a pad of paper from the inside coat pocket. "Well, Martin, what do you think of this?" He gestured toward the protesters.

"I don't know what to think," Will said as if in a daze. "I had no idea they'd be here." He blinked his eyes. "There's no wetland here."

"Oh? What about the pond back there?" Randell pointed across the field.

"Pond?" Will replied. "You mean that little puddle in the back corner?"

Randell flipped over several pages in his notebook, "That 'little puddle,' as you call it, is fed by Telford's well. It has considerable historical significance, as well as being a free-flowing artesian well. I hardly think it is a 'little puddle.' "

Will stared at the newspaperman. "The last time I looked at that corner there was just a rusty pipe sticking out of the ground."

"Oh? Then how did you know about your 'little puddle'?" Randell asked with his pencil poised above the notepad.

"The last time before this morning is what I meant to say. While I was walking the boundaries of the property just now, I discovered somebody had opened the valve on the pipe."

A half dozen cars were arriving, raising more dust, and Will was relieved to see David Jobb's Lincoln among them. The protesters increased the volume of their chant as people began to emerge from their cars. A television van pulled past Will and Lloyd Randell, and its crew began setting up equipment. David Jobb waved, then hurried down the road to Will's side.

"Sorry to be late," he said, shaking Will's hand. He turned to the newspaperman. "How are you, Lloyd?" he asked.

"Fine as frog's hair," Randell replied. "Just wondering why your boy here didn't know about the wetland on the property."

"Wetland?" Jobb asked.

"There's an old rusty pipe in the back corner," Will said.

"Somebody has opened the valve in the last few days and there's a puddle about an inch deep that's draining into the irrigation ditch. Mr. Randell tells me it's a capped artesian well."

Jobb shaded his eyes with his hand and looked across the field. "I'd hardly call that a wetland, Lloyd."

The newspaperman shrugged his shoulders, turned with a slight bow, and walked toward the protesters. Over his shoulder he said, "I guess we'll just have to see, won't we?"

Will shuddered slightly. "I don't like that man."

"Nor do I," Jobb replied, "but what's with the chanting and the signs?"

"They pulled up a few minutes ago. They're against destroying wetlands and creating urban sprawl. At least that's what their leader said."

"I wonder who hired them." David stroked his chin.

"Hired? What do you mean?"

"Oh, I think they're a bunch of professional protesters. We call them the PANE . . . People Against Nearly Everything. If there's no controversy, there's no paycheck. Somebody put them up to this demonstration. Wetland, my foot." The lawyer suddenly spun on his heel and walked briskly to where the large bearded protester led the chant. They engaged in a conversation that appeared to Will to become increasingly heated. Will started to join David Jobb when Charles Merrill drove up in his van and opened the rear doors. He spotted Will and beckoned to him.

"What's all this?" he said when Will reached the back of the van.

"Protesters," Will replied. "David thinks they've been hired."

"Well, it will liven things up a bit, I suspect. How about giving me a hand with these easels? I've brought two of them."

Will carried the two easels through the line of protesters to the edge of the property and set them up. Charles Merrill followed behind, carrying the two large renderings of the Martin's Glen project, both carefully draped with navy blue cloth. He placed one of them on each easel. The television crews hoisted their cameras to their shoulders as Will stood between the two draped pictures, with David Jobb on one side and Charles Merrill on the other.

Several more cars arrived, and people climbed out of them to join the growing crowd on the edge of the field. The protesters increased the volume of their chant.

"How do we get them to be quiet?" Will asked David Jobb.

"Let me handle it," he said as he left Will's side and walked quickly to the bearded leader of the group. After a few quick words were exchanged, the unkempt man lowered his sign and the chanting stopped. David made his way back to Will's side with a sly smile on his face. "Go ahead," he whispered to Will.

"Friends," Will began, "thank you for coming to the unveiling of what I think will be a great development for our town. We've carefully tried to avoid the problems that other, unplanned developments have run into. We've integrated homes, businesses, and open space into a beautifully designed, planned community." Will spotted Hunter Hoggard and Ray Spellman standing near the back of the crowd.

"I want you to know we couldn't have done this without the help of some very skilled and professional players. Hunter, Ray, would you please join us up front?" Both men made their way through the small crowd to Will's side. "I'm sure all of you recognize Hunter Hoggard and Ray Spellman and are familiar with the excellent work done by these two fine contractors."

A few people in the crowd clapped their hands. Will continued, "We want to assure you that both the homes and businesses built in this community will be of the highest quality." He indicated Charles Merrill with his right hand. "Many of you know the excellence associated with Charles Merrill's architectural designs. In a moment I'm going to ask him to unveil the drawings he has done that will show you the scope and beauty of this project." He paused and looked over the crowd. The protesters remained quiet but appeared ready to begin at a moment's notice. Lloyd Randell was busily taking notes. Suddenly Will saw a face in the crowd that surprised him. Julia Welsch, a woman he had dated when he first returned home, was standing on the back fringe, next to one of the television cameramen. Will had broken off their relationship and had not seen Julia since. *Why in the world is she here?* he thought.

The crowd began to murmur slightly. David Jobb turned

to Will and said quietly, "You'd better show them the renderings before the protesters start again. The crowd's getting restless."

With a slight nod Will turned to Charles Merrill. "Why don't we show these people what they've come to see?" With a flourish Charles and David flipped the navy blue covers backward over the easels and the crowd moved forward to get a better look. "We give you Martin's Glen."

Immediately the protesters hoisted their signs and began chanting. One of the television reporters waved over the crowd and beckoned to Will. He melted back through the crowd until he stood on the fringe with the reporter who thrust a microphone in front of him and then nodded to her cameraman.

"We're at the site of a new project that was announced this morning. I have with me Mr. Will Martin, who is overseeing the development of Martin's Glen." The camera panned to Will. "What are you hoping to accomplish, Mr. Martin?"

Will looked at the reporter. "Well, we're trying to build a community that will serve the needs of its residents and be mindful of the environment."

"How quickly will we see this empty field transformed into your dream?"

Will cleared his throat. "We expect to break ground within the next few months and have the first homes ready to occupy by next summer at the latest."

"Why the protest?"

"I'm really not sure," Will responded.

"Thank you," she finished and the smile slid from her face as the camera was shut off. "Sam, get a shot of the picture," she pointed at one of the easels, "then let's get a statement from Myron . . . the big guy in the coveralls. He's usually the spokesman for the group." She turned back to Will and the smile reappeared. "Thank you, Mr. Martin."

"My pleasure," Will said. He watched the television crew work their way to the front of the crowd when he felt a hand on his arm. He turned his head and saw Julia Welsch smiling at him. "Julia," he stammered. "How are you?"

"Fine, just fine, Will." She pulled him to her and kissed him. "Good luck with your project. Shouldn't you be up front?" She pointed at the crowd gathered around the easels.

"Thank you," he said uncomfortably. "I've got to get over to the ball field. Justin's playing a game." He stepped back. "What are you up to nowadays?"

"Oh, not much," she said as she backed away from him. "I'll let you go." Then under her breath she said, "I'm just dabbling in a little politics."

Will had not noticed the photographer taking their picture. He glanced at his watch. It was quarter to twelve. He hurried to the Jaguar and sped to the ball game.

24

· · ·

WILL PULLED INTO THE PARKING LOT at the ball field and glanced at the dashboard clock. He was five minutes late for the start of the game, and he could hear the chatter from parents and players as he opened the door of the Jaguar. He trotted around the end of the aging stands and looked for Renee. He found her about halfway up the bleachers and made his way through the spectators to her side. He sat on the peeling forest-green-painted plank beside her.

"They just barely started, there's one out," she said. "How did the unveiling go?"

Will shaded his eyes with his hand and looked at the young boys on the field. Justin waved at him from his spot to the right of first base. "Okay, I guess. There were a few surprises."

The batter bounced a pitch back to the pitcher, who caught it and threw it to first base. Justin caught the ball and stepped on the bag.

Will jumped to his feet. "Good play, Champ!" he yelled. Justin swaggered a little as he walked back to his assigned spot. Will sat back down.

"What kind of surprises?" Renee asked.

"Someone had opened a valve on a pipe and flooded one area, and a bunch of protesters showed up to complain about ruining wetlands. It was bizarre. But the television people were there, and I think we'll be on Channel 8 tonight. That newspaper reporter, Lloyd Randell, was there, too, to cover the event." He thought about mentioning Julia Welsch and decided not to. "It was kind of a circus, but Charles Merrill has done some wonderful renderings of the whole project."

The next batter struck out and Justin's team trotted in from the field.

"All in all I think things went all right."

Justin came over to the backstop and stuck his fingers through the chain-link fence, "Hi, Will," he called.

"Hey, Champ. That was a great play at first," Will said enthusiastically. Justin ducked his head and grinned.

Renee stuck her arm through Will's, "It looks like all your practice paid off," she said, giving his arm a squeeze.

The game ended with Justin's team claiming a close victory, twelve to ten. Justin had managed to get two hits and score one run. He ran around the backstop and met Will and Renee at the bottom of the bleachers.

"Good game, Justin," Will said as he put his hand on Justin's shoulder.

"We won!" Justin exclaimed.

"Yes, you did," Renee said with a smile.

"I think we ought to celebrate with hamburgers at

Wendy's," Will said. "How about it?" Justin nodded his head and hurried toward Will's car.

Will took Renee's hand. "Why don't you leave your car here, and we'll run back and pick it up after we eat."

Fifteen minutes later they were sitting at a table eating lunch while Justin gave a play-by-play recounting of the game between mouthfuls of hamburger and French fries. Nearly an hour passed before they returned to the ball field, where another game was going on. Renee slipped out of the Jaguar. "Are you coming with me or are you riding home with Will?" she asked her son.

"I'll ride with Will," he said from the backseat.

"I'll see you at home, then," she said with a smile. Will backed his car out of the parking lot, while Renee walked to hers. There was a manila envelope tucked under the windshield wiper of the Chevrolet. Puzzled, she retrieved it, opened it, and removed the photograph from inside. It was a picture of Will and Julia Welsch, kissing. Renee's knees felt weak and she leaned back against the car, feeling as though she had been punched in the stomach. Blinking back tears, she unlocked the door of her car and sat down heavily. She inspected the picture more closely. It was clear that it had been taken this morning. She could see the small crowd of people in the background and recognized the location. *What is going on here?* she thought as her fingers felt the sticky note on the back of the photograph. She turned the picture over and read, "Tell your husband to withdraw from the race or we go public with this."

A flush of anger rose within her. She started the car and sprayed gravel as she shot onto the street. She was still fuming when she pulled into the driveway and parked next to Will's car. Grabbing the photograph she stomped into the house. Will was on the telephone as she entered the kitchen.

"David, I'm sorry," he said. "I had to get to Justin's ball game." He listened for a moment while Renee crossed her arms and leaned against the sink. "Well, I guess we'll just have to do what we can do. I'll talk to you on Monday. Good-bye." Will hung up the phone, walked to a chair and sat down wearily. It suddenly registered with him that his wife was standing across the kitchen. "That was David Jobb," he said by way of explanation. "Apparently, after I left Martin's Glen, there were several people who wanted to talk with me. David had to field the questions, and I don't think he was very happy."

"I'm not very happy, either," she spat. "Look at this." She handed Will the photograph.

Will looked at the picture and blanched. "I should have told you about Julia being there," he said, embarrassed.

"Yes, you should have," Renee said acidly, "but that's not the problem. Turn it over."

Will read the note. "What in the world . . . ?"

"You were set up! That little witch set you up!"

"Why?" Will asked. "I haven't had anything to do with her in well over a year. I haven't even seen her around town. I don't understand."

Renee sat down opposite Will, still fuming. "I think I do. I think your competition is worried. Maybe it's time we paid him a visit." She leaned back in her chair. "Have you ever met Milton Phillips?"

"Not personally."

She stood up, picked up the phone book, and began looking through it. "Do you have any idea where he lives?"

Will shook his head. "No idea." He looked at the picture again. "Maybe we ought to call David and let him know what's happening."

"Good idea," Renee said. "Maybe he knows where Milton Phillips lives, since apparently he has an unlisted phone number."

Will picked up the phone and called David Jobb's number. When the attorney answered, Will filled him in on the details of what had transpired.

"I'll be right there," Jobb said.

Will hung up the phone as Justin ran into the kitchen. "Can we go practice, Will?"

Renee looked at her son and said, "Will and I have some business to attend to, sweetheart. Maybe you two can practice later."

"Aw, Mom," he whined.

"Justin, that's enough. This is something we have to do." Her voice had an edge to it.

"Later, Champ," Will interjected. "But your mom's right. We have something we need to do right now." He picked up the phone and dialed his grandmother's number. When she answered, he said, "Grams, this is Will. I hate to ask this on such short notice, but is there any chance you could come over and watch Justin for an hour or so? Renee and I have an emergency we need to deal with." He listened to her answer. "Thanks. I'll run over and pick you up."

"I don't need anyone to watch me," Justin said petulantly.

"I'm sure that's true," Will said, "but just humor us on this one." He hurried out of the house.

David Jobb was pulling up to the curb when Will returned with his grandmother. The three of them walked into the house together.

Renee met them at the door and thrust the photograph into Jobb's hand. "Take a look at this," she snarled.

Ruth Martin looked over David's shoulder at the photograph. "Why, that's Julia Welsch," she said.

"Look at the note on the back," Renee commanded.

David turned the picture over, read the note, and his face turned grim. "I told you they'd do anything to win," he said. "But I didn't think they'd stoop this low." He peeled the note from the back of the photo. "The question is, how do we handle this?"

"Will and I were just going to go visit Milton Phillips," Renee said. "If you know where he lives."

Jobb sank down on the couch. "I'm not sure that's the wisest course," he mused. "Let's think about this for a while." He inspected the photograph again. "What happens if they do go public? . . . How will they do it?" David tapped the edge of the photograph on the side of his hand. "I suppose the only way they can is if they get it published in the newspaper."

Ruth Martin had remained quiet, but now she spoke up. "You know, dear, I think it's marvelous that Julia is so excited about your new project. Wouldn't it be wonderful if everyone knew how excited she was?"

"What?" Will said.

Renee stared at the silver-haired woman and smiled. "Your grandmother is absolutely right," she said. "Why don't we publish the picture first?"

David Jobb's face broke into a big smile. "Ruth Martin, you're a genius." He stood up quickly. "Why don't you let me take care of getting the press release to the paper . . . if I can have this photograph."

"Of course," Will smiled. David started toward the door. "Can I ask you something, David?"

"Of course."

"How did you get the protesters to stop chanting this morning? While I was speaking, I mean."

"Oh, that was easy. I just asked Myron . . . the big, shaggy character . . . how much he was being paid and offered him a hundred dollars if they'd be quiet for ten minutes. It seemed like a simple enough solution."

Will smiled thinly and shook his head. "I guess you can get anything you want with money."

Jobb frowned. "I really should have seen this coming," he said, flourishing the photograph. "Myron told me that the

CCG had hired him to turn on the tap to create the 'wetland' and then start demonstrating."

"And how much did that information cost you?" Renee asked.

Jobb smiled as he walked out the door. "Never mind, we'll take it out of your campaign contributions."

Ruth Martin stood up. "Well, it seems that you don't need my help," she said with a smile. "It's a beautiful day. I think I'll walk home."

25

· · ·

RENEE TOOK WILL'S HAND AS HE helped her from the car. They could hear organ music through the open doors as they entered the chapel and searched for a seat. The church was nearly full with a large portion of the center section roped off. They found a spot near the front on the left side of the chapel where a woman in a black pantsuit and a large-brimmed black straw hat was occupying most of a pew. A small man with a florid complexion sat on her other side.

"Is this seat taken?" Will whispered.

She shook her head and slid closer to her husband, making room for Will and Renee.

"Thank you," Renee said as she sat down next to the woman. Will squeezed in next to his wife and placed his arm around her shoulders. "This has been a hard two months," she said quietly. "I'm surprised he hung on this long. At least it has given us a chance to get to know Louise better." Will nodded his head.

They sat silently listening to the music for nearly half an hour before three men walked into the chapel and made their way to the raised stand. Two of them sat down and the third walked to the pulpit.

"Would you all please stand?" he said in a quiet voice.

The audience arose, and two funeral directors guided a coffin on a wheeled carriage to its place in front of the pulpit. The coffin was gunmetal blue with an American flag draped over it. Louise Barrow, dressed in a black floor-length dress, followed the coffin until she was led to a seat on the second pew. She was followed by well over a hundred men and women who filled in the reserved section of the chapel. When they were all seated, the speaker announced, "Thank you. You may all be seated."

There was rustling of fabric and a muted cough as the crowd complied. Louise Barrow sat straight-backed, her silver hair gleaming against the blackness of her outfit.

The speaker cleared his throat, "Thank you for being here and acknowledging the accomplishments of a remarkable man, Creighton Langston Barrow. My name is Lyle Warburton, and I've been asked by Louise to conduct these services."

"He's the Speaker of the House," Will whispered to Renee. "I think all of those men and women over there are members of the House and Senate."

"Next year you'll be among them," she whispered back, squeezing his arm.

"Maybe."

"Shhh," the hat next to Renee said.

Lyle Warburton began his eulogy of Creighton Barrow, "He was an ordinary man who did extraordinary things. This community has few men of his stature. He was a very private man, who sought not for the honor of men but to serve men. In the ten years I had the opportunity and pleasure to serve with Creigh, I found him to be honest, forthright, and a voice of reason. He will be sorely missed." He grasped the sides of the pulpit and struggled to compose himself. When he could finally continue he said, "Louise—wonderful, beautiful, stalwart Louise—who stood beside him and gave her unwavering support. How bitter this separation must be, yet how wonderful it must be to see this faithful companion free of pain." He looked into Louise's eyes.

His remarks continued for another ten minutes, then he relinquished the pulpit to one of the other gentlemen sitting on the stand. He was thin, almost cadaverous, and spoke with a high reedy voice.

"Creigh Barrow was one of a kind," he began. "A man who held an enormous amount of power in his hands and never misused it." He coughed softly into his handkerchief.

"Who is he?" Renee whispered to Will.

"I don't know," he whispered back.

As if in answer to their question, the man said, "My name is Roland Ainsworth, and I had the opportunity to serve with Creigh on a number of projects over the past thirty years." He looked down at Louise. "Louise, what a great man you were married to. And what a great woman you are." He continued speaking for several more minutes.

The third speaker concluded, and the congregation followed

the coffin out of the church. A light drizzle had begun during the service, and people scurried to their cars to form a cortege to the cemetery. By the time they arrived at the memorial gardens, the heavens had opened, bright flashes of lightning sparked, and ominous thunder rebounded from the hills. Will retrieved an umbrella from the backseat of the car and held it over the two of them as he and Renee stepped through the wet grass to the graveside where two large canopies had been erected. Only a few of those at the funeral had traveled to the cemetery, but even so they had to crowd together under the canopies to avoid the drenching rain. Then, as quickly as it had come, the rain stopped, and the sun split the clouds.

David Jobb led Louise Barrow to a folding seat under the canopy as the coffin was lowered by the pallbearers onto the canvas straps spanning the grave. She looked at the handful of mourners who stood nearby, saw Will and Renee, and with a sad little smile beckoned to them to join her. She patted the seats on both sides of her and the two of them sat down.

"Thank you," she said. "I need your support."

The mournful sound of a single bugle began playing "Taps." An honor guard removed the flag from on top of the casket, folded it, and presented it to Louise. A prayer was offered and the service was over. Will and Renee helped the widow to her feet as people began passing by to offer their final condolences. The last in line was Lyle Warburton, Speaker of the House. He took her hand between both of his and said, "Louise, this is not really the time or place, but I do hope you'll consider our offer." He leaned over and kissed her gently on her cheek.

"Lyle," she said softly, "thank you so much for all you did today. I appreciate you more than you know."

"My pleasure," he replied. "I'll call you next week."

Louise nodded her head gently. "That will be fine."

Lyle Warburton let go of her hand and extended his toward Will. "I'm Lyle Warburton," he said.

"Will Martin." He took the Speaker's hand.

"Ah. Yes," he said. "And this is your pretty wife. Creighton and I knew your grandfather well. They were two of a kind. If you are anything like your grandfather, I can understand why Creigh was so strong in his endorsement of you." He let go of Will's hand and took Renee's between his own two hands. "Well, I'd better be going."

David Jobb joined the three of them, and Louise handed him the folded flag. "Are you ready to go?" he asked.

Louise Barrow sank back onto the chair and stared empty-eyed across the cemetery. "David, I'm not thinking very clearly right now, and Lyle has made me an offer I'm not sure I'm ready to accept."

Jobb sat down next to her. "What kind of an offer?"

"He wants me to finish out Creigh's term."

"I see."

Suddenly she looked up at Will and said, "I suggested they appoint you, Will, so you can run as an incumbent, but he balked." She reached for David's hand. "I'm not much of a political animal, my old friend. I'm asking for your advice."

David Jobb ran his hand over his nearly bald head. "You'd be wonderful, Louise. There are only a handful of meetings left and you'd find them interesting." He looked up at Will with a puzzled expression on his face. "I'm sure they'll appoint someone else to serve as majority leader, so you won't have to worry about that." He squeezed Louise's hand. "Of course the decision is yours. But if I can be of any help, just know that I am here."

"Thank you, David." She reached out for Will's hand and pulled herself to her feet. "I'm ready to go now," she said, glancing at the grave. Tears once again began to course down her cheeks as David led her across the grass toward his Lincoln.

An hour later the phone rang on Will's desk. "Martin Real Estate, Will speaking."

"Will, this is David Jobb. Are you available? We need to talk."

"I have an appointment in about ten minutes that will last about an hour, then I'm free. Will that work?"

"Could you come to my office when you've finished?"

Will checked his calendar for the rest of the day. "Sure. I'll be there before four o'clock. You sound awfully serious, is there a problem?"

The attorney sighed. "I'll tell you when you get here. I'll see you around four."

26

• • •

I'M NOT SURE WHAT THE CCG HAVE threatened, but I can't get Lyle Warburton to budge on your nomination," Jobb ran his hand across his head. "Louise is a fine woman . . . don't misunderstand me . . . but she doesn't have a political bone in her body. With his influence, he could have the party send your name to the governor and have him appoint you to finish out Creighton's term. But for some reason he won't do it. And the only reason he gives is that he wants to honor Creighton by appointing Louise." He paced back and forth across the office.

"What makes you think the CCG are involved?" Will asked.

Jobb stopped his pacing. "Well, we've come up with another little problem," he said, pointing to the couch. "Have a seat."

Will sat down. "What kind of a problem?"

David Jobb sat down on the corner of his desk. "You know I've been trying to raise money for your campaign. Nearly eight thousand dollars came in quickly and then it was just as if the tap was turned off. I've been to some of the people I felt would gladly contribute to you and I started getting a bushel full of excuses. I finally nailed down . . . well, perhaps I shouldn't mention names . . . anyway, I finally found out that Milton Phillips and the CCG have threatened to boycott any business that contributes money to you." He spread his hands on his desk. "So there we are. I've approached a few individuals for contributions, and we'll be all right, but we're not going to have as much as I expected."

"Why would they do that?"

Jobb stared into Will's eyes. "Because they see you as a threat, Will. And they'll do anything, and I mean *anything,* to win."

"I guess it's a good thing we have the signs and flyers printed."

David nodded his head. "And I've paid those bills. But after we pay the postage on one mailer, the kitty will be pretty empty." He stood up and began to pace again. "We'll be all right, but it would sure be a boost if Warburton would get you nominated instead of Louise. She doesn't really want it, and it would give you some additional exposure. Come November, I think you're going to need every vote you can get."

Will massaged his temples. "I'm not cut out for this, David."

The lawyer stopped pacing, walked to where Will sat, and looked into his face. "Yes, you are, Will Martin. I can't think of a better person for the job. Creighton and I can see your grandfather in you. I didn't tell you these things to discourage you. I just wanted to give you a heads-up."

Will sighed. "If you say so." He lowered his eyes. "Any other bad news?"

Jobb shook his head. "Not really. What can I do to help you?" He stroked his head. "This has kept you pretty busy. Have you gotten any further on your adoption plans?"

Will stood up abruptly, "No, I still haven't found Gary Carr, but aside from an initial attempt, I haven't had time to search for him." He started toward the door. "But if there isn't anything else, I'd better get going. Justin's team is playing this afternoon, and if they win they get to play for the championship."

"Of course," Jobb said. "Can I ask you something, Will?"

Will stopped with his hand on the doorknob. "Sure."

"Have you talked to your wife about this?"

Will froze in place. "I can't, David. I've got to find Gary and get his permission. Then I'll talk to Renee."

The lawyer cleared his throat. "She might have information that would help you find him. I can't believe she'd oppose the adoption. Gary might be difficult to locate."

"David, you might be right, but I just don't feel good about it. I've got to find Gary Carr."

"As you wish, Will. Would you mind a suggestion?"

"Not at all."

"Why not try setting a date? A time when you'll have definitely resolved this problem. I've learned that when I write down a goal, or share it with a friend, then I tend to accomplish what I've set out to do. An unwritten goal is nothing more than a wish."

Will let go of the doorknob, turned, and leaned against the door. "There is so much going on in my life right now, David. With the election just a couple of months ahead and the groundbreaking of Martin's Glen, I don't know when I'll have time—"

"To do what's really important?" Jobb put his hand on Will's shoulder. "I'm not trying to pressure you, but I think you're going to find more and more excuses not to spend the time on the adoption. Will, families are what this life is all about. I know you've got heavy responsibilities with the Martin's Glen project, and I know I've placed a big burden on your shoulders with your campaign, but you need to solve this problem because it's always in the back of your mind gnawing at you. Will, it's a worthy quest you're on, and at the risk of offending you, let me ask you again, when are you going to spend enough time to go ahead with the adoption?"

Will stammered, "By Christmas . . . by the end of the year."

David Jobb smiled and patted Will's shoulder. "Now that wasn't too hard was it? I feel confident that you'll be able to get the answers you need." He opened the door. "Now hurry so you're not late to the ball game. Oh, and I'll be checking from time to time to see how things are progressing."

Will hurried out of the office, jogged across the square to his Jaguar, and drove across town to the ballpark. He realized, with some satisfaction, that he had arrived before Justin and

Renee. The bleachers were nearly half-full as he climbed up the splintered green seats. He shook hands with several of the people he recognized from the baseball season. *I need to do that more often. These people are going to be the ones who go the polls in November.* He blinked. *Whoa, I'm starting to think like a politician.*

He saw Renee's Chevrolet bounce into the parking lot, and he stood and waved. Renee and Justin waved back. The boy ran ahead of his mother. "You're here!" He bounced up the seats to where Will stood.

"Wouldn't miss it, Champ." He put his arm around Justin and gave him a hug. "Go play a smart game."

"Think we'll win?" the boy said as he skipped back down the seats.

"You bet! But if you don't, we'll still love you."

Justin stopped, looked back at Will, and grinned. Renee reached Will, unfolded a blanket on the bleachers, and sat down. "Busy day?"

Will kissed her on the cheek. "Kind of a discouraging one, actually." He told her of the conversation he'd had with David Jobb. When he finished she sat quietly fuming.

"Play ball," the umpire shouted as he pulled the mask over his face and squatted down behind the catcher.

Justin's team had lost the toss and was up first. As the lead off batter stepped into the box, Renee swiveled on the blanket and looked directly into Will's eyes. "Will, from the moment you decided to get involved in this insanity I told you I'd support you. I've tried to do that." He nodded his head. "But this kind of shenanigan is nothing more than dirty politics and it means war!"

"Y're out!" the umpire called as his thumb jerked over his shoulder.

"Sweetheart, I'm not sure what we're going to do, but we're not going to stoop to those kinds of tactics," he said.

The next batter hit a shallow fly toward left field, and the fielder caught the ball. The third batter walked to the batter's box.

Renee's face was rigid. "I don't know what we're going to do, either, but this means we come out with both guns blazing!"

The batter hit a ground ball between the shortstop, and the third baseman and ran, as fast as his short little legs could carry him, to first base. Justin was up next.

"I think we're going to be okay," he said. "David's working on it." He pointed at Justin. "Come on, Champ. Just meet the ball, don't try to kill it. Easy does it."

Justin let the first two pitches go by . . . one a ball, one a strike. He swung at the third pitch and sent the ball bouncing past the pitcher. The second baseman grabbed the ball and stepped on the base. Justin ran over to the bench, grabbed his mitt, and looked into the stands.

"Good hit, Champ," Will said. "You'll get 'em next inning."

Justin grinned and ran to his position at first base.

"Aren't there laws against what Milton Phillips is doing?" Renee asked.

"Apparently he's very clever with what he's saying," Will replied. "David's working on a plan of attack." He patted her hand. "Let's watch the game."

Will watched while Renee gnawed on her knuckle. The game was scoreless at the start of the final inning, and Will realized Justin was the first batter. He stepped into the box and looked at the pitcher. The first ball was low and bounced into the catcher's mitt from just in front of home plate.

"Ball one," the umpire called.

The second pitch floated toward the plate and Justin made contact, sending a soft liner into left field. The ball dropped between the shortstop and the fielder, and Justin ran as fast as he could to first base.

"Way to go, Champ!" Will leapt to his feet and yelled. Justin waved at him from his perch on first base. The next batter, Bob Gold, was the oldest boy on the team. He glared at the pitcher, swung at the first pitch, and sent it deep into center field. Justin took off and reached third base before the coach signaled him to stop. They had runners on second and third.

"What do you think David's going to do?" Renee asked.

"I don't know, sweetheart. I'm just leaving it up to him." He pointed at Justin on third base. "Look where Justin is."

The next two batters struck out. Jeff Lewis, the smallest

member of the team, stepped to the plate. The pitcher threw the first ball so high the catcher had to stand to catch it.

"Ball one."

The next two pitches were so low that they nearly hit the plate. The opposing coach called time out and walked out to the pitcher's mound. Jeff Lewis looked for help from Coach Morris when the umpire said, "Play ball."

The pitcher threw a pitch low and outside. Jeff reached for it and hit it. The ball dribbled toward the third baseman. As Jeff hit the ball Justin started for home. The third baseman ran toward the ball, grabbed it, and turned to throw toward first base. Out of the corner of his eye he saw Justin running for home, Bob Gold running for third, and the batter running for first. He hesitated, trying to decide where to throw the ball, and Justin crossed home plate. Too late, the third baseman threw the ball to first base.

The next player struck out, stranding two men on base. Justin's team led one to nothing.

"Good work, Champ," Will stood up and called as Justin gathered up his mitt and trotted to first base. "Three outs and the game's over."

"What if we talked to Louise Barrow and asked for her help?" Renee said as Will sat back down. "Maybe if she told the Speaker she wasn't interested, he'd nominate you. What do you think?"

"I guess it couldn't hurt, but I think she's already told him that." The first batter stepped into the box. "Easy out!" Will yelled.

"I think we ought to go see her this evening," Renee persisted.

The batter hit the first pitch and bounced it back to the pitcher, who threw it to Justin at first base. One out.

"Do you want me to call her and see if she's free?" Renee asked.

"Sure," Will replied. "Two more outs are all we need," he called toward the field.

The second batter struck out and the third hit a pop fly that the shortstop caught. Will jumped to his feet, bounded down the bleachers, and ran to join the players and parents on the field. He lifted Justin off the ground and hugged him. "You did it, Champ! Great game!"

Justin threw his arms around Will's neck and hugged him back. Will set him back on the ground as Coach Morris signaled for his team to surround him. "Let's give a cheer for the Badgers," he said. "Hip, hip, hooray, Badgers!"

Will slipped back through the crowd and leaned against the backstop. The Badgers returned a cheer for the Mustangs, gathered up their gear, and walked dejectedly off the field. Coach Morris raised his hand and tried to get his team to quiet down. After some time he was able to be heard over their cheers.

"All right, team, I'm proud of you. One more game and you've won the championship." The boys cheered and jumped up and down. Coach Morris looked at the parents who were either on the field or standing in the bleachers. "I'm proud of your boys," he said loudly. "You've raised fine sons." He lifted the cap from his head, slicked down his hair, and replaced it. "The final game is next Saturday at noon. We play the Diablos. They're a good team, as you know. We've played them twice this season and we've split. Each of us has won one game, so this will be a tough one." The boys had grown quiet. The coach spread his arms as if to envelop the entire team. "But with this great team, I'm confident we're going to win. You guys are awesome!" he shouted. And the boys erupted into cheers.

Renee came down from the bleachers and stood behind Will on the opposite side of the backdrop. She stuck her fingers through the fence and poked him gently in the back. "Thank you," she said.

He turned around and touched her fingers with his. "For what?"

"For helping Justin," she said with glistening eyes. "For loving both of us."

Justin ran over and threw his arms around Will's waist. "Are you riding home with me or your mom?" Will asked.

Justin looked through the chain-link fence at his mother, "Is okay if I go with Will?" he asked.

"Sure, sweetheart," she said. "That would be just fine."

Will put his hand on Justin's shoulder and said through the backstop, "We'll see you at home." He gave Renee a wink and turned to Justin. "You scored the winning run, Champ."

. . .

27

"I HAVE NO POLITICAL ASPIRATIONS, none at all. Surely you know that," Louise Barrow said. "I've told Lyle Warburton he ought to nominate you, but there's some problem . . . I have no idea what it is . . . and he says he can't do it."

Renee, Justin, and Will sat together in the living room of the Barrows' home. Renee spoke quietly, "Thank you, Mrs. Barrow, you were kind to allow us to visit on such short notice. Thank you for already approaching the Speaker about nominating Will."

Louise Barrow looked past them and out the window into the garden. The sun had set, stitching a fringe of gold on the edge of rose-tinted clouds. Accent lights had come on in the garden. "You know this is the part of politics that Creigh hated. He was there to work for the people he represented. I never heard him speak an ill word about any other member of the House . . . from either party. He felt strongly that you had to stoop pretty low to pick up mud." A frown crossed her face. "I'm sorry, Will. I'm not sure what is going on. There must be some threat I'm not aware of, but I'm afraid I can't help you, much as I want to."

Will stood up from the couch. "Thank you, Mrs. Barrow. You've been most kind."

"Nonsense. It's the least I could do after all your grandfather did for us."

"Oh?" Will waited patiently.

Louise Barrow sat quietly for several seconds, then said, "When Creigh first decided to go into politics he approached your grandfather for advice. Warren was emphatic that if Creigh was going to take this important step he'd have to be very careful that he remain an honest man. Then he gave Creigh a check for enough money to begin his campaign in style. Every year he ran for reelection, Creigh knew he could count on your grandfather for support. He, David Jobb, and Creigh were the three musketeers. Three supermen, and now David's the only one left." She stared vacantly out the window. "Creigh saw your grandfather in you, young Will. That's why he asked David to get you to run for his seat. He needed an honest man." She drifted again into silence.

Will helped Renee to her feet, and the three of them followed Louise Barrow to the front door. "Thank you," Renee said.

"For what? I wish I could be of more help." She was not much taller than Justin, and she took his hand in hers. "Thank you for visiting, young man. You come back again." Justin nodded his head. She shook Will's hand then reached for Renee's and held it between hers while Will and Justin continued toward the car. "Can I ask a rather indelicate question?" she whispered.

"I suppose," Renee answered warily.

Louise Barrow pursed her lips, "I suppose there's no politically correct way to ask this, but weren't you married to Gary Carr?"

Renee's eyebrows raised. "Yes, I was," she said quietly, "several years ago. Why do you ask?"

"Just an old woman's curiosity. I thought I recognized you, and I hope I didn't offend you."

"Of course not," Renee replied as she started down the steps to where Will and Justin waited.

"Do you know how he is doing?"

Renee looked back to where Louise stood on the porch. "I haven't seen or heard from Gary in nearly five years, Mrs. Barrow. I'm afraid I'm not much help."

"Oh, my, I'm sorry, my dear, I didn't mean to revisit unpleasant memories." Louise fluttered her hands.

Will took a step back toward the porch. "Mrs. Barrow, what did you mean, 'How is he doing?'"

Louise looked very uncomfortable. "Perhaps it's not my place to say anything. I'm really not much of a gossip, you know."

"I'm sure you're not," Will responded.

The silver-haired woman fussed with her collar before finally saying, "When I first took Creigh back to Sloane-Kettering, we thought it was interesting that two other people from our little community were there as well. Mr. Carr . . . Gary . . . was one of them." She twisted her hands together. "I was just wondering how he was. I haven't seen him since."

Renee looked perplexed. "How long ago was that?"

Louise Barrow thought for a moment. "My goodness, that must be nearly five years ago. Time does fly, doesn't it?"

"Yes, I suppose it does," Will interjected.

"I've kept you too long," Louise said. "I'd better let you go." She waved her hand and went back into the house.

"Did Gary have cancer?" Will asked as he opened the door for Renee.

"Not that I know."

"Maybe he was there doing computer networking for them," Will suggested. He started the car and drove toward home.

"Maybe," Renee said dubiously. "If so, he never told me about it." She sank down into the seat.

"Are we going to get ice cream on the way home?" Justin asked from the backseat.

"Sure, Champ. It's the least we can do to celebrate your victory."

Fifteen minutes later they sat outside the ice cream shop on white vinyl chairs, eating banana splits. Renee twirled a curl of her hair around her finger while she sucked on a maraschino cherry. The stem stuck out from between her lips like the tail of a mouse, and Will reached over and tugged on it. Renee swatted at his hand.

"Is it possible Gary had cancer?" Will asked.

Thoughtfully Renee chewed on the cherry. "I don't think so. He's no older than you," she said. "Why? You seem awfully interested."

Will raised his hands defensively. "No reason. Just wondering."

Renee chewed on the cherry and dropped the stem onto a napkin. "Still, I wonder when he was at Sloane-Kettering. It must have been after he left for Paris, but why would he come clear back to New York? It just doesn't add up."

"Will, are you coming to the game on Saturday?" Justin asked as he scooped a chunk of pineapple into his mouth.

"What? Oh, wouldn't miss it, Champ."

"Do you think we can win?"

Will smiled broadly at the little boy. "Absolutely. Especially when you have the best first baseman ever to play the game." He tugged Justin's ball cap down over his eyes.

Justin grinned. "Aw, I'm not that good," he said.

"I think you are." Will spooned the last bit of banana into his mouth. "Are we about ready to go home?"

"Two more bites," Renee replied. She looked at Justin and Will and smiled. "What's on the docket for Monday? Will you have time for lunch?"

"I'm headed over to Charles Merrill's Monday morning. He says he has the final plans drawn, and I need to get them over to the county courthouse. The commission was generous to give conceptual approval to the project, but they won't give final approval until they see the plans. Would you like to ride over with me? We could grab lunch on the way."

"Sounds good to me," she said with a smile. "I guess we'll be back in time to meet Justin when he gets home from school."

"Yeah," Justin said, "school."

"Great! It will be a good way to start out the week."

28

. . .

Hunter Hoggard and Ray Spellman were waiting at Charles Merrill's office when Will arrived. The three men had the plat plan rolled out on the conference table and were inspecting it when Will walked into the room.

"Good morning, gentlemen," Will said brightly. "How does it look?"

"Charlie always does good work," Hoggard said.

Ray Spellman nodded his head in agreement. "It really is a good plan, Will. You'll be pleased." The two developers stepped aside and Will joined Charles Merrill at the edge of the table. Will quickly scanned the drawing. On the south side of the property a grocery store was set back far enough to provide a parking lot with access from the road. A strip mall ran north and south along the west side of the parking lot. Merrill had carefully designed it so that the row of cottonwood trees was preserved behind the buildings. The rest of the acreage was divided into residential lots by a series of sweeping curved streets. In the northeast corner a small park and playground were designed, utilizing the water from Telford's well to feed a fountain and wading pool. Several other parks were scattered throughout the development.

"I'm impressed," Will said. "You do remarkable work, Charles."

The architect beamed. "You're too kind. I hope it's what you wanted."

Will turned to the two developers. "What do you two think?" Both men nodded their heads.

"When do we break ground?" Hoggard asked.

Will began to roll up the plans. "I'm taking these to the courthouse to get final approval, then I think we ought to get going as soon as we can."

"Super," Hoggard said. "I'd like to get a bunch of the homes dried in before the snow flies." He turned to his rival, "What about you, Ray?"

Spellman sat down on the edge of the table. "We're ready to go as soon as we know who's going to occupy the stores. Any word on that yet, Will?"

Will shook his head. "I'm meeting with the LaPoint Group later today. The funeral kind of stopped things for a while."

"I understand, but I hope you realize I can't start building without specific directions from a tenant." Spellman put his hand reassuringly on Will's shoulder. "But I'm sure you're going to rectify that problem shortly."

"I hope so, Ray."

"Sold any of the homes?" Hoggard asked.

"We have some interest in six of them," Will replied. "Not

as many as we'd hoped, but I think once the first one pops out of the ground we'll see increased interest. We need to see some income as soon as possible."

"Pro'ly right," Hunter said. "Anyway, you're going to have to have a model home or an office or something there, and we might as well do it right."

Will inserted the rolled-up plans into a cardboard tube. "Well, I'd better be on my way. I'm glad this is all starting to come together." The others nodded their heads in agreement.

Will had started for the door when Hunter Hoggard said, "How soon do you think you can get final approval?"

"The county commission meets tomorrow night, and they've already made this an action item on the agenda. I think we'll be good to go on Wednesday, unless there's some unexpected problem." Will tapped the cardboard tube against his leg.

Hoggard smiled broadly. "What if we had a ground-breaking this weekend? I could bring over a backhoe and dig a hole. We won't have it all staked out, but Charlie here has a couple of big maps of the property painted on plywood and we could get them on some posts at the corners of the project and make it look pretty good. Might generate some interest. What do ya think?"

Ray Spellman put a restraining hand on Hoggard's shoulder. "I really think we ought to have the lots laid out before we do anything that dramatic."

Hoggard lowered his head for a minute, then looked at

Spellman with a wolfish grin. "I'll tell you what, old man, if I pull my whole crew over to the property and you pull yours, I'll bet we can have it laid out by Saturday morning."

"Two hundred acres? You're nuts!" Spellman said.

"Guess I'll just have to do it myself," Hunter said.

"There hasn't been any site preparation," Spellman said emphatically.

"It's nearly flat, Ray. All we've got to do is run a blade over it to knock down the weeds and we can lay the whole thing out." He plopped his hard hat back on his head. "We're going to get approved . . . you know that . . . and I can have equipment over there this afternoon. We can have it cleared easy by Wednesday, and I've got two good survey teams that can start puttin' stakes in ten minutes later."

"It sounds like you're challenging me," Spellman said.

Hoggard smiled again. "Old man, we can do it ourselves. I was just trying to let you have some of the fun . . . in our new-found spirit of cooperation." He doffed his hat.

"I'll have my crew there, too," Spellman said gruffly. "You start on the southeast corner and we'll start on the northwest."

"Whatever you say," Hoggard said with mock civility.

Will smiled at Charles Merrill. "Well, like it or not, it looks as if we're under way." He held up the cardboard tube. "But, I'd better get these over to the county." Quickly he walked out of the building and drove away.

Charles Merrill watched him go, then said to the two developers, "Do you want me to put something together for

Saturday? I'd be happy to create a media release and get it delivered to the right people."

Ray Spellman nodded his head. "That would be great, Charles."

"How about noon on Saturday? That work for you?" Hoggard asked. "That'll give us three and a half days to get everything laid out."

"That works for me," Ray said, and Charles nodded his agreement.

"I'll send a truck over this afternoon to pick up those big signs you done," Hunter said to Merrill. "Soon as we clear the corners we ought to get those in place so that people know what's goin' on." Hoggard stuck the hard hat back on his head. "Well, time's a-wastin'. I'd better get my crew movin' on this."

Charles Merrill and Ray Spellman watched him go. "He's quite abrasive, but he does good work," the architect said.

"I have to admit you're right . . . on both counts," Spellman said with a smile. "I hope we don't have any glitches between now and Saturday." He lifted his jacket from the back of the chair and shrugged it onto his shoulders. "I guess I'd better get hold of my crew and tell them what we're doing."

Charles Merrill walked him to the door. "You know, Ray, I didn't think we had a chance in the world of breaking ground by October first, and it looks as if we're going to beat that date by a week."

"Pretty amazing."

"I guess if it had been Will's grandfather, Warren, I wouldn't be so surprised, but I have to admit I wasn't sure Will could handle all of this," Merrill said.

"I'm becoming more and more impressed with this kid, Charles. He just might turn out all right."

Will picked up Renee and delivered the plans to the county offices. They stopped for lunch on the way back. "Have you talked to David Jobb this morning?" she asked.

Will looked at the clouds gathering over the mountains to the east. The wind had picked up and a definite hint of fall was in the air. "No, I haven't," he finally answered.

"Would you mind if I called him?"

"Of course not," Will said. "I think you've almost become more involved in this race than I have."

"Just trying to be supportive," she replied.

He dropped her off at home and drove to his meeting with the LaPoint Group. Half an hour later he returned to his car and called Ray Spellman on his car phone. Ray's secretary answered and indicated that her boss had gone to the Martin's Glen site. Will turned the Jaguar around and headed for the project. When he arrived, two large, yellow scrapers were at work clearing off the weeds and leveling the ground. Hunter Hoggard and Ray Spellman were huddled around the tailgate of Hoggard's truck. Will parked behind them and hurried to the two men.

"Ray," Will called when he was still several steps away, "I have good news." He nearly sprinted to the truck. "Dee's

Markets has agreed to locate a store at Martin's Glen. Their staff wants to meet with you as quickly as possible to finalize the floor plan and design."

"Great!" Spellman said.

Will handed him a card with a name and phone number on it. "Apparently they've been here already and they've looked at Charles Merrill's designs. They seem pretty pleased to be part of Martin's Glen. And we have a lot of interest in the smaller buildings."

"I'll call as soon as I get back to the office." Spellman gestured toward the earthmovers. "Well, what do you think?"

Dust plumed up behind the two machines like columns of smoke. "I'm excited and nervous," Will finally said.

"So am I," Spellman said, "So am I."

29

. . .

WILL WATCHED THE MACHINES for nearly an hour. The sun had dropped below the western hills, bathing the entire scene in a dusty, rose-colored glow. The men who had been leveling the ground finally shut down the deep diesel drone of the machines, walked to their trucks, and left. Will was suddenly enveloped in an intense silence. Then, as twilight deepened, a cricket chorus began. He walked leisurely back to his car and winced at the thick coat of dust that had settled on it. When he opened the door an avalanche of dirt cascaded down the window. He got in, started the car, and turned on the windshield wipers to clear the dust. A full moon was just peeking over the hills as he reached an intersection and turned toward home. *A harvest moon. The days are definitely getting shorter.*

"David Jobb wants you to call him," Renee said when he got home. "You're late."

"Ray and Hunter began clearing the land. I was out at Martin's Glen and kind of lost track of the time. I'm sorry."

He shuffled off toward the bathroom and met Justin coming down the hall. "Hi, Champ."

"Hi, Will," the boy replied. "You know how to do fractions?"

Will nodded his head. "I think I have a pretty good grasp of them." He tousled the boy's hair. "Need some help?"

"Stupid math. Never gonna need this stuff anyway."

Will smiled to himself. "Let's take a look at it after dinner." He went into the bathroom and shut the door behind him. Five minutes later he walked into the kitchen, picked up the phone, and dialed David Jobb's number.

The lawyer answered on the first ring. "Hello?"

"David, this is Will. Renee said you wanted me to call."

"Thanks, Will. Would you have ten minutes tonight that I could talk to you about getting your signs out? The election is six weeks from tomorrow, and we need to talk about what we're going to do."

"Sure," Will said, glancing at the clock on the wall. "We're just sitting down to dinner. How about in an hour?"

"Fine. I'll see you then."

Will returned the phone to its cradle and sat down at the dinner table. "David's coming over in about an hour to talk about putting up signs," he said to Renee.

"I thought you were going to help me with homework," Justin said.

"You're right, Champ. I'll help you right after dinner, before David gets here."

"What if it takes longer than that?" the boy asked.

"Justin," Renee said a little sharply, "don't be so demanding. Will has said he'll help you, but we need to meet with Mr. Jobb for a little while."

"Okay," Justin said in a quiet voice.

"We'll get your homework done, Justin," Will said. "But we might have to take a break for a few minutes while David's here. Okay?"

"I guess."

"Tell us what's happening at Martin's Glen," Renee interjected brightly. She glanced at Will and then at Justin.

"They started clearing off the weeds and leveling the land." He focused on Justin. "I need to take you out there—you'd love the machines they're using."

"They gave you final approval that quickly?" Renee said.

"Well, actually, not yet, but I'm sure they will tomorrow afternoon."

"Isn't it risky to start working before the project's approved?"

Will shifted uncomfortably on his chair. "Probably, but Hunter wanted to get started with the leveling. He's really anxious to get some houses dried in before Christmas."

"Dried in?" Justin said. "What does that mean?"

"It means they need to have the roof on and all of the windows and doors in place so that the inside stays dry."

"Oh," said Justin.

They finished eating, and Renee stood up and began

clearing the table. "I'll take care of the dishes," she said. "You two can get started on that homework. David's due here in about fifteen minutes."

Will and Justin walked down the hallway to Justin's bedroom. A single piece of paper lay on the table. Justin jabbed at it with his finger. "Dumb fractions." He picked up the page and handed it to Will.

"Hmm, adding fractions." He inspected the problems before sitting down next to the boy. "Remember when we had pizza the other night?"

Justin nodded his head. "Yeah, pepperoni."

"When they put the pizza in front of us, how many pieces were there?"

Justin screwed up his mouth. "Eight, I think."

"I think you're right," Will said. "How many pieces did you eat?"

"Two," the boy replied, "plus a piece of garlic bread."

"Forget the bread for a minute. What fraction of the pizza did you eat?"

"Huh? I didn't eat a fraction, I ate two pieces of pizza."

Will tried again. "What part of the pizza did you have?"

"Two slices," Justin said.

"Okay. Each slice is one eighth of the pizza, right?"

Justin nodded his head but looked puzzled.

"You ate two pieces. So how many eighths did you eat?"

"Two," Justin said, "but that doesn't help."

Will drew a circle on the bottom of the paper and divided

it into eighths. "Is there another way you could describe what you ate?"

"What do you mean?" Justin asked.

"Maybe this will help." Carefully Will erased the line that divided two of the wedges he had drawn in the circle. "Isn't that the same as the two pieces you ate?"

"So?"

"What fraction of the whole circle is that piece of pie?"

Justin studied the drawing for a minute. "One fourth?" he asked timidly.

"Right. So if you add one eighth and one eighth you get two eighths, which is the same as one fourth." He picked up the pencil again and wrote "$\frac{1}{8} + \frac{1}{8} = \frac{2}{8} = \frac{1}{4}$."

"But how'd you get the one fourth?" Justin asked.

"Well, one eighth plus one eighth is two eighths. Then you can divide the two and the eight by two and get one fourth. The two is what's called 'the lowest common denominator'— the smallest number that can be divided equally into two and eight. Does that make sense?"

Justin shook his head. "No." He studied the diagram and the problem again. The doorbell rang.

"Will," Renee called, "David's here."

"It's really easy, once you catch on. We'll work on it some more. I'll be back in a few minutes."

"Okay," Justin said despondently.

Will walked quickly to the front room where Renee and

David stood talking. He shook Jobb's hand and led him to the couch. "Please, have a seat."

"Thank you," David said, sinking into the cushion. "I thought we'd better go over a strategy for getting your lawn signs placed." He snapped open his briefcase and pulled out a yellow legal pad. "I've invited about a dozen people to meet with us on Saturday. They're eager to meet you, by the way. Anyway, I've drawn out a plan that Creighton and I used that seemed to work." He reached back into his briefcase and retrieved a map. "As you can see, I've divided District 85 into twelve areas. And I've marked the critical intersections where we ought to make sure we have signs." He pointed with the tip of his pen to a number of black crosses he'd made on the map. "Usually we put up about fifty signs this first weekend and then we add another fifty each weekend, until all three hundred are in place the Saturday before the election." He sat forward on the couch. "That way your signs appear in different spots, and people don't get used to seeing them and ignoring them." He extended the map toward Will. "What do you think?"

Renee slid close to Will and looked at the map he held. "You've obviously given this a lot of thought," she said.

"It worked for Creighton," David said. "I think it will work for you. And, with a dozen people, that means each one has to put up only four or five signs each week. I thought we'd put up the large ones ourselves."

"Sounds good to me," Will said. "When are we meeting them?"

David returned the legal pad and the map to his briefcase. "I told them to meet at my office at noon on Saturday. You ought to be prepared to say something to them. You know, express thanks for their willingness to help out, give them a little pep talk. That sort of thing."

Will nodded his head. "Okay. Who are these people, anyway? And why are they willing to help? Are they expecting anything?"

"They're faithful members of the party. They believe in what we stand for. Most of them have been involved for years and are long-time supporters of Creighton. Like us, they don't want to lose the seat he's vacated."

"I see," Will said.

"Incidentally, I've delivered the brochure to be addressed and mailed. Every home will have it delivered sometime next week."

"Where does that leave us financially?"

David's face turned serious. "Well, that's the other thing I wanted to show you." He pulled a sheet with typed figures on it from his briefcase. "Here's an accounting of what we've taken in and a listing of our expenses so far. As you can see, we have only a few hundred dollars left. But we'll be okay if we don't run into any unforeseen complications."

Will and Renee studied the page, then handed it back to David, who put it back into his briefcase and snapped it shut.

"You make me feel a little guilty, David. You've done so much. I really appreciate you."

"My pleasure, Will." He smiled. "Now, I'd better get out of your hair and let you have the rest of a pleasant evening. I'm afraid you're going to be pretty well occupied during the next six weeks." He turned to Renee. "Thank you for being so understanding, Mrs. Martin."

Renee smiled wanly, "I try, David." She walked him to the door and let him out. A cold breath of air swirled around her ankles as she watched the Lincoln back out of their driveway.

"I'd better get back to helping Justin," Will said. "He's struggling a bit with fractions."

Renee nodded her head and watched her husband hurry down the hall toward her son's room. *Saturday at noon.*

30

. . .

ENID COOK RAPPED ON WILL'S DOOR, pushed it open, and stuck her head into his office. "Mr. Spellman is here to see you."

Will stood up from behind his desk and said, "Send him in."

Ray Spellman entered with a beaming smile on his face and began speaking at a rapid pace. "Will, I met with the Dee's Market people yesterday afternoon and showed them the plans Charles has drawn. They have a stock floor plan they use, and it will fit nicely into the space we left for a grocery store. They like the façade that Charles developed and are having their graphics man work on how to incorporate their logo on the front of the building." He stopped and took a deep breath, then sank down into one of the chairs near Will's desk. "I've got to be completely honest with you, Will, I didn't think you could bring all of the loose ends together so quickly. There's a great deal of your grandfather in you. I'm proud to be part of this team."

"Thank you," Will said. "So, how soon do you start building Dee's Market?"

"Right after the groundbreaking ceremony on Saturday," Ray said. "Hunter wants to start digging a hole for a house and we'll get started on the market." He scratched the side of his head. "I think we'll have them into the store by next June, although they realize there won't be many homes finished by then. I think they're hoping to draw people from town to keep them going until all the homes are built."

"I hope so, too," Will said. "I'm asking them to take quite a gamble, aren't I?"

Spellman nodded his head in agreement. "Yes, you are, but I just have a feeling in my gut that this is going to turn out all right." He launched himself from the chair. "I'd better get going, I've got to get out to the Glen and make sure things are progressing." He started toward the door. "Have you heard from the commission on final approval? I'm a *little* nervous about pushing dirt around, but I'm *real* nervous about starting to excavate."

"I'm going to attend the county commission meeting this afternoon, in case there are any questions. So I ought to know this evening." He walked to the door, shook Spellman's hand, and said, "Thanks for believing in me, Ray. I appreciate it more than you know."

"Thank you for believing in all of us," Spellman said.

"What time on Saturday?" Will asked as Ray started down the stairs.

"We're going to meet at Martin's Glen at noon. Charles has invited the media and quite a few of the people who've expressed interest in the other business locations. It's going to be a good opportunity for you to meet these people and help them feel the vision of the project." He hurried down the stairs.

Enid Cook followed Will back into his office. "Mr. Martin, have you begun looking for my successor? I know you've been very busy, but I really am planning to retire as soon as you can replace me."

"Enid, no one could replace you. Are you sure you want to do this?"

"Yes, I am, Mr. Martin."

"When is the drop-dead date?"

"I suppose I could wait until after the election or even until the end of the year, but I have been planning a number of things I want to do, and the longer this stretches out, the less time I have left to do them."

Will regarded the gray-haired woman seriously. "Enid, if I promise you I'll find a replacement by Christmas, will that do? That way you can help me again with the Christmas bonuses."

"Yes, Mr. Martin, that will do." She turned and marched from the room.

Will closed the door to his office, sat down in the swivel chair, and looked out the window toward the square, enjoying the view he never tired of. The leaves were changing to red and gold, and a few had already fallen to the ground. He closed his eyes and rested his head on the back of the chair.

He could hear his employees in the outer office talking with one another in unintelligible sounds. *I've put those people's lives at stake with Martin's Glen. I can't let it fail.*

He opened his eyes and thought about a replacement for Enid Cook. *Just one more piece of the puzzle that has to be solved by the end of the year.* He pulled open his desk drawer and rummaged for the telephone directory when a thought hit him. He shoved the drawer shut and walked out of his office to Enid's desk.

"Could I speak to you again?" he said.

"Of course, Mr. Martin," she said. She followed him into his office.

Will leaned against his desk. "I just wondered if you had any ideas of someone to replace you."

A smile creased Enid Cook's usually stern countenance. "Why, Mr. Martin, of course I do. I didn't think you'd ever get around to asking." She brushed an imagined wrinkle from her skirt. "If I might be blunt, you don't do that as often as you should . . . letting other people help, I mean."

"You're probably right, Enid," he said, suppressing a smile.

"I usually am. Now, if you'll talk to Carol Wanless at the bank, I understand she's looking for a new position. She is an excellent bookkeeper and could learn the ropes here very quickly. If you approach her soon, I'll be able to train her before I leave." Abruptly she rose, opened the door, and left Will's office.

"Thank you for the suggestion," he said as the door closed. *I wonder how Hal Jenkins would feel if I stole one of his people from the bank?* he mused.

A few minutes later he picked up his briefcase and coat and drove to the Martin's Glen site and watched the machines continuing the grading of the land. While he sat observing from the comfort of his Jaguar, a pickup truck with a camper shell pulled onto the shoulder of the road near the southeast corner of the lot and two men climbed out. They quickly found the government corner and set up a transit over the spot. After a few moments of adjustment they began taking measurements and driving stakes into the ground. After referring to the map, they tied brightly colored ribbons . . . some red, some orange, some blue . . . to the top of the stakes. Will was so engrossed in the process that he almost forgot to look at his watch, and when he did, he realized he'd have to hurry to be at the courthouse on time.

Will was surprised to see a crowd outside the courthouse when he arrived and searched for a parking place. He finally found one on the margin of the parking lot, retrieved his briefcase from the backseat, and headed toward the commission chambers. As he approached the crowd he recognized a shaggy-headed man. *What was his name?* he thought. *Myron, that's it. He was there when we announced Martin's Glen.*

Will threaded his way through the crowd and entered the courthouse. The phalanx of protesters followed him inside the building and down the hallway to the commission chambers. Will found a seat near the front of the room. The five members of the county commission had padded swivel chairs nearly hidden behind a curved walnut table on a raised platform. A few minutes later the five members of the commission entered the room and took their seats. The chairman rapped his gavel, and the meeting formally began.

There were three items on the agenda. Martin's Glen was the last one, and the first two were disposed of quickly. The chairman looked over the top of his half-moon glasses at the agenda and said, "We gave conceptual approval to the Martin's Glen project at our last meeting. Is there any further input before we vote on the matter?"

He looked quickly to his left and to his right at the other four commission members. None of them said anything. "I suppose we are ready for a motion."

In the back of the room a man raised his hand and said, "No public input, Commissioner?"

The chairman stared at the man over the top of his glasses. "We took comments last meeting," he said gruffly. "It moved to an action item on this agenda."

The man stood up and walked toward the portable lectern near the front of the room. He was just shy of six feet and dressed in a navy blue, chalk-striped, three-piece, expensive-looking suit. "I don't wish to disagree, Mr. Chairman, but I believe there are quite a few people who are here today to comment on this agenda item." His black hair glistened, and the part appeared to have been made with a knife. "Certainly you're not going to trample our First Amendment rights, are you?"

"We aren't trampling on anybody's rights, Mr. Phillips. This item was discussed fully at our last meeting. And, as you well know, that agenda was posted for public view well over the required twenty-four hours." The rumble grew louder. The chairman removed his glasses and wiped them with the tail of his tie. "However, if there is pertinent information we ought to know about, we'll be happy to hear it." He replaced his glasses. "But please keep it short."

Milton Phillips gave a slight bow. "Thank you, Mr. Chairman, members of the commission. Before you give final approval to this project, I think you ought to be aware that Martin's Glen will disturb some very sensitive wetlands, although someone has gone to a great deal of trouble to erad-icate them. Telford's well was a free-flowing artesian well for nearly a century before it was unceremoniously and probably illegally capped. The area lies on the winter migratory flight path of a number of species of waterfowl."

Will could feel anger beginning to boil, and he struggled to keep his face impassive.

Milton Phillips continued, "But that may not be the most egregious of the problems with Martin's Glen. There is also significant evidence that toxic waste is buried on the site. There is an area that is totally devoid of vegetation." Phillips turned toward where Will sat and pointed his finger.

"Now we have a man who wants to endanger us all by dig-ging up this potentially dangerous site so he can feather his own nest, a man arrogant enough that he has begun work on the site before he even has approval to do so. A man who not only threatens our very well-being but then has the unmitigated gall to run for public office where he can place himself in a position to protect his own selfish interests."

Phillips turned back to the commission. "I cannot believe that you gentlemen could possibly approve this . . . this . . . ill-conceived and self-serving project." He spun around and marched back to his seat. The protesters erupted into wild applause. The chairman banged his gavel.

"Is there anyone else who'd like to speak?" he asked gruffly.

Will sat immobilized for a moment, then turned and looked at the crowd assembled behind him. No one else seemed inclined to speak. He turned back and caught the eyes of the five commissioners all staring at him.

Gathering his thoughts, Will stood and walked to the podium. A buzz sounded through the audience. "Gentlemen, I'm sorry to take your time, but I think you deserve an answer to the charges that have just been leveled at Martin's Glen. First, let me address Telford's well. I have no idea who capped it, but it must have been quite a long time ago. The pipe is rusty and the valve requires a wrench to turn it. There has been no water coming out of that pipe in at least a decade. However, recognizing the significance of that well, our architect has incorporated it into a fountain in a playground that will be in one of several parks at Martin's Glen.

"Second, as for the supposed toxic site, it is true that there is a small knoll that has nothing growing on it. If we discover anything suspicious, we will take the appropriate measures to mitigate the problem.

"And, finally, the charge that I am running for office so I can take financial advantage of this situation. That charge is so absurd that I won't even dignify it with a response. Martin's Glen will provide needed residential growth for our community, as well as an increased tax base. I certainly hope you haven't been swayed by these baseless accusations." Will snapped open his briefcase. "I have copies of the architectural renderings and other information, if it is of interest to you." He walked to the dais, stepped up and dropped the drawings onto the end of the platform. He could feel himself beginning to tremble as he walked back to his seat. His face was flushed, and he could feel sweat running down his back. *Just control your temper,* he thought.

A chorus of boos rose from the back of the room, and Milton Phillips began to come to the lectern again. The chairman banged his gavel. "That will be enough demonstrating," he declared. He pointed his gavel at Milton Phillips and said, "We've heard from you, Mr. Phillips. Sit down!" He looked at the other commissioners. "I'm waiting for a motion," he said.

One of the commissioners glanced at Milton Phillips, then raised his hand. "Mr. Chairman, I move that we approve the Martin's Glen project."

"Do I hear a second?"

"Second," said the man next to him.

"Approval has been moved and seconded. All in favor signify by saying, 'Aye.'"

The two commissioners who had previously spoken, said, "Aye."

"Opposed?" said the chairman.

The other two commissioners said, "Nay."

A murmur went through the crowd. Will felt the sweat forming a river down his backbone.

"Imagine that," the chairman said sarcastically. "A tie vote. As you know, I only vote in the case of a tie." He looked directly at Milton Phillips with his lips compressed so tightly they formed a white slash across his face. "I vote 'Aye.' Mr. Martin, your project is approved."

A louder chorus of boos filled the room. The chairman rapped his gavel and when the booing grew louder he turned to the man on his right, who immediately shouted out, "I move we adjourn."

"Nondebatable. All in favor?" The five men stood and walked through the door behind the table.

Will gathered the materials into his briefcase and looked for an exit other than the one at the back of the room. There was none, so he took a deep breath and pushed his way through the crowd. Milton Phillips followed him out the door.

"Well, Will Martin, congratulations on your victory in there," he said with a sinister grin. "I hope it's your last."

Will bit his tongue, took a deep breath and said, "I'm sure you do. Good-bye, Mr. Phillips." He strode across the parking lot to his Jaguar and sped from the parking lot.

31

. . .

THE BACKHOE SCRAPED UP A bucketful of dirt, raised it and deposited it on the pile next to the hole in which it sat. A crew was working with a power posthole digger near the southeast corner of the property. They had already cemented three four-by-four posts into the ground and were preparing to set the fourth and final one. Ray Spellman tipped his hard hat back on his head. "They'll let the concrete harden overnight, then put up the picture of Martin's Glen that Charles Merrill painted on those sheets of plywood." He pointed toward the southwest corner. "When they're finished here they'll go down there and put up another set of posts." He put his hand on Will's shoulder. "So, the approval process didn't go as smoothly as you thought?"

Will shook his head. "I was afraid it wasn't going to get approved." He reached for his jacket and slipped it on. "But at least we know who the enemy is," he said. "I can't believe how this has changed in just the last couple of days." He looked across the field toward the far corner. Several workmen were visible in the distance.

Spellman saw where he was looking. "That's my crew out there. They're laying out the park and the four cul-de-sacs that surround it. I didn't think we could really get this done by Saturday, but I have to admit Hunter's crew is pretty good. They've darn near laid out a third of the residential lots and even though we're supposed to be working on the commercial property, my men are out there working right along with Hoggard's, getting the lots laid out. We're really going to be ready by Saturday."

Will shook Ray's hand. "I'd better head back to town. I've got a meeting with Hal Jenkins at the bank. He'll be relieved that the approval came through." He climbed into the Jaguar, ran the window down, and said, "When Hunter gets here, tell him how much I appreciate him, too." He closed the window, made a U-turn, and headed back toward town.

Will watched the dust rising above Martin's Glen until it was out of sight in his rearview mirrors. As he approached the intersection that led him back to town he noticed two four-by-eight-foot signs that had been attached to the fences on two of the corners. *Vote for Milton Phillips, a Man for the People.*

"Great," Will said to himself, "now every time anyone comes out to Martin's Glen they're going to see Milton's campaign signs. We should have gotten ours up sooner." His opponent's campaign signs greeted him at every corner. Frustrated, Will parked his car and climbed the stairs to his office. Enid Cook handed him a note as he passed by her desk.

He unfolded it and saw David Jobb's phone number. He stripped off his jacket, sank into his chair, and picked up the phone. Jobb answered on the second ring.

"I just walked in," Will said. "I've been out to Martin's Glen."

"I hear the commission meeting was . . . interesting."

Will snorted, "That's one word for it. So you've already heard we have approval to go ahead with the Glen, and this morning we broke ground. Of course, now I can say I've finally met Milton Phillips."

"I imagine that was a thrill," Jobb said with a chuckle.

Will's voice turned serious. "What's worse, he's put campaign signs on every corner leading back to town from the Glen."

"He must be scared," David mused, "or he wouldn't be putting this much effort into his campaign this early."

"I suppose," Will said. "Why did you need me to call you?"

"Ah, yes. Well, I don't quite know how to ask this—after all I'm supposed to be your fund-raiser—but do you have any money you could put into your campaign?"

Will tugged on his lower lip. "I could come up with a thousand dollars or so, I suppose. Normally I could draw an advance from the company, but I'm afraid I've extended Martin Real Estate about as far as we can go." He thought for a minute. "Why? Is something wrong?"

"Well, not exactly. It's sort of a feeling I have that we might need to have some money in reserve in case there's a reason to expand your campaign." There was a long five seconds of silence. "It's probably nothing . . . just a premonition. I'll get busy and raise some more money, just in case. I'd put more in, but I've reached the legal limit."

Will turned slowly in his chair and looked out the window. "David, I feel as if I'm putting an enormous burden on you."

"No, no. I didn't want to imply that at all. Oh, incidentally, I'll be out of the office until late Friday night. I have some depositions I have to take in Sacramento. I'll call you Saturday morning, after I return."

"Have a good trip," Will said.

"Thank you, I will. I'll see you Saturday."

Will replaced the phone in its cradle, rocked back in his chair and crossed his legs. His shoe, sock, and pant leg were covered with dirt. Briskly and unsuccessfully he tried to brush the dust off. He stood up, grabbed his jacket, and walked out the door.

"Miss Cook," he said, "I'm going to run home and change clothes." He indicated the dirt on his feet and legs.

"Very good, Mr. Martin," she replied.

A few minutes later he pulled the Jaguar into the driveway next to Renee's Chevrolet. He walked around the corner of the house and found his wife on an extension ladder, leaning against the house. She waved guiltily and made her way down the ladder.

"I didn't expect you home," she said with a smile. She

pulled the gloves from her hands and placed them on a rung of the ladder.

"Obviously," he said. "What are you doing up there?" He jabbed his finger toward the roof.

"Cleaning out the rain gutters."

"Why didn't you wait for me to do it? I don't want you risking your life!"

"Calm down. I've climbed a lot of ladders before, and you don't have much time lately." She brushed a stray strand of hair off her forehead. "I'm just trying to help, Will."

"I know, but still, I wish you'd let me do that." He leaned against the ladder and rubbed his forehead with the heels of his hands. "I'm sorry I've been so busy."

"I think it's going to get worse," she said, reaching for his hand. She led him to the lawn swing and sat down.

He sat down beside her and took her hand in his. "I don't see how it can get worse," he murmured. They rocked silently for a few minutes before Will remembered the dirt on his shoes and slacks. "I came home to change clothes." He pointed with his free hand. "I was out at Martin's Glen. They've started to dig the hole for the first foundation."

"That must be exciting," she said softly. "I'd like to see what's going on."

He thought for a moment. "Yes, it is. I hope we have a good turnout on Saturday for the groundbreaking."

"I'm sure it will be wonderful," she said somewhat sadly.

"What's the matter?"

"You've been so busy, I think you've forgotten what else is happening Saturday."

Will rocked a few more times before it finally registered. "Nuts! I'm suppose to be meeting with David and the people who are putting up signs at the same time as the ground-breaking!"

"That's true," Renee said.

Will took his head in his hands. "What am I going to do?" he said.

"I don't know," she said, "but I'm sure you'll think of something." She stood up abruptly from the swing and marched into the house. Will watched her go and then followed her into the kitchen.

"What did I do?" he asked as he saw the tears running down her cheeks.

Renee just shook her head. "You'd better get changed and get back to work," she said.

Confused, Will made his way to the bedroom, changed clothes, and walked back into the kitchen. Renee stood at the window looking into the backyard. Will kissed her cheek, walked out the back door, and drove back to the bank and his meeting with Hal Jenkins. After bringing the banker up to speed on what was happening at Martin's Glen, Will hurried back to his office. Enid Cook greeted him at the top of the stairs.

"I was just leaving for lunch, Mr. Martin. Your grandmother would like you to call her. I left a note on your desk."

Will dropped wearily into his chair, picked up the phone, and called his grandmother.

"Will, dear," she said cheerfully, "how are you?"

"Just fine, Grams. What can I do for you?"

"Oh, I just wondered if you'd mind if I hitched a ride to the ball game. I'd like to support Justin in this final game of the year."

"That would be great, Grams. We'll pick you up about . . ." Realization hit home. "Oh, nuts!"

"What's the matter, dear?" Ruth Martin asked sweetly.

"I . . . well, I'd sort of forgotten, I mean, well, there are some conflicts that have come up."

"What kinds of conflicts?"

Will rubbed his forehead. "There's a groundbreaking for Martin's Glen, and I'm suppose to be meeting with some campaign workers at the same time as the game. Man, how could I have forgotten that?"

"I know you've been busy. These things happen. But I'm sure you'll find a solution."

"I wish I could see one, Grams. It just seems like I'm running from place to place, trying to put out fires."

Ruth Martin waited for a moment, then said, "You haven't asked for my advice, and you might think me a meddlesome old woman . . ."

"No, no, Grams, go on."

"Do you have a Bible handy?"

"What?" Will glanced at the picture of his grandfather

hanging on the wall. "A Bible? I don't think I have one here at the office. Why?"

"Oh, nothing. I just think there's a story in Exodus that might help you with your problem. There really are a lot of solutions in the scriptures, you know."

Will took a deep breath and tried to calm himself. "I'm sure there are, Grams. What does it say in Exodus?"

"It's in the eighteenth chapter, when Moses' father-in-law comes to visit him. It might make interesting reading. I'm sure Enid has a Bible if you can't find one. Well, I've taken up too much of your time. Why don't you get back to me and let me know what's happening on Saturday. Have a pleasant day, dear."

Will hung up the phone and walked to Enid Cook's desk. He looked for her Bible and found it on top of her file cabinet. He glanced around the office. No one was paying much attention to him, so he picked up the book and walked back to his desk. He leafed through Genesis, noting that many of the verses were underlined, until he reached Exodus. He glanced at the note he had scribbled on his calendar pad . . . "Exodus 18." When he reached that chapter he noticed that Enid had already underlined several lines of scripture. His eye was drawn to them.

And when Moses' father in law saw all that he did to the people, he said, What is this thing that thou doest to the people? why sittest thou thyself alone, and all the people stand by thee from morning unto even?

And Moses said unto his father in law, Because the people come unto me to enquire of God: . . .

And Moses' father in law said unto him, The thing that thou doest is not good.

Thou wilt surely wear away, both thou, and this people that is with thee: for this thing is too heavy for thee; thou art not able to perform it thyself alone.

Will leaned back in his chair and stared at the ceiling. He had never felt more worn away in his life. Finally, he turned back to the phone, picked it up, and dialed David Jobb's number. After several rings, David's secretary, Patricia Ames, answered the phone.

"Patricia, this is Will Martin. Is David still there?"

"I'm sorry, Mr. Martin, he left a few minutes ago to go to the airport. He has to fly to California."

"He told me," Will said despondently. "I was just trying to catch him before he left. I'll call him Saturday, after he returns."

"Very good. I'll leave him a message that you called."

"Thank you." Will read the rest of the eighteenth chapter of Exodus, closed Enid's Bible, and returned it to the file cabinet.

32

. . .

"CAN YOU GET OUT HERE TO THE GLEN?" Hunter Hoggard said over his cell phone.

Will could hear the sound of machinery in the background. "Why? Is something wrong?"

"Maybe. I think you ought to look at it yourself."

"I'll be right there." Will raced out of his office and sped across town and out to Martin's Glen. Hunter Hoggard and Ray Spellman stood by a pickup truck awaiting his arrival.

"What's up?" Will said apprehensively.

Hunter pointed across the field. "You know that knob of ground where nothing was growing?" Will nodded his head. "We've uncovered some stuff there that you ought to see." He started walking briskly toward the spot he indicated. Ray and Will struggled to keep up with him. When they reached the spot, Will could see a front loader that sat idling with its bucket full of dirt. Hoggard led them to the front of the machine and pointed into the bucket. "See that."

A bleached bone was sticking out of the dirt. It appeared to be a rib. "Where did it come from?" Will asked.

Hoggard pointed to the knob of ground. "We ran over this with the blade a couple of days ago and loosened it up and we was just kinda knocking the top of this little knoll and Bart spotted this bone." He jerked his head toward the other side of the machine. "It ain't the only one."

Will skirted the front loader and saw the ends of what appeared to be several ribs sticking out of the recently disturbed earth. He squatted and looked at the white bones without touching them, stood and looked back toward the road. The knoll was barely ten feet in diameter and rose less than a foot higher than the rest of the ground.

"I called 911 after I called you," Hoggard continued over the noise of the machine. "I guess that's what you wanted me to do?"

Will nodded his head. "Not what we wanted to find, what with the groundbreaking ceremony tomorrow," he said.

Ray Spellman crouched next to the raw earth. "I wonder what else we'll find?" He stood up in time to see the county sheriff's Ford Explorer pull to a stop on the road. He extended his arm and waved his hand. The SUV bucked its way across the field toward them. "Good thing we filled in that irrigation ditch," Spellman said.

Half an hour later Will sat in the backseat of the sheriff's car. A number of survey pegs had been driven into the ground and yellow plastic tape isolated the knob of ground. "You're the owner of this land?" the deputy asked.

Will nodded his head. "Yes, sir. I bought it from Gordon Burningham."

The deputy wrote down a comment on the clipboard he was carrying. "How long ago did you purchase it?" he asked.

"About six months ago," Will answered. The deputy added a comment to his notes.

"I don't suppose you have a phone number for him?"

"I'm sorry," Will said. "I have it back at the office, but not with me."

The deputy picked up the microphone. "This is Deputy Anderson, would you see if you can reach a . . ." he looked at the notes, "Gordon Burningham on the phone and patch him through."

The radio spat back, "Ten-four, that's Gordon Burningham. Do you have an address, Deputy?"

The deputy cocked an eyebrow toward Will. "He just lives about a mile further down the road," Will said, as he pointed to the west.

"Somewhere on Spring Canyon Road," the deputy said into the microphone. He turned his attention back to Will. "Any idea what's buried here?"

"None," said Will. "We've just begun to develop the property. When Hunter Hoggard's man discovered this, he stopped and called you."

"Well, they don't look too recent," he said, sliding his dark glasses back into place. "But you never know. We've got the medical examiner coming. I'd appreciate it if you didn't disturb the area until he's finished his investigation."

"How long is that going to take?" Will asked. "We're suppose to have a groundbreaking at noon tomorrow."

"Depends," the deputy replied. "Here he comes now."

A second white SUV bumped across the field to the side of the knoll, and a short, rotund gentleman walked toward them. "What do we have here, Deputy Anderson?"

"We don't know, sir," he replied. "It appears to be some remains."

The medical examiner stepped over the yellow tape and peered at the bones. "Interesting," he said. He opened the satchel he carried with him and pulled on a pair of latex gloves.

The radio squawked from the police car and Deputy Anderson popped open the door and grabbed the microphone. "Anderson here. Go ahead."

"We have Gordon Burningham on the phone. Just a sec and I'll patch him through." A buzz and a number of clicks were heard. "Go ahead."

"Mr. Burningham? This is Deputy Sheriff Anderson."

"Are you Junie's boy?" Gordon Burningham asked.

"Yes, sir. I am."

"Fine woman. What can I do for you?"

"We're over at the piece of property you sold to Will Martin."

"Is there some problem?"

Anderson thought for a minute. "Well, sir, would it be possible for you come over here?"

"No problem. How's your mother doing? Haven't seen her in some time."

"She's just fine, sir. How soon would you be able to join us?"

"I'll be right there."

A cloud of dust announced the arrival of Gordon Burningham's truck. He left it on the road and walked to where the men waited. He smiled at Will and shook his hand. "What's the problem?" he asked.

"I'm Deputy Anderson."

"Junie's boy," Gordon replied.

"Yes, sir. We've uncovered some bones," he continued as Gordon walked around the end of the front loader. "We're wondering if you could offer any explanation as to why they'd be here."

Burningham pushed the brim of his Stetson until the hat rested precariously on the back of his head. "Reckon that's what's left of them two deer we buried here," he said. "Came to take a watering turn one morning and found 'em lying here in the middle of the field. They'd been dead four, five days. Stunk up the place real bad and flies all over 'em. Me and Karl just brought the tractor out here and buried 'em."

"How long ago was that?" Anderson asked.

Gordon fiddled with the brim of his hat, "'Eighty-three . . . no eighty-four, right after the floods. Back when we was still farmin' this piece of ground." He pulled the hat back on his head. "Hope it ain't caused any trouble."

The medical examiner looked at the bone sticking out of the load of dirt in the front loader. "It's an animal bone, all right," he said. He slipped the fragment of bone into a plastic bag. "I'll take a little closer look at it back at the lab. Let me know if you uncover anything else." He stripped off the latex gloves and walked back to his van. "I'll see you boys later."

Deputy Anderson began pulling down the yellow plastic ribbon, and a few minutes later the sheriff's car bounced away over the field. Bart climbed back onto the front loader and gingerly continued leveling the knoll. The next scoop uncovered the skull, confirming the remains were that of a deer. "I think we'll haul the bones away," Hoggard said. "Some people might be a little spooked by them." They watched the leveling efforts for a few minutes until the land was fairly smooth. No other bones appeared.

The three men began walking back to the road, and Spellman said, "That's the last little piece we have to lay out and then we're ready for tomorrow's celebration." He patted Will on the shoulder. "Excited?"

Will nodded his head as Hunter exclaimed, "This is gonna be a great development. Thanks for makin' me part of it."

"The thanks really belongs to you," Will replied. "Without the two of you none of this would be possible."

They reached the road. "Nonsense," said Spellman, "You deserve all the credit." He clapped Will on the shoulder again.

"Tomorrow will be a landmark day. I've been thinking this will be good for your campaign, too. All of this publicity, you know."

Will dragged his toe through the dirt at the side of the road. "What if I just leave the groundbreaking up to the two of you . . . and Charles, of course."

"I really think you need to be here," Spellman said. "Is there a problem?"

"I have a conflict that's come up. Something I can't change. I really do need to let you two take the credit, anyway."

"I don't know," Hoggard said, pushing his hard hat back on his head. "Who's gonna be the spokesman?"

"Charles can handle that," Will said. "I'll call him." He watched Hoggard tug his hard hat back in place. "I've counted on you two this far and I can't see any reason to change." Will climbed into his car and drove away.

Ray Spellman watched him drive off, then turned to Hunter, "He's getting more and more like his grandfather. Warren Martin wouldn't have been here, either. He did all he could to avoid the spotlight."

Daylight was fading as Will drove into the driveway. Renee's Chevrolet was gone from its usual spot. When he got in the house, he called Charles Merrill's office and asked him if he would take charge of the groundbreaking, then sat down wearily in the recliner and dozed off. He awakened to the sound of his wife trying to open the backdoor. She was balancing a grocery sack with one hand while she turned the doorknob with the other. Will shook the sleep from his eyes and hurried to help her.

"More groceries in the car," she said as she lowered the sack onto the kitchen counter.

Will carried the rest of the groceries into the house. "Where's Justin?"

Renee brushed a strand of hair back with her hand. "He's staying over at Billy's for the night. I left him there while I went shopping." She kissed him lightly. "I thought you might need a little time by yourself," she said with a smile.

"After what happened today, I think you're right." While they put the groceries away he told her of the discovery of the bones at Martin's Glen.

"I don't suppose it will delay the ceremony?"

He shook his head. "No, it will go on as planned."

"I see," she said quietly. "Have you worked out the conflict with David? He's pretty insistent that you be there to meet your campaign helpers."

"He's in California and won't be back until late tonight. I'll just have to call him in the morning."

Renee finished putting the last of the produce in the refrigerator. "Well, those are two very important parts of your life right now," she said with a shake of her head. "What do you want for dinner?"

"Why don't we drive over to Cassidy's for dinner. Just the two of us."

"What's the occasion?" Renee said with a smile.

"Because I'm lucky enough to have such a beautiful wife," he said, pulling her to him and kissing her.

"It's a deal, Mr. Martin," she said, kissing him back.

33

• • •

WILL STRETCHED, ROLLED OVER, and looked at the clock on the nightstand. It was nearly nine o'clock. He blinked his eyes, stretched again, and yawned and pushed himself to a sitting position on the edge of the bed. He pulled on his robe and shuffled to the bathroom as quietly as he could. Renee continued to sleep, her auburn curls framing her face.

He dialed David Jobb's home number. "Hello?" a sleepy voice answered.

"I hope I didn't wake you, David."

"I needed to get up anyway," he said. "The flight was delayed coming back last night, and I didn't get home until about two in the morning."

"David, I have a favor to ask of you."

"Oh?"

"Can you take care of the distribution of the signs for me? I know you have it all mapped out, and I have a conflict today."

David cleared his throat. "I suppose that will be possible,

but we're going to ask these people to work hard for you, and I'm sure they're counting on meeting you. Isn't there any way you can come for just a few minutes?"

Will pondered for a moment. "I might be able to be there for a short time, but please, please handle this for me. You're much more politically astute, and I'm sure you can do just fine without my bungling."

David sighed. "I suppose I can, if I have to. I'll talk to you later."

As quietly as possible, Will heated a griddle while he mixed pancake batter. He placed a frying pan on the stove and began cooking strips of bacon. Within a few minutes a delicious aroma filled the air. He heard Renee stirring as he dropped some batter on the griddle. Quickly he set the table, poured glasses of orange juice, then flipped the pancakes. "Breakfast is ready," he called down the hall.

Renee emerged from the upstairs dressed in a pale pink robe. "What's this all about?" she smiled. "Trying to sweep me off my feet?"

"Just thought you'd enjoy having someone else do the cooking," he smiled. Will placed the plates of food on the table and they began to eat.

"I could make this a habit," Renee said with a shake of her curls.

"I wonder how Justin got along at Billy's last night," Will pondered. "That's the first time he's been away from home for the night."

"I'm sure he's just fine," she said, "but I'd better hurry and shower. He needs to be over at the diamond an hour before the game. Coach Morris wants to talk to the boys and warm them up before the game." She refused to meet Will's eyes with her own. "And I suppose you need to get on with your activities of the day," she said with a tight smile on her lips.

"Yes, I suppose I do," he said. "You go ahead and shower and I'll clean up the kitchen," he said. "I can shower after you're finished."

At a quarter to eleven, Renee kissed Will good-bye and drove away in the Chevrolet. Will hurried to the Jaguar and sped out to Martin's Glen. A canopy had been erected over a raised platform that had bunting draped across its front. Banners fluttered from ropes attached to the canopy and stretched to the ground. A backhoe had dug a trench and refilled it with soft soil into which a dozen shovels had been stuck. Everything appeared to be ready for the ceremony. He turned around and drove past David Jobb's office. A stack of campaign signs rested against the outside wall. Will stopped long enough to take a good look at them. *Will Martin, A Vote for Responsible Government.* And beneath it in small type, *House of Representatives, District 85.*

"They look good, David," he said quietly as he shifted into gear and drove toward the ball diamond. He guided the Jaguar into a spot next to Renee's car. Coach Morris had gathered the boys around him near third base. Will searched the stands and saw Renee and his grandmother sitting on the next to the top bleacher. His wife had a camera to her eye and was focusing on the group of boys. He climbed the forest green planks and sat down quietly between the two of them. She finished taking the picture and looked at Will in surprise.

"Don't you have other things you need to do?" she asked.

He shook his head, "Nothing that someone else can't do. But no one can replace me here."

Tears sprang to her eyes, and she wiped them away with the back of her hand. She reached over and squeezed his hand. Ruth Martin smiled.

The Diablos had been warming up in right field. Their coach left them and came to where Coach Morris was talking to his Mustangs. The two men shook hands and the two teams jogged to home plate. The Mustangs won the toss and elected to be the home team. The Diablos took their seats on the bench, and the Mustangs ran onto the field. While the pitcher warmed up, Justin took his assigned spot near first base and looked into the stands, searching for his mother. When he saw Will he waved furiously.

"I told him you weren't going to be able to be here," Renee said. "I should have asked."

Will put his arm around her shoulders. "And I should have told you," he replied, "except I wanted it to be a secret."

"Play ball!" the umpire shouted.

Five scoreless innings passed before a Diablo batter hit a fly ball deep into center field and made it to second base before the fielder could retrieve the ball and throw it to the infield.

The next batter advanced him to third with a ground ball hit to the shortstop, who threw it to Justin at first base in time to put out the runner. The next batter hit a foul ball deep down the left field line. Coach Morris called time out and walked to the mound. He knelt down next to the pitcher and talked to him. Then he patted the boy on the shoulder and walked off the field. On the next pitch the batter hit a looping fly into shallow left field and made it safe to first base. The runner on third scored.

As it turned out, that was the only score in the game, and the Diablos won 1–0. Coach Morris gathered the Mustangs around him and they gave a cheer for the Diablos. He then handed each boy a small certificate and told them he hoped they'd all be together again next summer. Justin kicked at a clump of morning glory with his shoe as he walked around the end of the backstop. Will, Ruth, and Renee met him at the bottom of the bleachers.

Justin looked at the ground and then at Will. "We lost, Will," he said dejectedly.

"Sometimes that happens," he said. "Whenever someone wins, someone else loses. But, Champ, it's just one game. There'll be a lot more games in the future."

The tears began. "I wanted to be a champion," Justin complained.

"You'll always be a champion with me," Will said, hugging the boy. "Now, I think it's time to celebrate."

"But we lost," Justin repeated through his tears.

"Just this game, Champ. Let's go celebrate a winning season."

Justin wiped at the tears and managed a tight smile.

"I'm starved," Will exclaimed. He winked at Renee and his grandmother. "Where shall we go?" He turned back to Justin. "You pick, Champ." He took Renee's hand, "Leave your car here and we'll pick it up on the way back."

They drove through the city and saw Will's campaign signs attached to a number of fences and on stakes on several lawns. Milton Phillips's signs were also visible. "There's your name," Justin said excitedly as he pointed to one of the signs. "That's cool."

After lunch they drove to Martin's Glen, where a crew of men were disassembling the platform and loading the pieces into a large stake bed truck. They spotted Hunter Hoggard engaged in a conversation with someone near his truck. Everyone else had left. They pulled to the side of the road and got out of the car.

Renee looked across the field where all of the lots were identified by stakes with various colored plastic tape tied around them. "I can't believe what they've accomplished in such a short time," she said to Will. "You must be very proud of the two of them."

"I am," Will said. "Actually, they've learned to work together, and I didn't think I'd ever see that day."

"I always said you were a miracle worker," his grandmother said with a broad smile.

Hunter Hoggard spotted the four of them, shook hands with the man with whom he had been speaking, and ambled over to where they stood. He removed his hard hat and bowed slightly toward Renee and Ruth.

"How did it go, Hunter?"

A smile split his leathery face. "Man, we had over a hun'erd people here," he said. He jerked his thumb over his shoulder. "That guy I was talkin' to, he wants to build a home clear back by Telford's well. I told him we wouldn't have the road paved for at least six months, but he don't care. He wants to live back there. I told him to come see you Monday and you'd take care of him."

"Good! I knew you men could handle it."

"Must be about twenty or thirty people who said they wanted to buy lots. Ray talked to a lot of 'em. Ya' know, he's a better talker than me. I hate to admit it, but I kinda like the guy."

"Well, it sounds as if we're going to have plenty of work to keep you busy, Hunter," Will said, reaching to shake the contractor's hand. "Thanks for handling this today. I think you know my grandmother." Hunter nodded his head. Will presented his wife, "Have you met my wife, Renee?"

Hunter nodded his head. "We've met before . . . quite some time ago."

"And this is Justin. His ball team came within one run of being the city champions. He's quite the first baseman."

Justin looked shyly at the ground in front of him. Hunter

Hoggard knelt down in front of him. "Will, here, was quite the player, too. Congratulations." He reached for Justin's hand and shook it before he returned to his feet. He plunked the hard hat back on his head. "Monday, we're gonna form up the footings on the Walburgs' house. I figure we can have the foundation in place by next Friday and have the walls going up the following week." He pointed in the general direction of the lot. "Next question is, do you want to build a house here to use as an office? We can build it as a spec home, use it as a field office, and then sell it later on. Whatta ya think?"

"Good idea, Hunter. Where do you think it ought to be built?" Will looked over the field of flags.

Renee put her hand on Will's arm. "Over there," she pointed. "It will have good visibility from the road, but will be far enough back that the shopping center won't block the view."

"Good choice, Mrs. Martin," Hunter said. "Can I take that as a 'yes'?"

Will thought about the financial situation of Martin Real Estate. "I suppose it makes sense," he finally said.

"Good! We'll get going on it next." Hunter smiled, "Oh, and I seen somebody puttin' up one of your signs." He pointed toward the intersection. "I noticed your opponent has already put up some of his."

"That's the way the process works, Hunter."

"Ya got any real big ones? I mean, man, you could put one

up right below the picture of Martin's Glen. You got posts in the ground already."

"Good idea, Mr. Hoggard," Renee said. "We might be back out this evening to do that."

Hoggard gave a salute, turned, and walked back to his truck. The platform had been completely taken apart and loaded into the waiting truck. "It's a big gamble, sweetheart," Will said, rubbing his forehead. "I just hope it turns out all right."

"Have faith," she said.

34

. . .

"THEY'RE ALL GONE?"

"Every one, Will. I can't believe that even Milton Phillips would stoop this low." David Jobb paced the floor in Will's front room. "Sometime overnight someone stole every one of your signs."

"And no one saw them doing it?" Renee asked.

"Apparently not. They must have done it in the early morning hours." Jobb continued to pace. "The question is, how do we respond? We can put another fifty out, but I suspect they'll disappear as well."

"What about going to the media with it?" Renee pondered. "If only Will's signs are being taken, that looks pretty suspicious."

"We might get some coverage . . . probably on the bottom of page 13. I just want to keep it from happening again. We've got to get your name out there if you're going to have a chance." Jobb ran his hand over his head.

"Thank goodness we didn't have the large ones up yet.

Renee and I were just getting ready to go out to Martin's Glen and hang up a couple of those," Will said.

Jobb stopped pacing. "Maybe that's a good idea. You've got enough people around there all day that the signs might be safe."

"Not if they're stealing them at night," Renee said. "Still, I think we ought to put a couple up and see what happens."

Will rubbed his jaw. "What if we take a couple of signs out after dark and put them up at the Glen. That way nobody will even see them until tomorrow."

"Then what?" Jobb asked. "Do we place somebody out there tomorrow night to see if someone comes to steal them?" He began to pace again. "The simple fact is we've got to get your name in front of the people. That's especially true in Page's Landing and in Mossburg, where they don't really know you."

"Are you sure those signs are gone as well?" Renee said.

Jobb nodded his head. "The people I have in those two communities were the first to call me this morning with the news." He sank down onto the couch. "I think we've got to risk another fifty signs. We still have two hundred and fifty, and we ought to concentrate them in those two little communities. What do you think?"

"Well, they won't do any good sitting in your garage, David. Let's do it!" Renee said forcefully.

The attorney struggled to his feet. "I'll go home and start organizing the troops." He turned to Will. "I assume you'd be able to meet with them tomorrow night. I think it would help a great deal to have you there . . . face-to-face with them."

"Of course."

"Then I'll be off." He grabbed his briefcase off the end table and headed for the door. "Seven o'clock tomorrow night? My office?"

Will and Renee both nodded their heads.

"Good! I'll see you then," he said as he let himself out the front door.

It was nearly ten o'clock when the three of them arrived at the Glen. Justin was fighting to keep his eyes open while Will untied the four-by-eight-foot signs he had lashed to the top of Renee's car. By the headlights of the Chevrolet, Renee held the foam board in place while Will secured it to the posts with roofing nails. When they finished on the southeast corner, they carried the second sign to the northwest corner and repeated the task. Justin fell asleep on the drive home.

"I guess we'll see what happens," Renee said as she followed Will into the house. Will carried Justin in his arms to his bedroom, where he deposited him on his bed. Carefully he removed Justin's shoes and pulled the blanket over the sleeping boy.

The following evening the three of them arrived at David Jobb's office ten minutes before the meeting. As people arrived, Will greeted each one. Fifty signs were divided among those who had come and David Jobb distributed new maps showing where the signs needed to be placed. Before they left,

Will took a few minutes to thank them for their support and to pledge himself to represent them well.

By Tuesday afternoon all of the signs were in place. By Wednesday morning they were all missing, including the two large signs at Martin's Glen.

"This is preposterous!" David Jobb said. "I think it's time we paid a visit to Milton Phillips."

"I agree," Will said angrily. The two men walked out of David's office, sat down in his Lincoln, and cruised across town. "What does Milton do for a living?" Will asked.

"He's a consultant," David answered with a shrug. "Who he consults with is anybody's guess. And he's been a lobbyist for the CCG."

"Where's his office?"

"He works out of his home in Page's Landing."

They took the freeway on-ramp and drove on in silence, anger festering like a boil, until David exited into the county seat and turned into the driveway of an impressive home. "David," Will said, "I just remember something Creighton told me. He said that Milton would work hard to make me angry so that I'd do something stupid. Let's be careful."

"Good advice," David said, punching the doorbell with his forefinger. A few moments later Milton Phillips answered the door.

"Mr. Martin, what a delight. And Mr. Jobb. What can I do for you?" he oozed. He stood in the doorway but did not invite them into the house.

David squared his shoulders. "Milton, Will has put up over a hundred signs in the past week and all of them have been stolen."

"What a shame," he said with a frown. "Certainly you don't think I have anything to do with that, do you?"

"It entered my mind," David retorted.

Phillips shifted his gaze to Will. "Someone must not like you very much. Isn't that too bad?"

Will could feel the anger beginning to boil, but he clenched his teeth and remained silent.

"I just wanted to warn you, Milton, that the police have been alerted and are increasing surveillance. The total value of the signs is such that this would constitute a felony."

"Oh, dear me. You know it would only be a felony if one individual had taken all those signs. If a number of people, say fifty, each took a sign, it would hardly register as a misdemeanor, let alone a felony." He turned back to Will. "Haven't you ever heard, young man, that nice guys finish last?" He turned on his heel, and slammed the door behind him.

"But they're still nice guys," David muttered. "I hate to make an idle threat, Will. Let's go report this to the police."

Half an hour later they sat in the county sheriff's office. Deputy Anderson greeted them. "Find anything else on your property, Mr. Martin?" he asked.

"No, nothing like that," Will responded. "We're here on an entirely different matter. We've put up over a hundred campaign signs in the last few days, and every one of them has been stolen."

"You're kidding me," the deputy said.

"I wish we were," David interjected. "We put them up in Page's Landing, in Mossburg, in the county, and here at home, and every one of them has been removed."

"It sounds as if somebody is out to get you," Anderson said. "Let me get a formal report and I'll gather some information." He left the small office and reappeared a couple of minutes later with a clipboard and report form. "Incidentally, the medical examiner called yesterday. That piece of bone he took was from a mule deer." He sat down with the clipboard on his lap. "How many signs did you say were stolen?"

"A hundred," David said through clenched teeth.

Anderson tapped the tip of his pen on the report sheet. "Do you plan to put up any more?"

"Oh, yes," Will said, "about two hundred more. Why do you ask?"

"I was just thinking, what if you put up a sign in a location where we could hide a police car? I've got a couple of new reserve officers who would be happy to sit there all night if they thought they could collar someone. Is that a possibility?"

Both Will and David nodded their heads. "You tell us where, Deputy Anderson, and we'll get a sign installed."

Anderson tapped the pen against his front teeth. "On the east side of Page's Landing there's a spot where the road curves. There's a big thicket of scrub oak, where we often conceal a car to catch speeders coming into town. Right across from that thicket is a stretch of fence. I'll bet you could get permission to hang a sign on it."

"David, we'll have to put up more than one sign or it's going to be obvious that we're trying to catch someone."

"I know, Will. I guess we'll sacrifice another fifty, but it'll be worth it if we can catch our thief."

"All right," Anderson said. "When are you going to put them up?"

"Let's see," David thought out loud, "what if we do it on Friday night? Saturday would be the next time we'd normally put them up."

"Don't break your pattern," Anderson warned. "If you normally put them up on Saturday, wait until Saturday. I don't think one day is going to make a difference."

Will and David stood up to leave. "Deputy, we'll distribute them Saturday morning, and they'll all be up that afternoon."

"Good. That will give me time to get hold of my two reserve officers and make sure they're in place."

David took the long way back to town. They passed dozens of Milton Phillips signs, several of them located where Will's signs had been located the day before. "I told you he was a force to be reckoned with," David said as he dropped Will off in front of Martin Real Estate.

"Thanks for your help, David. Let's hope this plan works." Just as he started to close the door he stopped. "It's hard to imagine someone being that blatantly determined to sabatoge our campaign."

"It happens. Now you know what you're up against. Politics can be a ruthless business."

Will shook his head. "Makes me wonder if it's worth it."

"Oh, it's worth it. Even if it's just to prevent someone like Phillips getting elected." With that, Will closed the door and watched the Lincoln drive away.

35

. . .

SUNDAY MORNING WILL ROLLED out of bed, blinked his eyes, stretched, and yawned. *I wonder if they caught anybody?* As quietly as possible he dressed and slipped down the hall to the living room. He put on his shoes, tiptoed out the back door, and backed out of the driveway. Will cruised down the street past his grandmother's home and saw one of his signs attached to a chain-link fence on the corner. Two blocks further he saw another one. He headed for the freeway entrance and ten minutes later took the Page's Landing exit. He slowed down as he approached the curve and experienced a wave of mixed emotion when he saw his sign was still attached to the fence. In a way, he had hoped someone might have been caught stealing it. He stopped on the side of the road, got out of his car, and looked across the top of his Jaguar. He could see a sheriff's car partially hidden in the growth of brush and trees. He crossed the road and approached the vehicle and the two uniformed reserve officers seated in it.

"Good morning, gentlemen," he said. "Been out here long?"

One of the officers ignored his greeting, but the one in the driver's seat responded through his open window. "Long enough. What is your business here?"

"I'm Will Martin. That's one of my campaign signs. I came to see if it had been stolen."

"Obviously it hasn't," the officer said.

The officers were clearly not enthralled by the vigil they had been asked to keep, and their irritability showed.

"Well," Will said, "I appreciate your efforts." He waited for a response that didn't come, then added, "I guess I'll head back home."

Feeling somehow chastened, he got into his car and drove the rest of the way through Page's Landing, noticing several of his signs, along with those belonging to Milton Phillips. *Maybe he got the message,* Will thought as he turned the car around and headed back to the freeway.

By Monday morning all of Will's signs had disappeared.

"I feel like going out and taking all of his signs down," Renee said angrily.

"As soon as we try that, we'll get caught," Will responded. "Although I have to admit the thought has crossed my mind."

"If we can't fight dirty, we need to fight smart. Do you agree?"

Both David and Will nodded their heads.

"How do we turn this into a positive?" She stood up from the couch, walked into the dining room, and returned with the newspaper. "Can we get press coverage on this?"

"How?" David asked.

"I don't know. But somehow we need to let people know what's happening." She folded the newspaper and thumped it against her arm.

"Maybe we ought to ask your grandmother," David suggested. "She was the one with the idea that turned the Julia Welsch photograph into a win."

"It couldn't hurt," Will said, "Or how about Louise Barrow? Certainly Creighton must have had things like this happen to him."

"Well, all I know is that we have four weeks until the election, and if we don't do something, my husband is going to go down in flames and all because of a pumped-up phony named Milton Phillips!"

"I'm open to suggestions," Will said. "Why not invite Grams and Louise Barrow to meet with us tomorrow night? It's for darn sure we're not going to put up any more signs before then, and maybe they can give us an idea."

"I'd be happy to invite Louise," David said.

"Here, tomorrow night, at seven o'clock," Renee said. "Will, go call your grandmother."

"I'll be going, then," David said.

The following evening David Jobb arrived with Louise Barrow. Will had already picked up his grandmother, and the five of them seated themselves in the living room. Will went over what had gone on with his signs.

"That must be discouraging," Ruth Martin said. "After the

expense and hard work to get them in place and then to have them all taken."

Louise Barrow frowned. "I can't remember when Creigh ever had *all* of his signs taken. There were always a few that disappeared, but never all of them."

David Jobb cleared his throat. "Well, it has happened, and the question is, what do we do about it?"

"Have you gone to the police?" Louise asked.

"Oh, yes," Renee said. "But they haven't been successful in catching anyone."

Ruth Martin straightened her skirt, "What about the newspapers?"

"We didn't think it would get much coverage," David answered.

"I see. Could we buy some coverage?"

David glanced at Will. "I suppose we could, Mrs. Martin, if we had more money to spend. Unfortunately the campaign fund is almost used up."

"How much would it cost?" Ruth asked.

David mulled it over for a minute before Louise Barrow said, "If I remember correctly it costs about ten thousand dollars for a full-page advertisement, but I suspect a half-page would do, don't you, David?"

"I'm sure a half-page would do nicely. But if I remember right, that costs about six thousand dollars, and we don't have nearly that much in the bank."

Louise Barrow brightened. "Well, I do. Since I've been

sworn in as Creigh's replacement, I have access to his campaign funds, and since I'm never planning to run for reelection, I can't think of a better way to spend them than on my successor."

"I can't let you do that," David said. "There may be other places you'll want to spend that money."

"Nonsense." She stiffened on the couch. "I'll pay for the ad, and I'll place it so there isn't any question about exceeding the legal limit of contributions from one person. All that we have to do is decide how to word it. It will be my opportunity to speak out against dirty politics."

Ruth Martin turned to Louise Barrow and said, "What are we really trying to do?"

"Keep Milton Phillips and the CCG from stealing Will's signs," Louise responded, "and maybe this seat in the House."

"Maybe that's exactly what he'd like us to do," Ruth said.

"What do you mean, Grams?" Will asked.

"Maybe this is a red herring . . . something that will take up so much time and energy that you won't have any left to spend on campaigning." She shifted in her seat. "Are there better things you could do with your time and money?"

Louise Barrow smiled at Ruth. "You know, I think you're on to something. If we make a big thing out of this, Milton Phillips will respond that he is innocent and that Will is trying to smear him. The whole thing could backfire. You're a wise woman, Ruth Martin."

"Not wise, just old," Ruth smiled back. "Perhaps you could

spend the money on advertisements that promote Will rather than focusing on the stolen signs. Isn't that what you really need . . . to let people know who you are and what you stand for?" She turned to Louise. "I'll be happy to contribute to the cause, as well. Isn't that the code we've tried to live by . . . the individual is responsible for himself, then he turns to his family before going elsewhere?"

Louise nodded her head. "Well said, Ruth. So, what do we put in these advertisements? Do you have a picture we can use? A recent one?"

Renee stood and walked into the hallway. She returned shortly with a photo album, sat down, opened it, and removed a picture. "I think this is a good picture of Will. It's the one his old firm used in promotional materials."

"You look very handsome, dear," his grandmother said. Then she pointed to another picture in the book. "What about that one . . . the one with you, Renee, and Justin?"

Renee removed the picture. "Well, it isn't nearly as formal. It's the one that Coach Morris's wife took after one of the ball games."

"I like it," Ruth Martin said. "What do you think, Louise?"

"Much better," she said, "it shows Will as he really is . . . kneeling down next to Justin . . . and it doesn't hurt that your pretty wife is in the picture as well."

Renee blushed.

David Jobb had been writing notes on a legal pad while the women were talking. "May I see the picture, please?" He examined it and nodded his approval. "How does this sound? 'A vote for Will Martin is a vote for strong families!'" When the others nodded general agreement, David continued, "We can put that simple phrase, the picture, and then 'House of Representatives, District 85' at the bottom of the ad." He handed the sketch he had made to Louise Barrow. "How much money do you really want to contribute, Louise?"

The silver-haired woman looked at the sketch on David's legal pad. "Creigh left nearly fifteen thousand dollars in that account. Feel free to use all of it. It will be worth it to defeat Milton Phillips." She smiled sweetly. "Why don't you and I go over to the newspaper tomorrow and place the ads? That is, if you can give me a ride, David."

"I'd be delighted," he said in return.

Will interrupted. "Are you sure about this, Mrs. Barrow?"

"Never more sure in my life," she replied.

"I can't thank you enough," he said. Will stood up and walked to the mantel. "We still haven't solved the problem with the signs, though," he said glumly.

"That's true," David agreed.

Ruth Martin and Louise Barrow glanced at each other and then Ruth spoke. "What if you didn't put any of the rest of your signs up until the day before the election? Do you have enough help to do that?"

Jobb looked at her in amazement. "Well, yes. We could do that, I guess, but why?"

"I think people get used to seeing the signs if they're put up too soon. If they were all put up on the day before the election . . . and I'd put them up during the day so people see them being put up . . . then, if someone tries to remove them, it will be quite a formidable task."

Louise Barrow nodded her head. "We'll run ads in the papers for the next three weeks and then have the blitz of signs just before the election. Ruth, you're a wonderful strategist, it's too bad Creigh didn't have you to work on his campaigns."

"It certainly is a different strategy," David said. "I hope it works."

"Have faith, my friend," Louise said. "Now, I think we've accomplished all we can this evening. How about giving me a ride home?"

"Of course," David said. He extended his hand and helped Louise Barrow to her feet. "Ruth, would you like me to drop you off, as well?"

"That would be splendid," Ruth said. Renee retrieved their coats from the hall closet, and Will helped his grandmother put hers on while David helped Louise with hers. Renee waved good-bye from the front door while Will walked the three other people to David's Lincoln. He opened the rear door for his grandmother and helped her into her seat.

"I think this was a productive night, dear," she said. "Don't you?"

"Very," Will replied. He closed her door, then opened the front one for Louise Barrow. "I can't thank you enough, Mrs. Barrow."

"Nonsense. It's what Creigh would want done." She took his hand in hers. "You're the kind of man we need in politics," she smiled.

He helped her into her seat while David started the car. Will ducked down and looked across the car at his lawyer friend. "Thanks for everything, David."

"My pleasure, Will." Almost as an afterthought he said, "How are things coming with the other projects in your life?"

"I haven't had much time, David," he said. As he stood up a thought crossed his mind and before he shut the door he said, "Mrs. Barrow, you once said there were two other people from our town at Sloane-Kettering with your husband. I know that Gary Carr was one of them. Who was the other?" He heard a small gasp from the backseat.

Louise Barrow shifted uncomfortably on the soft leather seat. She glanced at David Jobb out of the corner of her eye and then said softly and reverently, "Why, David's wife, of course."

36

· · ·

RENEE SAT IN THE SWIVEL CHAIR in Will's office nervously tapping her foot on the floor. She looked out the window onto the town square. October had come and gone and most of the leaves had fallen from the trees. In the late afternoon sunlight two men were preparing to place lights on the gazebo in anticipation of the Santa Claus parade the day after Thanksgiving. Winter weather had descended upon the town, and the men were wearing bulky parkas. *Hurry, Will!* she thought as she watched the men untangling strings of lights. She glanced at the clock that hung on the wall next to Warren Martin's portrait. *We're supposed to be at Louise Barrow's in ten minutes.*

She saw Will's Jaguar pull into view and disappear into the parking lot at the side of the building. A minute later she heard him running up the stairs, two at a time. He opened the door of his office and spotted his wife sitting in his chair. His face split into a grin.

"Ready to go?" he said, rubbing his hands together to warm them.

"Ready as ever," she replied. "I'm glad I got here when I

did. Enid was just leaving when I arrived and she let me in. If she hadn't, I'd be sitting in my car with the motor running, trying to keep warm."

"Good old Enid, I'm going to miss her," Will said as they hurried down the stairs. "I've finally reached an agreement with Hal Jenkins at the bank. He's going to let me have Carol Wanless a couple of days each week, so Enid can train her before she leaves next month."

They reached the car and Will opened the door for his wife. "Things went well out at the Glen today. Hunter's really working overtime on that model home, and he thinks he'll have it done before Christmas." Will glanced at Renee as he closed her door. He hurried to the driver's side, climbed in, and pulled the car onto the road surrounding the square. "He'd like you to come over and choose paint colors and cabinets and carpet sometime."

"Me?" she said. "Why?"

"I think he believes you have good taste," he replied. "The electrical and plumbing work will be finished next week, and then they'll be ready to put the sheet rock on the walls." He glanced sideways at his wife. "So I think he wants your opinion about the kitchen cabinets and the paint colors."

"I guess," she said dubiously. "I'll give it my best shot." She reached over and turned the heater fan to a higher speed. "I can't believe how cold it has gotten."

"We might have an early winter. Maybe we'll have a white Christmas."

The Jaguar purred on quietly for several blocks and then

Renee said, "How many people has David arranged for? Do you know?"

"I have no idea. I've left that up to him, but I do know that Louise has been encouraging him to have quite a few." Will turned the corner that led to the Barrow home. "It's hard to believe that the election is next Tuesday."

"Worried?"

"A little. I think the newspaper ads have been wonderful. They've been simple and to the point. They've probably given me more name and face recognition than a thousand signs and, yet, I'm glad we're going to put up the remaining hundred and fifty signs on Monday."

"Maybe when this is over, we can get back to our Friday night dates," Renee said.

"Maybe." Will glanced at her again. "Are you sorry we've gotten involved in all of this?"

"I have mixed feelings," Renee responded, "I'm proud of you, sweetheart, and I'll support you completely, but some of the things that have gone on leave an awfully bitter taste in my mouth."

"I know what you mean." He guided the car to a parking place near the curb. More than twenty cars were parked around the Barrow residence. Will and Renee walked to the front door and rang the bell.

"Come in, come in," David Jobb said. "We're just about ready to distribute the materials to these good people."

About fifty people were assembled in Louise Barrow's

family room. Every chair and couch was taken, and a number of people either sat on the floor or remained standing. An electric snap went through the room and the conversations ended when Will walked in.

"Thank you so much for volunteering," Will said, shaking hands with a few of the workers. "We couldn't pull this off without your help." Several people began to applaud and soon others joined in.

David Jobb raised his hands and quieted them. "As Will said, we appreciate you coming here tonight. I know it's been discouraging, putting up signs only to have them stolen, so we've tried to make this fairly easy for you. I have a map showing where each of you will need to put up five signs, sometime between noon and dark on Monday. We're purposely doing this during the daylight hours. The more people who see you putting up the signs, the better." There was a bit of chatter among the people. "I know it would be a lot easier for many of you to put them up on Saturday—tomorrow—but we need to have you wait until Monday. We've spread the signs out all over the district, but we especially want to concentrate them in Page's Landing and Mossburg, since Will isn't known as well in those locations. He's been out knocking on doors and introducing himself, but he's still not as well known in those two towns as he is here at home."

One of the women in the group raised her hand. "I've been talking to my neighbors," she said. "I think you're better known than you know."

"Thank you for that," David replied. "Still, that's where

we've concentrated the signs. If there are some of you who just can't work it out to get those signs in place on Monday, please let me know and we'll find someone else to handle it."

The workers started to talk among themselves, and David raised his hands again. "I think you'd like to hear from Will, wouldn't you?"

The crowd began to clap and David thrust Will forward.

"You people are what this is all about," he began. "There really is government by the people, of the people, and for the people. I want you to know that I'm not on some power trip or out to garner personal honors. If I had known what running for office was going to require of me and my family, I might have rejected the idea. But my agenda remains what it was in the beginning—to help promote responsible government, to be a part of a legislature that really is responsive to the needs of the people."

There was more applause.

"If you succeed in helping me get elected, I want you to know that my door will be open to you . . . all of you . . . as well as to every other one of my constituents, whether they agree with me or not. Thank you again, my friends."

Renee began a chant, "We want Will . . . We want Will." The others picked it up until David Jobb raised his hands again and said, "If you'll follow me out this backdoor we can go directly into the garage. Then, if you'll tell Renee your name she'll find your map and Will and I will get you your signs. Any questions?"

An elderly gentleman who was sitting on a stool raised his hand. "Between noon and dark on Monday, right?"

"That's right, Arnold," David said. "Is that a problem?"

"Nope. And I'm retired, so if some of you can't get yours up, call me."

David pushed open the patio door and the crowd streamed into the side door to the garage through the frosty night air. Half an hour later they had all left with their allotment of signs, and Louise Barrow invited David, Will, and Renee back into the house.

"Where's your dear little boy?" she asked.

"Grams is taking care of him," Will said. "Although I think he thinks he's taking care of her."

"I understand," Louise said. "She's very lucky to have such a wonderful great-grandson. I'm afraid I've missed out on so much," she said wistfully. "Please have a seat." Louise gestured toward the couch. "How are you feeling about the race, Will?" she asked.

"It's hard to say," he replied. "I've talked to so many people and so few of them actually know who's running or anything about the issues. I owe a debt of gratitude to my grandfather, I've discovered, since so many people knew him . . . and felt so positively about him. Still, it's hard to know where I stand. Next Tuesday will tell."

"You sound just like Creigh," Louise said. "He used to be a basket case during the last week before every election. He'd swing back and forth between being sure he'd win and equally sure that he was going to lose. He was pretty hard to live with." She turned to Renee. "Has this young man been the same way?"

Renee nodded her head. "Except that I haven't seen him a whole lot this past month. He's been out walking the district and knocking on doors."

"I couldn't have done it without you, sweetheart," he said.

David Jobb stood up and began pacing the floor. "Well, to tell the truth, I'm worried," he said.

"About what, David?" Louise asked.

"Milton Phillips and the CCG have been too quiet for the past couple of weeks. I realize we took away their fun with the campaign signs, but they haven't done anything. There haven't been any advertisements to counter Will's . . . nothing. I can't believe they've given up."

"What could they possibly do?" Renee asked.

Louise Barrow patted the seat next to her. "Sit down, David, you're making us all nervous." She captured Will's eyes. "Often this group will make one big effort just before the election. David may be right, but I guess we'll just have to wait and see and be ready."

Will felt a cold chill in the room. "We'd better get over to Grams's and pick up Justin before it gets any later," he said, extending his hand to Renee. "Thank you, Mrs. Barrow and David, for all of your help and encouragement."

"You're more than welcome," she answered, while David nodded.

By the time Will and Renee arrived at Ruth's house, Justin had fallen asleep on the couch in front of the television set. Will picked him up and carried him to the car. He slept all the way home. Will carried him from the car to his room and placed him on his bed. "This is getting to be a habit, Champ," he whispered quietly as he removed the boy's shoes.

A crisp wind was blowing the next morning when the telephone awakened Will from a sound sleep. "Hello?" he said groggily.

"Have you seen this morning's paper?" David Jobb said.

"Not yet. Why?" he said yawning.

"I'll be right over," Jobb said.

The tone of David's voice awakened Will. He shrugged himself into his robe, walked down the hallway, opened the front door, and picked up the newspaper. He slipped off the red rubber band and unfolded the paper on the dining room table. He thumbed quickly through the first section, discarded it, and started on the second section. A full-page advertisement screamed at him.

WOULD YOU VOTE FOR A CHILD MOLESTER?
WOULD YOU VOTE FOR A WIFE ABUSER?
WOULD YOU VOTE FOR A DRUG USER?
WOULD YOU VOTE FOR A CONVICTED FELON?
No!

VOTE FOR MILTON PHILLIPS
EXPERIENCE, HONESTY, INTEGRITY
HOUSE OF REPRESENTATIVES—DISTRICT 85

Will felt his hands start to shake. He crunched the newspaper into a ball and flung it against the wall just as Renee appeared in the dining room.

"Will!" she said. "What's the matter?"

"That slimy toad!" he yelled.

Renee retrieved the wadded paper and began to smooth it out. Before she had finished, she realized what it said. "That conniving little weasel." She wadded the newspaper back into a ball and threw it to the floor. The doorbell rang.

"I take it you've seen it," David said as he walked into the living room. Will's hands were still shaking badly. He merely nodded his head.

Renee's voice was edged with ice. "All right, David. What do we do?"

"You have to respond," he said to Will. "The only question is how you do it."

"What are our options?" Renee asked.

"I suppose we can try to get a flyer printed and call our distribution network together to get it delivered."

"You sound unsure," Renee said coldly.

"The problems are that we'd have to get it printed quickly and we'd be asking the same people who are putting out your signs to canvass an area. I'm not sure we can count on them to get it all done."

Renee began to pace as she drew her robe tightly around her. "What other options do we have?"

The phone began ringing, and Will walked to the kitchen

to answer it. "Hello?" He perched on the corner of the table. "Yes, Mrs. Barrow, we've seen it." He listened to her response for a moment. "David's here now trying to figure out what we're going to do." Another pause. "I'll tell him. Thank you." He hung up and returned to the living room. "Louise Barrow is willing to help any way she can," Will said to David. "She wanted you to know."

David nodded his head. "I think the only other option is to fight fire with fire. I'm pretty sure I can get an ad placed in Monday's paper with your response to these baseless allegations. May I use your phone?"

Renee nodded her head as she continued to pace. David walked into the kitchen and dialed a number. Renee walked to where Will stood, still trembling with rage and disbelief. "What are you thinking, Will?"

"I'm trying to control myself, so I don't do something stupid! But it's darn hard."

David came back into the living room. "The *Examiner* will let us run a full-page response in Monday's paper. That's the good news. The bad news is that they want twelve thousand dollars up front to print it, and we've got to have both the copy and the money to them by two o'clock this afternoon." He sank heavily onto the sofa. "The copy isn't a problem . . . the money is."

"Twelve thousand dollars?" Will sank to the sofa beside David. "Where could we possibly come up with that kind of money that quickly?"

David shook his head. "We've used nearly everything Creighton had in his campaign account on the ads we've run this past month. There's only about five hundred dollars left. I don't dare approach Louise for more." He hung his head, "I just don't know where to go."

Renee had stopped her pacing. "I'll give you the twelve thousand dollars," she said quietly.

"You?" said David.

Will was staring at her. "Where would you get twelve thousand dollars?" he asked.

"I suppose that does require a little explanation," she said. "After we were married, I didn't need the child support checks from Gary that came each month. I've been putting the money into an account for Justin's education." She avoided Will's eyes. "I probably should have told you."

After an uncomfortable silence, David said, "Well . . . regardless, it is very welcome news."

Will stared at his wife in disbelief. "You have twelve thousand dollars?"

"Actually it's a little closer to fifteen," she admitted. "I'm sorry, sweetheart, I should have told you."

Will stood up from the couch and walked toward the stairs leading to their bedroom. Renee and David watched him go and then Jobb said, "I suppose that was quite a surprise to your husband." She nodded numbly.

Will reappeared a few minutes later. He avoided Renee's eyes and walked to where David was sitting. He had a pad of paper and a pen in his hand. "I suppose we'd better decide how to write our answer to that . . . that baloney."

"Yes, I think you're right." David followed him to the dining room table where Will began to write on the pad. *I have avoided completely any negative campaigning,* he began, *but the unwarranted and completely false allegations of last Saturday must be answered. To suggest that I have molested a child, abused my wife, or done any of the other things that were implied in the advertisement paid for by my opponent, Milton Phillips, is so ludicrous that I hate to dignify them with a response. It is this kind of smear campaign and innuendo that gives politics a bad name.*

I hope that you can see past the inflammatory rhetoric to the truth and cast your vote for someone who has made this an issues-only campaign.

A vote for Will Martin is a vote for responsible government.

He handed the pad to David Jobb and said, "What do you think?"

"Honestly, Will, I think it's too wordy. I don't think anyone will read it."

Renee said timidly, "Could you just say, *Scrape away the lies and vote for Will Martin?*"

David said, "I think that's a little too brief. Would you mind if I took your ideas to Louise and let her work on them a little bit? In spite of her insistence she knows little of politics, I know she often helped Creighton with his press releases."

"That would be fine, David," Will said.

"I'll call you for your approval on the final copy." He looked at Renee, "I don't want to bring up a sore subject, but I don't suppose you have that money where you can get to it today?"

"No, I don't, David. It's in the bank in a savings account. But I can write you a check and first thing Monday morning I'll go to the bank and transfer the money, if that's all right."

"I'm sure that will do nicely," he said, avoiding Will's eyes.

Renee walked into the kitchen and returned a few minutes later with a check. She handed it to David Jobb. "Thank you," she said to him, then turned to Will. "I'm sorry, sweetheart."

Will nodded his head and walked upstairs to their bedroom.

37

. . .

SUNDAY DAWNED SLATE GRAY AND WINDY. Will rolled out of bed and padded down the hall to the living room. Rain pattered against the windows as he blinked his eyes in the early morning gloom, sat on the couch, and rested his head in his hands. The furnace clicked on, and a few minutes later Will felt warm air creeping under the couch and licking at his feet. He heard sounds from the hallway, looked up, and saw Justin standing there.

"Hi, Champ."

Justin yawned and waved his hand, "Hi, Will." He walked to where Will sat and bounced onto the couch beside him. "Are you and Mom mad at each other?" he asked.

Will shifted further back on the couch. "Not mad . . . just disappointed."

"What does that mean?" Justin asked. "You didn't talk to each other all day yesterday."

Will tried to sort through yesterday's revelation and how to explain it to an eight-year-old boy. "It's a little hard to explain, Champ, but your mother kept a pretty big secret from me, and when I found out about it I was disappointed. Does that make any sense?"

Justin pondered for a moment, then said, "Do you keep any secrets from her?"

Will began to shake his head, then stopped. "I guess we all keep a few things secret. Especially if we think they might hurt the other person."

"Did Mom keep her secret because she didn't want to hurt you?" he said innocently.

"I don't know, Champ."

"Does this mean you're going to go away?"

Will slipped his arm around the boy's thin shoulders. "No, Champ. I'm not going away."

"That's good to know," Renee said from the doorway.

Will jumped, startled. "I didn't hear you."

"I tried to be quiet. It seemed as if the two of you were having a serious conversation." She sat down next to Justin. "Will, I'm sorry about yesterday. It was wrong of me to have kept that money secret. It's just that . . . oh, never mind. There really isn't a legitimate excuse."

Will reached past Justin and squeezed her shoulder with his hand, "I'm the one who should apologize. I've been acting like a spoiled brat." He leaned over and kissed her.

"Ooh, mush," Justin said disgustedly as he slid out from between them and ran down the hallway to his room.

Will pulled Renee close to him and kissed her again. "I'm sorry, sweetheart," he said as he stroked her back. She snuggled against him and drew her feet up beneath her on the couch. They sat together in silence listening to Justin slam the bathroom door and start water running in the bathtub. "Any other secrets?" Will asked.

"None from me," she said. "What about you?"

Will sucked on his bottom lip. "There is something I've been meaning to talk to you about," he said barely louder than a whisper. He could feel her suddenly tense in his arms. "This is really hard for me, Renee, because I'm not sure how you feel, and I don't want to risk hurting you—but I'd like to adopt Justin."

He felt the tension release and suddenly she put her hands behind his head and pulled him to her. She kissed him deeply. "You don't know how I feel?" She kissed him again and tears spilled over and ran down her face. "I've been afraid you wouldn't want to . . . Oh, never mind."

"Can I take that as a 'yes'?" He hugged her tightly. "Renee, the reason I haven't brought it up is that I've been trying to find Gary to get his permission. And I can't locate him."

"He's in Paris," she said simply. "At least that's where I thought he was."

"What about the child-support payments? Where do they come from?"

"They're deposited directly into the bank. They just show up on a statement I get each quarter." She looked puzzled. "I haven't had any direct correspondence from Gary in a long time." She listened to Justin splashing in the bathtub. "But he has sent Justin a birthday card every year." She rose from the couch, walked down the hall, and returned shortly with an envelope in her hands. "This came for his birthday a couple of months ago." She handed it to Will.

"It's postmarked Fort Lee, New Jersey," Will said. "That's a long way from Paris, France." He tapped the envelope against his hand. "Where in the world is he?"

"Maybe Hal Jenkins at the bank knows," she offered.

Will thought for a moment. "And maybe David knows something."

"What makes you think that?" Renee queried.

"Louise Barrow told me that David's wife was with Creighton and Gary at Sloane-Kettering."

"Sloane-Kettering? What would Gary be doing there—" Suddenly Renee held her hand to her mouth.

Will lapsed into thoughtful silence. "If David knows something, why hasn't he offered any help?"

"I'm confused," Renee said. "It sounds as though Gary may have been sick. But why would David know anything about you trying to reach Gary?"

Will ducked his head. "Actually, I've been looking for him for quite some time, and I approached David about what might have to happen for me to adopt Justin if we couldn't locate Gary. So he's known what I've been planning for some time."

Renee crossed her arms and stared at Will, "And you accuse me of keeping secrets," she said.

"Wednesday morning, as soon as the election's over, I'm going to spend more time trying to resolve this problem. I promised David I'd have it all worked out by Christmas."

There was a thump on the front door. Renee freed herself from the couch and returned a few minutes later with the newspaper. Fearing the worst, she thumbed her way through the first two sections until the paper fell open to another full-page ad. This one featured the photograph of Will kissing Julia Welsch prominently displayed; however, Julia was now wearing a brief bikini and Will was dressed only in swimming trunks. The background had been changed to a beach with no one else in sight. At the bottom of the page was Milton Phillips's picture. In huge type were the words, *Lechery or Leadership?*

Vote for Milton Phillips.

Will felt rage welling up inside him. "I'm going over and punch his lights out," he snarled.

"That's just what he wants you to do! And you can bet he'll have witnesses to tell the story. Just ignore it, Will. Your ad will run tomorrow, and then it will all be over."

Will paced furiously up and down the room and finally grabbed the phone book from the countertop. He thumbed through until he found the name he was looking for, then snatched the phone from its cradle, and punched in the number. The phone rang several times until someone picked it up at the other end.

"I'm sorry to wake you, Les," Will said, "but I need your

computer expertise." He listened for a minute. I'll be right over." He hung the phone up and raced up the stairs to his bedroom.

"Where are you going?" Renee said when she caught up to him.

"To Les Jardine's. He's the computer whiz who found the actual boundaries of Martin's Glen. Several months ago he demonstrated some pretty slick forging on his computer. I'm betting he can show me how Milton Phillips manipulated that photograph." He threw on slacks and a sweatshirt and struggled into a pair of tennis shoes.

"I'm coming with you," she said. He started to shake his head, but something in her eye warned him.

"What about Justin?"

Renee pulled on her sweatshirt. "Justin," she called, "get out of the tub. We've got an errand to run."

Something in her voice told him not to argue, and five minutes later the three of them were in the Jaguar and heading toward Les Jardine's home.

A pizza box was still on the table in the front room, whether the same one Will had seen previously, he wasn't able to determine, but the computer room was still as pristine as a hospital operating room. Will handed Les the newspaper and said, "How did he do it? That picture was taken out at Martin's Glen and both of us were fully clothed."

Jardine's face split into a smile. "Never trust a photograph," he said. "I'll show you. Let's work with this dude on the bottom of the page." He placed the picture of Milton Phillips on his flatbed scanner. A few seconds later the picture appeared on the computer screen. "This isn't a great picture to begin with. Probably eighty-five or one hundred line," he mumbled. "Let's clean it up." He pulled down a menu with his mouse and the picture became noticeably clearer. "That's better."

Renee had been peering over Jardine's shoulder. "That's amazing."

"You ain't seen nothin' yet." Quickly he outlined the picture and isolated it and discarded the rest of the image of the newspaper. "Is he the bad dude who's been givin' you grief, Mr. Martin?"

Will nodded his head. "You could say that."

"I think it's time his true character is revealed." Quickly he opened another window and brought up a picture of a cow and bull standing in a field. With a few deft strokes he copied the bull's horns and a moment later had them installed on either side of Milton Phillips's head. Several more manipulations added a beard and mustache and a pitchfork. "Speak of the devil," Jardine cackled. He added some color and sent the picture to his printer. "If you want me to do a real professional job it might take half an hour," he said proudly as he handed the print to Will and Renee.

"That's unbelievable," Renee said.

Jardine was inspecting the newspaper ad with a critical eye. "Whoever did this did a pretty sloppy job. He pointed to a place near Will's arm where part of his blazer was still visible and another spot on Julia's leg where the pattern of her dress remained. "If you want quality work, you've got to find somebody who really knows what he's doing." He pointed to the background. "Look, they've just pasted in the beach and the shadows go the wrong way."

Will took the newspaper page back. "I knew you could explain this," he said. "I'm sorry I dragged you out of bed."

"It's all right, man. I need to be checking on my servers anyway." Jardine led them to the door. "If I can ever help, you know where I live." He started to close the door, then stopped and said, "Is this dude really hassling you, Mr. Martin?"

Will nodded his head. "I guess you could say that."

Les Jardine stepped onto the porch. "Would you like me to waste his reputation?" he said conspiratorially.

"What?" said Renee. "What do you mean?"

Jardine looked around warily. "Well, I mean, he could suddenly max out all his credit cards, he might develop a bunch of outstanding warrants . . . you know, just some stuff to let him know you can take him out anytime you want to."

Will smiled. "Tempting, Les, but no thanks."

Jardine shrugged his shoulders, then walked back into the house. "If you change your mind, just give me a call."

"That guy is scary," Renee said, once they were back in the car.

"I think I want to keep him on my side," Will replied.

"Will?" Justin said from the backseat.

"What, Champ?"

"Can we get a computer like his?"

38

• • •

Monday's paper carried Will's full-page ad. Louise Barrow and David Jobb had written the copy:

> **Weigh honesty against deceit**
> **Weigh the truth against lies**
> **And you'll decide**
> **Where there's a weigh, there's a Will**
> **VOTE WILL MARTIN**
> **Where there's a Will there's a way**
> **toward honest government!**

The type flowed around an enlarged picture of Will, Renee, and Justin. "I hope it works," he said to his wife.

"So do I," she replied. "Did you have a rough day at work?"

"I've never been so tired in my life," Will replied. "I'll be so glad when this is over."

She kneaded his shoulders. "So will I."

"On the bright side, the walls are almost up on Dee's

Market. I had quite a conversation with the owner today. He's more than satisfied with Ray Spellman's work. And Hunter Hoggard's really pushing me to have you choose colors on the model home. He has twenty or so others under some stage of construction. So things seem to be moving along at Martin's Glen."

She continued to massage his shoulders and back. "Now if you can just get this election behind you."

"Tomorrow it is behind us, one way or another." He closed his eyes. "After dinner let's take a ride and see if all the signs have been put in place."

An hour later the sun had set completely as Will, Renee, and Justin took a drive through Will's district. Everywhere they turned, a Will Martin sign popped out at them. They returned home encouraged. "It may be unorthodox, but who knows, it might work," he said as he parked the Jaguar in the driveway. "Tomorrow we'll know."

Election day dawned clear and cold. Will had spent a near-sleepless night worrying and wondering what else could have been done. He slipped out of bed as noiselessly as he could and stumbled into the bathroom. He showered and shaved and inspected the dark circles under his eyes. When he emerged he found Renee was in the kitchen preparing breakfast. He kissed her and sat down at the table.

"Nervous?" she asked.

"Mostly tired," he replied as he glanced at his watch. "The

polls have been open for half an hour. I think I'll vote on the way to work."

"I'll get there after I drop Justin at school." She sat down opposite him. "Have you planned a victory party for this evening?"

He shook his head. "I just thought we'd go over to the courthouse and wait for the results. David told me that's where he'll be." Will finished his breakfast, kissed his wife good-bye, and drove to the elementary school where voting was taking place. He was surprised to see ten or twelve people waiting to get their ballots and all of the voting booths filled. He had just taken his place at the back of the line when a woman in one of the voting booths stepped out and deposited her ballot in the locked box. She looked up and recognized Will.

"Will Martin," she said cordially, "good to see you here. I guess I know whom you'll be voting for." She chuckled. All of the other people in line turned and looked at him. He smiled at them, some smiled back, some turned away.

"Good luck," the woman said as she walked past him and out the door.

A few minutes later Will finished voting and drove to his office. The sun had crept over the eastern mountains and turned the frost on the lawn in the town square to a silver sheen. All of the pine trees were decorated with lights as was the gazebo. Will opened the door of the agency and climbed the stairs. Enid Cook met him outside his office.

"Good luck, Mr. Martin," she said primly.

"Thank you, Miss Cook. I'm glad that it's nearly over."

She followed him into his office. "And how are you feeling?"

"Tired, but fine." He hung his coat on a coatrack. "And hopeful that we'll win."

Enid leaned over his desk. "I saw the ads that despicable man put in the newspaper. I can't think anyone will believe that drivel."

"I hope not. This election has really opened my eyes."

"I don't see how he can live with himself, spreading all those lies."

"The most frightening thing, Miss Cook, is that he apparently believes that it's all right to do those kinds of things if it helps him win. In his mind, the end justifies the means."

"I suppose," she sniffed, "but I hope you drub him." She smacked her fist into the palm of her other hand, something so uncharacteristic that Will laughed out loud. She looked embarrassed, then added, "Well, I hope you do!"

After Enid left his office, Will tried to concentrate on the work that had piled up on his desk during the past week, but his mind kept wandering. He played over and over the events of the past month and wondered what he could have done differently. There were many things that came to mind that he wished he'd done. He swiveled around in his chair and looked across the square. The sun was burning off the frost and the town was coming to life. He tapped his foot nervously on the floor and tried . . . unsuccessfully not to think of the election.

The day crept by as if on turtle legs until Will finally gave up and told Enid he was leaving for the day. He drove aimlessly though the streets where his spirits soared when he saw one of his campaign signs, then plummeted when he saw one of Milton Phillips's. He found himself near Martin's Glen. Construction crews were working hard, and storefronts were beginning to appear in a gentle curve in front of the cotton-wood trees that stood like silent sentinels, their naked branches pointing toward the sky. Will eased the Jaguar onto an unpaved road that led to where nearly two dozen homes were in various stages of construction. He continued past them, turned around, and had started back to the paved road when Hunter Hoggard stepped out of the front door of one of the homes and waved. Will eased the Jaguar into the driveway.

"Good luck, boss," Hoggard said loudly as Will opened the door of the car.

"Thanks, Hunter. How did you know it was me?"

"There aren't many silver Jags driving around this town," he laughed. "When's your wife comin' over to pick colors?"

"I've asked her a couple of times, but I think she's waiting for me to bring her out to the Glen. I'll try to get her out here in the next couple of days."

"I guess you've been pretty busy, boss. Today's your big day." He punched Will gently on the shoulder.

"I hope so. Well, I'd better get going."

Hoggard waved and walked back into the house and Will continued his aimless drive through the town. Eventually he took the on-ramp to the freeway and drove to Page's Landing. He drove past the polling place at the fire station and saw a line of people huddled inside. The same was true in Mossburg at the elementary school. He had to turn on his headlights as he wound down the road toward home. He passed the street where Les Jardine lived and saw that someone had attached a picture of Milton Phillips complete with devil's horns to the stop-sign post. Will read the words beneath the picture, *Speak of the Devil!* and burst into laughter. He looked at the dashboard clock and realized it was nearly six o'clock. He turned on the radio in time to hear the last bars of a song.

"And now KACH Radio brings you the news. This is Doug Norton. It appears that near record-breaking numbers have gone to the polls today. Pollster Brian Ford is here in the studio with us tonight. Brian, what do you think has caused the heavy voter interest in this election?"

"Clearly, the accusations made by the two camps in the race for the legislature have struck a nerve with the electorate and galvanized feelings on both sides. There have been some unusual strategies, including Martin's waiting until the last minute to put up the bulk of his campaign signs. In speaking to people at the polls there are few of them who are undecided. They are there to support their candidate."

"Brian, this seems unusual in a year when there isn't a

presidential or gubernatorial race to draw voters out. How do you see the race playing out?"

"Doug, we've been conducting exit polls all day, and now, with less than two hours until the polls close, it is too close to call. We're all going to have to wait to see who comes out on top in the race between Martin and Phillips."

"Thank you, Brian. Stay tuned to KACH for those results.

"Elsewhere, animal control officers were called today to a construction site near Silver Ridge where a coyote has apparently taken up residence in the crawl space under a home. Andrea Perkins is on the scene . . ."

Will turned off the radio. *Too close to call.* He reached his home and parked the Jaguar in the driveway.

Renee had dinner waiting and on the table when he walked through the back door. "You're late," she said with a smile. "Been out voting a few more times?"

He kissed her. "I wish. The radio says it's too close to call."

"You'll be fine," she said, "Now, go wash up and let's have dinner. Your grandmother wants us to pick her up on the way to the courthouse."

At five minutes before eight o'clock, Will parked the car in the parking lot at the courthouse. Several dozen other cars were already there. He opened the passenger door of the car for his wife and the back door for his grandmother. Justin scrambled out after Ruth. The four of them walked into the courthouse and headed for the county clerk's office. They could hear the rumble of conversation before they rounded the corner of the hallway. A throng of people was gathered in a conference room adjacent to the clerk's small office. Will recognized Milton Phillips and felt a lump of anger rise in his throat. He swallowed it down just as the election clerk, Marti Martinez, spotted him and waved in his direction. She pointed to a second conference room on the other side of the office.

"You can have your people meet in here," she said with a smile. "Good luck."

Will led the four of them into the conference room and flipped on the light. He could hear Milton Phillips's supporters talking noisily down the hall. A minute later David Jobb and Louise Barrow appeared at the end of the hall, spotted Will, and walked smiling into the room.

"Ballots will be delivered any time in the next few minutes," David said. "They'll probably be the ones from here in Page's Landing. The machine will count them rather quickly . . . they'll do it twice to verify the count . . . and then they'll write the votes on that white board." He pointed across the hallway at a board hanging on the wall. Someone had drawn lines on the board creating twenty-seven rows. A voting precinct number was written at the left margin of each row. At the top of the board "Martin" and "Phillips" had been printed.

David removed a calculator from his breast pocket. "The tricky thing is that they won't come in any particular order. We'll have precinct twelve, then precinct twenty-one, and so on. So, we have to keep a running total as they print the results on the board."

Les Jardine popped into the room carrying his laptop computer. "Hey, dude. This where the party is?" He placed his laptop on the table and popped it open. "I already created a spreadsheet," he said, "so when the votes come in, give 'em to me and I'll enter them in my computer. It'll tell us who's ahead." He smiled and booted the computer.

The seven of them chatted nervously for several minutes, and then two men turned the corner of the hall carrying a locked ballot box between them. Marti Martinez unlocked the padlock and dumped the ballots into a cardboard box on the counter in her office.

"I'm ready for poll watchers," she called out. David Jobb joined a short, heavy-set man who left Milton Phillips's supporters and walked into the clerk's office.

Deftly Marti gathered the ballots, tapped them into stacks on the counter, and rotated those that were upside down or backward. She then fed the packet of ballot cards into a counting machine. When the machine had finished feeding all of the cards into a hopper, she squared them up a second time and ran them through the machine again. A small tape printed out of one end of the machine. She showed it to the two men who both nodded agreement, then walked out of her office to the white board and found Precinct 17. She wrote *106* in Will's column and *111* in Milton's. A small cheer went up from the other conference room.

Les Jardine tapped the numbers into his computer and at the bottom of the screen two numbers began to flash, *106* and *111*.

Louise Barrow looked at a map of voting precincts that was hanging on the back wall of the conference room. "Seventeen," she said inspecting the map, "right here." She jabbed the map with her finger. "Right here in Page's Landing. I'd expect Milton to do well—he lives just down the street."

By ten o'clock all but two precincts had turned in their ballots. The totals at the bottom of Les's computer read *5,650* for Will and *5,703* for Milton Phillips.

"I can't believe that scoundrel has led all night," Ruth Martin said dejectedly.

David Jobb sat heavily on the edge of the table. "Louise, which two precincts haven't reported yet?"

Louise inspected the map and compared it with the missing numbers on the white board, "One from out in the country, near Silver Ridge, and mine," she said. "It's going to be close."

Milton Phillips knocked on the window of their conference room, then opened the door. "Well, Martin, are you ready to concede, yet?"

Before Will could answer, David Jobb said, "Not at all, Milton. There are still two precincts left to come in."

"Why delay the inevitable?" Phillips grinned knowingly.

Jobb took his elbow and led him out of the room. "It's not over, yet, Milton," he said.

A man and woman appeared with another ballot box. "We're from Silver Ridge," the woman said. "Sorry we're a little late." Marti Martinez opened the lock and dumped about fifty ballots onto the countertop. "We didn't have a very good turnout, I'm afraid," the woman continued. "There's been a lot of excitement up there today with a coyote, and I think people forgot to get out and vote."

Marti squared the cards and fed them into the machine. When the votes were counted she went to the white board and entered the two numbers, twenty-one for Will and twenty-six for Phillips.

Les Jardine punched the numbers into his computer. "He's ahead by fifty-eight votes," he said disgustedly. Wearily Will and Renee sat down on two of the straight-backed wooden chairs that lined the walls of the room. Will held his head in his hands. David Jobb patted him on the shoulder.

"You've put up a good fight. I'm proud to have worked with you," the lawyer said quietly.

Louise Barrow and Ruth Martin sat silently against the opposite wall while Les Jardine stared at his computer. Justin lay down across two chairs and put his head in his mother's lap. A feeling of gloom descended over the group. The noise from Milton Phillips's room increased with each passing minute. Will stood up and looked at David Jobb.

"Maybe it's time for me to concede," he said. Just then two men appeared in the hallway carrying the last ballot box.

"Precinct Three," one of them announced. "We're finally

here." They hoisted the locked box onto the countertop and when Marti Martinez opened it several hundred ballots spilled out. "I've never seen such a heavy turnout," one of the men said. "We're guessing nearly two-thirds of the voters in our precinct voted."

Ten minutes later the ballots had been counted and Marti walked to the white board. She consulted the paper tape and in Will's column entered *383*. Jardine entered the number into his computer. Marti then wrote *326* in Milton Phillips's column. Jardine's fingers flicked on the computer.

"No!" he screamed. "I can't believe it."

"What?" Jobb said.

Slowly Jardine turned his computer around so the others could see the totals. Will had received 6,054 votes and Milton Phillips had received 6,055. A cheer erupted from Milton Phillip's room.

"One *lousy* vote," Will said as Milton Phillips swaggered through the door.

"I suppose you'll want a recount," he said with a sneer.

Before Will could answer, Marti Martinez walked into the room. "I have to call the results in to the lieutenant governor," she said, "but you ought to know that we have nearly a hundred absentee ballots that have to be counted."

"Let's count them now," Phillips said.

"I have to wait until next Monday," she said.

"Why?" Phillips complained.

"The law says that absentee ballots may be mailed in and

must be postmarked before election day and must be received by my office before noon on the day of official canvassing. That day is always the Monday following the election," Martinez said simply. "So we will open all of those ballots next Monday, as soon as the mail has been delivered and we've checked to see if there are any more absentee ballots." She looked at both candidates. "I'm sure you'll want to have someone here to verify those ballots. The mail is usually delivered just before noon. Why don't we open those ballots at one o'clock in the afternoon?" She nodded her head slightly at the two men. "Will that do?"

"I suppose so," Phillips said coldly.

"That will be fine," Will said.

"Good! Now let's go home. Congratulations to both of you." She flipped out the lights.

39

. . .

WILL KICKED HIS SHOES OFF and slumped back in the recliner. Both David Jobb and Louise Barrow had called early that morning to assure him they were certain that when the absentee ballots were counted he'd be the winner. He wished he could believe them. The atmosphere around the office had been muted, as if people were unsure what to say. Lloyd Randell had written in the *Examiner* that Milton Phillips had won the race but had apparently had to file his story before the final two precincts were added in and had reported a much wider margin than a single vote. It had been a long, unproductive day. The only thing Will could recall that had actually been accomplished was that Renee had gone out to Martin's Glen, met with Hunter Hoggard, and selected the cabinets, colors for paint, tile for the countertops, and carpet for the model home. Now she and Justin had gone grocery shopping and Will was home by himself. He closed his eyes and tried to forget about the election results.

He awoke an hour later to the soft feel of Renee's lips against his. "Can you come help carry in the groceries?" she asked.

Will followed her through the kitchen door to the Chevrolet. Justin was wrestling two heavy plastic bags full of cans out of the backseat. "Hey, Justin, how ya doin'?" Will asked.

"Okay," the boy replied.

Will hung several bags from his fingers and followed Justin through the door into the house. "What's the matter?"

"Nothin'."

"Come on, don't try to kid me," Will said, hefting the bags onto the kitchen table.

"Me and Jeff kinda got into a fight," he said.

"About what?"

"I don't wanna say," Justin whined.

Will put his hand on the boy's shoulder, "I'd like to help, if I can."

Justin shook his head vigorously and began to cry quietly. Will looked at Renee, but she just shrugged her shoulders. The boy pulled away and ran down the hallway to his room.

"What was that all about?" Will asked.

"Beats me. He's seemed depressed ever since I picked him up at school, but this is the first I've heard about a fight. I think we ought to just leave him alone for a little while."

"If you say so," Will said as he sat down backward on a kitchen chair. He gripped the top of the back of the chair with both hands and rested his chin on his knuckles. "I talked to David today," he said. "I told him to go ahead with posting the announcement in the paper about me wanting to adopt

Justin. He said he'd have his associate, Haven Walker, draw up the legal notice." He watched his wife busily putting away groceries. "I hope that's all right."

"How long did he say it would take?"

"He hopes it can all be done by the end of the year." He stood up. "I'm going to see what's wrong with Justin." He walked down the hall and knocked on the closed bedroom door. "Can I come in?"

Justin's muffled voice replied, "If you want."

Will entered the room and sat down on the side of Justin's bed. The boy was lying on his stomach with his face buried in his pillow."

Will gently stroked his back. "Are you sure you don't want to talk about it?"

Justin lay quietly for a minute then said, "Jeff called you a loser."

Will snorted. "You know, sometimes I feel like one, but it's nothing to fight about."

Justin rolled over, sat up, and hugged Will. "You're not a loser," he cried into Will's shoulder.

"No, I'm not, as long as I have you and your mother."

Across town David Jobb flipped open his address book, ran his finger down the page, and punched a number into the phone. It rang twice and a woman answered, "Palisades Manor."

"Room 105, please."

"Thank you." David heard a number of clicks and then the

phone rang again. He hung up after the tenth ring and hit the redial button on the phone.

"Palisades Manor," the same woman answered.

"Yes, you rang Room 105, and no one answered. Do you happen to know where Gary Carr is?"

"I believe he's in the game room. Would you like me to bring him to the phone?"

"No, I'll call in the morning. Thank you." He hung up, then dialed Louise Barrow to see if she'd like to accompany him to dinner. David walked out to the Lincoln and drove to the Barrow residence with a smile on his lips.

Early the next morning, David Jobb steered his Lincoln into its usual parking place next to his law office. Overnight, the first snowstorm of the season had dusted the trees with powdered sugar and left an inch of frosting on the lawns and streets, and David walked gingerly across the slippery parking lot into his office. It was early enough that he was alone. Sitting down at his desk, he looked up the number again and punched the buttons on his phone. Although it was not yet quite seven-thirty, it was nearly nine-thirty in New Jersey.

"Palisades Manor," a man's voice said. "How may I help you?"

"Room 105, please."

The phone rang twice before someone answered in a quavering voice, "Hello?"

"May I speak with Gary Carr?" David asked.

"This is Gary," the man responded.

"This is David Jobb, Gary. I just thought you ought to know that Will and Renee are both trying to locate you. I learned last night that Will finally told Renee of his plans to adopt Justin."

"I see," the reedy voice replied. "I'll take care of it."

"Gary, you didn't ask for my advice, but I'm going to give you some. Why not contact them?"

There was a long pause before the voice said, "I just can't, Mr. Jobb. I think you understand why."

"I'm trying to understand, but I think you're wrong."

The voice faded to where David strained to hear the reply. "Just remember our attorney-client privilege. I don't want to see them, and I said I'd take care of it." He disconnected without saying good-bye.

David Jobb sighed and returned the phone to its cradle. He leaned back in his chair. "Why does everyone want to keep things secret?" he said to himself. Just then someone open the front door of the office, and David assumed it was Patricia Ames arriving, but a moment later there was a knock on his door.

"Come in," he called out. The door opened and Will appeared.

"Good morning, David."

"Good morning, Representative."

"I wish I was as sure of that as you seem to be," Will said wearily.

"Monday will tell, I suppose," David replied. "You're up early."

Will sat down in the chair opposite David's. "I'm just wondering if you can answer a question for me?"

The attorney spread his hands, "If I can."

"A few days ago Louise Barrow told me that when she and Creighton were at Sloane-Kettering, she saw your wife and Gary Carr there."

"Yes," David said almost in a whisper.

"I'm sorry about your wife's death, David. I suppose that happened while I was away in New York." Jobb nodded. "The question I have is, do you have any idea where Gary Carr is now?"

David thought quietly for a time then shook his head. "I'm sorry, Will, there's nothing I can tell you that will help you find him." He spread his hands again. "I've tried to help every way I could, but I'm just not much help on this." He brightened. "But I'm glad you're going ahead with the adoption plans."

Will rose slowly from his chair. "I just had to ask," he said. "Thanks for everything. Will you be going over to the courthouse on Monday?"

"You couldn't keep me away," David said with enthusiasm.

Will raised his hand in salute and left the lawyer's office.

The next three days dragged by, but Monday finally arrived. Will and Renee had kept Justin out of school for the day, and the three of them arrived at the courthouse just before one o'clock. They walked through the ancient hallway to the clerk's office, where David and Louise were waiting for them. Milton Phillips and several of his supporters were there as well.

Exactly at the stroke of one, Marti Martinez began slitting open the envelopes containing the absentee ballots and placing them in a stack on her desk. Within five minutes all of them were ready to count. Her assistant walked to the white board where less than a week before the votes had been tallied. All that remained on the board now were the final totals.

"Ready?" said the voting clerk. Her assistant nodded her head. "And are you ready?" she looked at Milton and Will. Both of them nodded.

"I hope you're not going to demand a recount," Phillips smirked at Will.

Marti lifted the first ballot. "Phillips," she said. Her assistant put a mark on the board under Milton Phillips's name. "Martin," Martinez said. Another mark.

Less than ten minutes later the ballots had all been counted. Milton Phillips had received thirty-eight votes and Will Martin had received forty-one.

Marti Martinez stood up and extended her hand to Will. "Congratulations, Mr. Martin. I'll call the lieutenant governor right now and certify you as the winner."

Milton Phillips exploded, "I demand a recount. We're well within the one percent requirement, and I'm formally requesting the recount. This is absurd!"

"Your request is noted, Mr. Phillips. I'll notify the appropriate people, and we'll contact you as soon as we're ready to do a recount. But for the moment, I'm certifying Mr. Martin as the winner. Thank you all for coming." She marched back into her office and closed the door.

Will stood in stunned silence. "We won?"

"It seems as if you have, by two votes," David said, throwing his arms around the young man.

Once David released him, Louise Barrow pulled on Will's arm and reached to kiss him on the cheek. "I told you not to worry," she said with a smile.

Will hugged Renee and kissed her soundly. "Congratulations, sweetheart," she said, kissing him back. Justin threw his arms around Will's waist.

Milton Phillips and his crew stormed down the hallway. Just before they turned the corner, Phillips looked back over his shoulder and snarled, "You haven't won yet, Martin."

Marti Martinez stepped out of her office. "I've certified you, Mr. Martin. We'll try to do the recount as quickly as we can, but, as you may know, the lieutenant governor is in Florida at a convention . . . they hold one every year following the elections . . . and I don't think he'll be back for at least ten days. I'm certain he'll want to be involved." She smiled, "But, you know, I have a lot of confidence in our counting machine, I'd be surprised if things change at all."

"Thank you."

"We'll be in contact as soon as anything is decided. Now, have a good day."

40

• • •

THE JAGUAR SLIPPED A BIT ON THE gravel road leading to the model home at Martin's Glen, but they reached the paved driveway and Will eased the car toward the open garage. Justin immediately scampered out of the backseat and ran into the garage.

"This is cool, Will," he said, spinning around in the empty space.

"I thought we ought to check out the house. Hunter Hoggard says the cabinets have been delivered and are ready to install." He unlocked the door that led from the garage into the house. They entered a little mudroom, and Renee looked into an adjoining space where a washer and dryer would eventually go.

"Nice," she said. "I'm impressed. Things have come a long way since I was here two weeks ago." She led them into a great room with a cathedral ceiling and windows that looked out at the mountains to the east.

"I'd say they're on schedule to have this finished by the end of the year," Will said as he walked down a hallway toward a suite of bedrooms.

"This one and the one next door," Renee said. She poked her

head into the master bathroom. "Look at that shower and Jacuzzi tub," she said with envy. "He does very good work."

"I'm impressed," Will admitted. "The cabinets are sitting on the kitchen floor and I guess they will get them installed within a day or two."

"Thanksgiving might slow them up a bit," she said.

"That gives them three days next week before the holiday. I think they can get them all in place by then."

Justin raced down the steps to the basement and they heard him slapping his feet on the floor to create an echo. "Maybe we need to get away when this is all over," Renee said.

Will took her hands in his. "You saw the announcement in the paper this morning? We have to give Gary . . . or anyone . . . seven days to object and then we have to place a second one before I . . . we . . . can go ahead with the adoption."

She snuggled against him. "Are you sure about this, sweetheart?"

Will cocked an ear, listening to Justin stomping around in the basement. "I've never been more sure in my life." He kissed her. "But it seems as if it has been an awfully long quest." He kissed her again just as Justin barreled up the steps from the basement.

"Yuck, mush," he said, holding his nose.

"Ready to go, Champ?" Will asked.

"I guess," he said. "Are we going to Gramma Martin's for Thanksgiving this year?" he asked as they walked to the car.

"Yes, we are, sweetheart," Renee said.

"Cool." Justin slipped into the backseat of the Jaguar. "She always has pie."

As promised, Ruth Martin had pumpkin pie as the grand finale for her usual sumptuous Thanksgiving feast. She had invited not only Will, Renee, and Justin, but David Jobb and Louise Barrow as well. "Your grandfather would have liked this company," she said with a smile.

David Jobb raised his glass. "To a gracious hostess and a good friend."

They all raised their glasses in a toast to Ruth Martin.

"Grams," Will said when the toast was finished, "it's time for me to ask my annual question, 'What do you want for Christmas?'"

"Heavens, when you're my age you don't need anything and you don't want much," she said with a smile.

"Nevertheless, there must be something you want for Christmas . . . we all have our Christmas wishes."

Ruth's face became serious. "I want you, Will Martin, to take your spot in the House of Representatives and remain as honest and true as you are today." She turned her gaze to Renee. "I want you to have the happiness you truly deserve."

It had grown totally quiet around the table. Ruth looked at Justin. "I want you to finally have a father who loves and cherishes you."

"Hear, hear," said David Jobb.

Ruth turned to where he and Louise Barrow sat. "And,

finally, I want the two of you to find companionship and comfort." She smiled. "That's not too much to ask, is it?"

The letter arrived the next day. It was an official-looking envelope, postmarked in Paris, France, and addressed to Renee Carr Martin. She slit it open and removed the single sheet of paper. It was a death certificate for Gary Carr from the City of Paris. Renee sat down on the couch and silently handed the paper to Will.

He read it, then looked at her. She was shaking her head sadly.

"I don't know what to say," Will said.

After a time, she spoke, but without looking at him. "When Gary left us so abruptly and we didn't hear anything from him for so long, it was easy to resent what he had done. I was so angry that I soon got over missing him. Instead of pain, I felt only loathing." She looked up at Will with tears brimming in her eyes. "This thing about Sloane-Kittering makes me wonder. What if he was sick and all alone? And now, to think that he's dead . . ."

Will said, "The certificate shows cancer as the cause of death."

Renee nodded her head. "I wonder what arrangements will have to be made . . ."

Will inspected the certificate more closely. "It appears he stipulated that he be cremated and his ashes scattered over the French countryside."

Then Will noticed the dithering.

41

. . .

T HE RECOUNT WAS COMPLETED the following Monday. Will now led by three votes. Milton Phillips immediately called a press conference and demanded that a manual recount of the ballots be done. "I think we've come to rely on technology too much," he said from the steps of the courthouse. "Just because a computer says something is so doesn't make it so. These machines make mistakes, too. I'm calling upon my worthy opponent to join with me in asking for a manual recount of the ballots. I'm sure he would not want to win a race fraudulently."

Marti Martinez called Will and David and asked them to come to her office. After they were seated she said, "I want to put this to you straight, Mr. Martin. We've done all that the law requires, and you are the clear winner. However, if Mr. Phillips continues his rampages with the press, you might not have a very easy time being an effective legislator because there will always be suspicion hanging over you. I want you two to discuss this and decide what to do. As I said before, you have no legal need to agree to a hand recount of the ballots.

Personally, I think the machine does a more accurate count than a bunch of people, but I will assure you that if you decide to agree to Mr. Phillips's demands, I will do everything possible to make sure we have an absolutely unbiased and accurate count." She stood up from behind her desk, "I'm going to leave for a few minutes so you two can have a private conversation." She left the room.

"What do you think, David?"

Jobb stroked the top of his head. "It's a no-win situation, Will. If we don't agree to the recount, we look like we're afraid. If we do agree, the manual recount might change the outcome of the election . . . not because it's more accurate . . . just the opposite. It's your decision, but I think we're going to have to agree."

Will sat silently staring out the window at the snow-draped trees outside the courthouse. "What do we have to lose? Let's get on with it."

The two men walked out of the office and beckoned to Marti Martinez, who walked down the hallway toward them. "Have you reached a decision, Mr. Martin?"

Will nodded his head. "Go ahead with the recount," he said.

She smiled. "Somehow I thought that would be your decision. As I said, we'll make sure no fraud enters into the count."

"When do you intend to start?" David asked.

"It will take me a few days. May I call you, as Mr. Martin's campaign manager, to agree upon the names of the people who will do the counting?"

David nodded his head. "Of course."

"That may be the most difficult task of all, because both you and Mr. Phillips's campaign manager will have to agree upon the counters. Then the lieutenant governor will have to certify them. It isn't an easy process. But one thing I can assure you, we have to be finished by the end of the year, so you can be ready to begin your first term in the legislature." She leaned close to his ear and whispered, "I'm supposed to be completely neutral, but we can't·let that hypocrite manipulate this process." She shook his hand and walked back into her office.

David and Will walked into the parking lot and got into David's Lincoln. He started the car and turned on the heater. "I'm sorry, Will. I had no idea this was going to drag on so long."

"It's not your fault, David." He leaned back into the soft seat. "But I'm about to the point where I don't care what happens."

David looked over his shoulder and began backing out of the parking space. "It matters a great deal to me," he said. As he pulled out of the parking lot, he changed the subject. "I'm assuming you haven't heard from Gary Carr. I'll place the second advertisement tomorrow."

Will stiffened. "Actually we have heard from Gary Carr . . . or to be more accurate, *about* Gary Carr. I should have told you sooner, but I've been thinking about this political race, and, well, you know."

David glanced at Will, "What did you hear?"

"He passed away, David. Apparently he died of cancer in Paris, at least that's what the certificate said."

Detecting the suspicion in Will's voice, David said, "But you're not sure?"

"David, the only other letter I've seen from Gary Carr was a computer forgery. Les Jardine showed me how easily it can be done."

"What made you think it was a forgery?"

"I didn't. It was Les who spotted the dithering on the letterhead."

"Dithering?"

"Little jagged edges on some parts of the logo, especially on curved lines."

"And this certificate from France has some of these same . . . problems?"

Will nodded his head. "And another thing, it's written in English. That seems peculiar to me."

David's hands tightened on the wheel, and they drove in silence for nearly a mile. "My advice to you, Will, is to accept it as being authentic."

"What?"

"Let me explain why. We've had an ad in the paper for a week with no response. Renee and Justin have had no communication from Gary in nearly five years. It's clear he doesn't want to have anything to do with his family. So, accept this as legitimate and let me have my associate, Haven Walker, file the papers with the judge." He looked straight ahead at the road. "Will, do you remember you promised me you'd have this whole thing wrapped up by Christmas? Well, the problems with voting have taken quite a bit of your time and—what I'm trying to say is that this will expedite matters and let you move ahead with the adoption. Quite frankly, once you show the judge that document from France, I don't think he's going to even know what dithering is and *he* will accept it as legitimate." He glanced at Will, who sat with his arms crossed.

"You're right, of course, David," he finally said. "It's just that I've never done anything in my life based on fraud, and I'm not sure I'm ready to start now."

The attorney exhaled sharply. "As you wish. I'll have the second notice printed in tomorrow's paper."

It took until the fifteenth of December for all the parties to agree upon the people who would hand-count the ballots. That same day, having had no response to the second notice in the paper, Haven Walker filed the necessary papers to allow Will to adopt Justin, and a hearing date was set for the morning of December twenty-fourth. The date of the recount was set for two days earlier, on the twenty-second.

That afternoon, three days before Christmas, Will looked out the window of his office toward the town square. Winter had arrived, and a foot of snow covered the ground. The pine trees drooped under its weight and piles of snow had accumulated around the gazebo, where snow had slid off the roof. Will had gone with David to the courthouse that morning and watched the first hour of the recount.

The pressure was palpable, and Will was a nervous wreck by the time he left the courthouse to drive back to his office. David remained behind and promised to call as soon as a total was available. From inside his office, Will could hear Enid Cook and Carol Wanless talking outside his door. *There's too much happening all at the same time. Enid's last day is Wednesday, Christmas Eve, the same day I go to court with Justin. Who knows how this election process will end?* He forced himself to turn away from the window and look at the portrait of his grandfather. *How did you do it? I'm just not cut out for this kind of pressure.*

Enid knocked on the door and entered Will's office, with Carol Wanless a step behind her. "Mr. Martin, I thought I'd show Carol how to figure the Christmas bonuses so she can handle it next year. Does that meet with your approval?"

"Of course, Miss Cook. Carol, we're happy to have you on board. I hope Hal Jenkins still feels all right about us pirating you away from the bank."

Carol was all smiles. "I think he's fine. Thank you for hiring me. Enid has been wonderful in explaining how the whole operation works."

Enid fidgeted with her lace collar. "May I have a moment in private, Mr. Martin?" Will nodded and Carol Wanless quickly stepped out of the office and closed the door behind her.

"What is it, Miss Cook?"

Enid sat uncomfortably on the edge of the chair in front of Will's desk, her hands folded in her lap. "I have a confession and an apology to make, Mr. Martin. I hope you'll understand how difficult this is for me."

Will felt as if the snow from the gazebo had been shoved down the back of his shirt. "I'm sure it is, Miss Cook."

She bowed her head and focused her gaze on the carpet in front of her. "Mr. Martin, I was less than supportive of you when you began the Martin's Glen project. I felt strongly that you had made a terrible mistake and that this agency was doomed to fall into bankruptcy or something worse." She finally raised her eyes and met Will's gaze. He could see that her eyes were glistening. "Mr. Martin, I was wrong. Late this morning I handled a transaction for the sale of one of the lots. When I added it to my ledger and totaled the income from Martin's Glen, it was clear that we have realized a fairly significant profit, even with fewer than ten percent of the lots sold." She pulled a tissue out of her pocket and blotted her eyes. "I was wrong, Mr. Martin. I had no faith in you and now it appears that this single project will probably make more money for this agency than your grandfather earned in thirty years." She blew her nose daintily. "Please forgive me, Mr. Martin. You have proven yourself more capable than I ever dreamed." She stood abruptly. "Thank you for listening to me. I wish I could rewind the clock and give you my support from the very beginning."

Will stood and came around his desk. "Enid," he said gently. "You weren't the only one with doubts. You have been invaluable here, and your hard work is what has kept this place going. You have no need to apologize." She was standing rigidly in front of the door, but tears were welling up in her eyes. He reached to take the gray-haired woman in his arms. She resisted his embrace for a moment, then surrendered and allowed him to hold her.

"I'll miss you, Enid," he said.

Choking back her emotion, she replied, "I'll miss you . . . Will." Then she slipped from his arms, opened the door, and escaped into the office, where she quickly took a seat at her desk.

Will closed the door and returned to his chair. He stared at the phone, willing it to ring, but it sat silent and immobile as a brick.

He nearly leapt from his chair as a snowball hit his window. Quickly he swung around and looked down into the street below. Renee and Justin stood there, wearing parkas and waving at him from the sidewalk. It was nearly dark, and the Christmas lights on the square and on the village shops sparkled brightly. Renee beckoned to him to join them. With a last look at the mute telephone, he shrugged on his overcoat, said good night to Enid and Carol, and descended the stairs to the front door. When he opened the door an icy breath stung his eyes and chilled his nostrils.

"What's wrong?" he asked.

"Nothing. We just came to kidnap you. We haven't seen much of you in the last few weeks, and Justin and I think it's time you paid some attention to us." She tugged him toward her car. "I left it running so we wouldn't freeze to death. We'll come back and get yours later." They tumbled into the warmth of the old Chevrolet with Renee behind the wheel.

"Where are we going?" Will asked, amused by the ambush.

"Just close your eyes and hang on or we'll have to blindfold you," she laughed while Justin chortled in the backseat. A few minutes later they stopped in front of Pallermo's. "You look like you could use some rest and a good meal," she said as they walked through the door into the fragrance of oregano, basil and garlic.

Will put his arm around her waist as they waited to be shown to a table. "You're right," he said, "except I'm waiting for a phone call from David. I still don't know how the recount went."

She took his face in her hands. "Will, whatever happens, I still love you. There's nothing you can do at this point to alter the outcome, so just relax for tonight. You deserve it." She kissed him.

"Yuck, mush," Justin said.

42

. . .

DAVID JOBB WAS SEATED IN WILL'S OFFICE. "You won, three to two," David said. "Three of the counting groups had you winning . . . each by a different number of votes, I might add . . . and two of them had Milton winning. Marti is re-arranging the groups this morning and having them do it again, plus she's running the ballots through the counting machine to see if anything funny has happened."

"When do you think we'll have a final answer?" Will asked wearily.

"Marti has told them they'll stay there until they're finished."

"Which will be when?"

"I suspect late tonight. She's turned into a pretty tough taskmaster."

Will rubbed his temples with the heels of his hands. "I'm on overload, David. I can't take much more of this. Tomorrow we have the court appearance on the adoption, the office Christmas party, and now this crazy election mix-up. I'm beside myself."

"I understand, Will, but all of it will soon be over." David stood up and walked to the window behind Will's desk. "Ever notice the people in the square, Will? They all move around completely oblivious to the others in the park. But they're all part of a bigger picture." He left his spot and walked toward the door. "A week from now you'll look back on this and wonder why you felt so much stress."

"I hope so, David. I hope so."

Jobb opened the door. "I'll call you as soon as we know something, regardless of how late it is." He smiled broadly. "And don't forget your court appearance at two o'clock tomorrow afternoon."

"You can count on that, at least," Will said. "I'll be waiting."

Will spent the afternoon mechanically going over sales figures and reviewing some listings. The day dragged on until closing time, when Enid Cook knocked on the door and entered his office. "I have the bonus checks ready, Mr. Martin." She handed him a stack of envelopes.

Will fanned the stack. "Thank you for preparing these."

"You're welcome," she said and backed out of his office. Will sorted through the envelopes until he found hers and removed it from the stack. He slit it open.

She gave herself one hundred dollars, he thought as he scanned the check he had removed from her envelope. He reached into his desk drawer and found a five-thousand-dollar check that Carol Wanless had prepared for him earlier that day and slipped it into a new envelope with Enid's name on it.

When darkness came he was still sitting at his desk waiting for a call from David. He picked up the phone and dialed the county courthouse. The phone rang five times and then an answering machine picked up and announced that the courthouse was open from ten in the morning until six at night, then hung up. Disappointed, he turned out the lights and drove home. Renee was even jumpier than he was through dinner. They watched the late evening news on television, but there was no report on the recount. Finally they gave up and went to bed.

The phone rang just after two o'clock in the morning. Heart racing from the unexpected sound, Will grabbed it on the first ring. "Hello?"

"It's David, Will. They've just finished the count for the final time."

"And?"

The phone was silent for several seconds before David said, "Congratulations, Representative Martin! I'll tell you about it tomorrow. Now get some sleep."

Will hung up, turned onto his back, and stared at the ceiling. Renee poked him in the side. "Well?" she said.

"I won," Will said. "After all this, I finally won."

She slipped her arm across his chest and hugged him. "Was there any doubt?" she smiled.

The next morning Will called David Jobb's office and

found that the attorney had not yet come in. Patricia Ames, his secretary, assured Will that Haven Walker would represent him in the adoption proceedings and that David expected to be there as well. At nine o'clock he walked out of his office into the main office of Martin Real Estate. Christmas decorations hung around the room, and a fragrant pine tree stood in one corner. All the agents and the entire staff had gathered. As soon as Will appeared, conversation stopped, and Janice Harr switched off the CD player that had been providing background Christmas carols. Will stood next to Enid Cook's desk.

"Gather 'round," he said. "It's time to start the annual Christmas party. The food is here . . . ordered as usual by Enid Cook . . . and ready to be eaten. I'd like to ask your indulgence, however. I'm not sure how many of you know that today is a very important day in my life."

Enid spoke up, "Have they reached a final decision on the election?"

"Yes, they have, Enid, but that isn't what is so important. This afternoon I have a date in court, and if all goes well, I will have formally adopted Justin. I thought you'd like to know. Maybe some of you have even noticed the announcements to that effect that were run in the newspaper last month. We've had no one object to the adoption, so I think it will go smoothly. And, by the way, I did win the election."

The office erupted into applause and cheers. After a moment, Will held up his hands for silence, and all of the heads turned in his direction. "I forgot one other very important thing. You've seen Carol Wanless working with Enid for the past month. Enid has wanted to keep this quiet, but she has decided to retire. Today is her last day with Martin Real Estate."

It was evident that Enid had done a poor job of keeping her secret from the other employees. Janice Harr broke away from the pack of people, walked to her desk, removed an envelope from a drawer, and approached Enid's desk.

"Enid, this is from all of us. We want you to know that we will miss you. And we wish you well." She handed her the envelope.

"Open it!" one of the salesmen called out. Embarrassed to be the center of attention, Enid blushed and with a trembling hand slit the envelope open. There was a card and inside of that a folded certificate. She saw what it was and put her hand to her mouth. "I can't possibly accept this," she said.

Will reached down and removed the certificate from her hand. It was a ticket for a Caribbean cruise.

Janice spoke up, "Yes, you can, Enid. I know this is something you've always wanted to do. Go, and have fun. You deserve it." Her coworkers broke into applause and came forward to shake Enid's hand and wish her well.

Will saw his grandmother, Renee, and Justin standing at the top of the stairs. He smiled at them, then turned back to his employees. "There's one other small thing. I have your bonuses here, so dig into the food, and I'll be around to give each of you your check." He gently pushed his way through the crowd to where his wife stood.

"We came a little early so we could have breakfast with you," Ruth said. "Unless you don't want us here."

Will grinned. "Of course I want you here—it wouldn't be complete without you." He kissed his grandmother on the cheek. "But right now I have to distribute these." He waved a fistful of envelopes.

It was nearly one o'clock before the party completely wound down and people began leaving for the day. Enid Cook, as usual, remained until the last to help clean up the office. She had not yet opened her bonus envelope. Will was carrying two large garbage bags down the stairs to the dumpster, when she sat down at her desk for the last time. A cardboard box lay at her feet, and she removed a framed picture of her parents from her desktop and placed it with the rest of her personal belongings in the box. Renee and Ruth were wiping off a tabletop, while Justin tried to find room for one more chocolate éclair, when Enid opened the envelope. She let out a gasp.

"This can't be right," she said emphatically.

"I wish it were more," Will said from the top of the stairs.

"Nonsense," she said. "This is too much."

"Merry Christmas, Enid. Thanks for everything. We've got to run to get over to the courthouse. Can I help you carry that box to your car?"

She sat without moving at her desk. "Thank you, Mr.

Martin, but no. I think I'd like to sit here for a few minutes before I leave. I'll lock the door on my way out."

"I understand." He went into his office and retrieved their coats and five minutes later they were sitting in the Jaguar as it sped toward the courthouse. There were a surprising number of cars in the parking lot when they slipped into an empty parking place. A few flakes of snow were falling as they walked into the building and found the door that led to the court-room. About three dozen people were sitting in the seats. Most of them were still wrapped in winter clothing. Two elderly women were dressed in identical black wool coats with red scarves around their throats. A man in a wheelchair was sitting in the back corner with his legs covered with a blanket and his face obscured by a cap with ear flaps and a scarf that covered his mouth. A half-dozen teenagers were sitting on the right side of the room dressed in ski parkas. Each of them had a notebook in his or her hand. It appeared to Will that they were there to fill an assignment for a school class. Four other couples were seated in various places in the room, each with a child between them. David Jobb and Haven Walker were sit-ting on the front row, and when Will's group entered, David waved them to seats they had saved. Louise Barrow was sitting directly behind David, and Ruth Martin quickly joined her.

David shook hands with Will and Renee and motioned them to take the empty chairs. He leaned over to Will, "Let me tell you about last night."

"Please do."

"We finished the recount at nine o'clock, and Milton won this time around. All five counting groups had him with either fourteen or fifteen more votes than you. Of course, he was jumping around trying to get Marti to certify him as the winner."

"I can see why."

"Except Marti wasn't born yesterday. She ran the ballots through the counting machine and guess what?"

"What?"

"Milton Phillips won."

"I don't understand," Will said. "I thought you told me I'd won, last night."

"Well, this is where it gets interesting. Marti was completely flabbergasted until she noticed one thing. The total number of votes cast was 12,206."

"That seems about right."

"*About* is the operative word. Thank heaven I had Les Jardine there. He immediately pointed out that there were only a total of 12,188 votes cast, including the absentee ballots. Somehow an extra eighteen ballots ended up in the stacks."

"But how?"

Jobb snorted. "As I said, Marti isn't that easy to fool. She'd drawn a line with a purple magic marker down the side of each stack of cards before she distributed them to be counted the first time. It took us nearly four more hours to go through every one of those cards and see if any of them lacked the purple stain. By then, the lieutenant governor had been called and was on the scene." Jobb was obviously relishing the tale. "Guess what? Eighteen of the cards lacked the purple mark. And, as you can imagine, all of them were votes for Milton Phillips!"

Will chuckled. "I wish I'd been there."

"So do I. Anyway, the lieutenant governor declared you the certified winner on the spot and told Milton that there'd be an investigation launched to see if it could be discovered who had inserted the phony ballots. He denied any knowledge of it, of course, but he and his henchmen were out of there like their tails were on fire." He clapped Will on the shoulder. "The official announcement will be made this afternoon. Congratulations!"

At that moment the bailiff asked everyone to rise, and Judge Andrew Bartholomew entered the courtroom through a door behind his chair.

The judge seated himself and opened the first folder on his desktop. "Are Mr. and Mrs. Gordon Burrell present?" he asked. One of the couples stood up. A small, blonde girl stood between them. "Are you represented by counsel?"

"No, your honor."

"Come forward." He motioned them to one of the tables in front of the bench. They took their seats and looked expectantly at the judge. The judge perused the documents in the folder. "It appears that all of the formal steps have been taken for you to adopt Julie," he said. "Is there anyone here who objects to this action?" He looked briefly around the court-room. "Seeing none, I'll approve this motion." He affixed his signature to the documents in front of him, closed the folder, and handed it to the clerk.

"Congratulations, Mr. and Mrs. Burrell, the adoption is approved. Merry Christmas."

The three people stood and hugged each other. "Thank you, your honor," Mrs. Burrell said.

"You're welcome." He opened the next folder, "Are Mr. and Mrs. Will Martin present?"

Will, Renee, Justin, and Haven Walker rose. "Yes, your honor," Haven said.

"I see you are represented by council," the judge replied. He worked through the documents in the folder. "You, Mrs. Martin, are the boy's birth mother, is that correct?"

"Yes, your honor."

"And the boy's father is deceased?"

Haven Walker spoke up. "That is our understanding from the certificate that is attached, your honor."

The judge made a small grunting sound as he looked at the document in the folder. "You, Mr. Martin, are the boy's step-father?" Will nodded his head. "Would you tell me why you want to formally adopt . . ."—he looked at the file " . . . Justin?"

Will cleared his throat. "I want to provide Justin a stable home," he began. "In the year and a half his mother and I have been married, the three of us have grown very close." Justin smiled at Will, reached up and took his hand. "The bottom line, your honor, is that I love his mother and I love him, and I want us to be a family."

"I see. Well, the paperwork seems to be in order. Is there anyone who objects to this procedure?" He looked around the room more closely this time. "Seeing none, I approve this action." He signed the papers and handed the folder to the clerk.

Will, Renee, and Justin walked hand in hand out of the courtroom. David Jobb and Haven Walker trailed behind them a step or two, followed by Ruth Martin and Louise Barrow. "I think it's time for a celebration," Ruth said. "I'm expecting all of you for dinner tonight."

"I'm sorry, Mrs. Martin, but I have another commitment," Haven Walker said.

"I understand," she said with a smile. "But the rest of you at seven o'clock sharp?"

The others all nodded their assent. "May I pick you up, Louise?" David asked.

"Of course," she replied.

"Until tonight," Ruth said as she looked through the window of the courthouse into the parking lot. Snow was falling in feathery flakes. "We'd better get home before this gets worse," she said. "I don't like driving in the snow."

All of them but David Jobb hurried across the parking lot to their cars. He turned back to the courtroom, entered, and seated himself next to the man in the wheelchair. "Ready to go?" The man nodded his head and David took hold of the handles of the chair and backed him out of the courtroom. "What time is your flight?"

The man reached up with a trembling hand and clawed at the scarf that covered his mouth. He wheezed, "Five o'clock."

"Then we'd better go." David wheeled him down the ramp behind the courthouse and helped lift him into the seat of his Lincoln. He opened the trunk of his car, folded the wheelchair, and placed it inside. A moment later they were headed toward the freeway on-ramp. "Are you sure you don't want to see them?"

"Absolutely," the man said in a high reedy voice.

"Why? What possible harm could it do?"

Gary Carr gathered his strength. "I don't want either of them remembering me this way. I know Justin probably doesn't remember me at all, but I'd rather have him remember a shadow than the way I am now."

"And Renee?"

Gary sat silently, and David saw a tear running down his cheek. "I'd rather have her remember me the way I was before . . ."

"He's a good man, Gary."

"I can tell that. He'll be a wonderful father for Justin."

"What is your prognosis?"

"Six months to a year. It isn't an exact science, you know. That's why they call it *practicing* medicine." He wheezed a dry, cackling laugh, then he turned somber. "In some ways I wish it had been quick, like Creighton Barrow's cancer. This one has grown more slowly." He coughed, turned his head, and looked out the window. "But I'm not going to be a burden on anyone like Dad was on Mom. It killed her, David, and then he died, too. I won't do that to Renee and Justin." He paused for several moments before he said very quietly, "I love them both too much."

"I'll respect your wish," David said quietly.

Gary sat still for several more minutes before he said, "If I'd stayed here, that's exactly what would have happened. It was only when I considered that job in Paris and had to take a physical that the cancer was detected. I decided, then and there, I wouldn't be a burden on either Renee or Justin. And if you look at me now, you know I would have been." He lapsed into silence for the rest of the trip to the airport. When they arrived, David helped him into the wheelchair and pushed him to the gate, where a customer service agent checked his ticket and took hold of the wheelchair.

"David," Gary said desperately, "thank you for everything." He struggled to hold his hand out and Jobb grabbed it in his. "I've put everything in a trust account, and made you the executor."

David leaned down and hugged Gary's frail frame. "Good-bye, Gary."

"Good-bye, David. Until we meet again." He motioned as best he could that he was ready to go to the plane that would fly him back to New Jersey.

David watched him go until he was out of sight, then pulled a handkerchief from his pocket and wiped his eyes. He returned to the Lincoln and drove back to the city.

43

• • •

THE TABLE WAS SET WITH SPODE CHINA and silverware bearing the family crest. Ruth Martin had prepared her traditional holiday feast for her family and friends. Promptly at seven o'clock they were seated, and she asked Will to say grace, then carve the turkey. David Jobb and Louise Barrow looked across the table at the portrait of Warren Martin on the wall. They turned in their seats and saw the accompanying portrait of Ruth on the wall behind them.

"Relieved, dear?" Ruth asked her grandson.

"More than you know," Will replied. "I never want to go through anything like this again."

"You won't have to for two years," David said with a smile. "That's when your term ends and you'll have to run again."

"But that isn't the biggest victory of the day." Will put his hand on Justin's shoulder.

"Are we goin' to have pumpkin pie?" Justin asked.

"Of course," Ruth answered. "A celebration wouldn't be complete without pie."

When the meal had ended, Ruth Martin looked down the

table from her position at the end. "Will, thank you for getting me the Christmas present I wanted. Assuming, of course, that you will be an honest politician." She looked at Justin. "And you fulfilled my other request," she said with a smile. "But now I have something for you." She rose from her chair and retrieved a neatly wrapped present from the sideboard beneath Warren Martin's portrait. She walked to where Will and Renee sat and handed the small box to Renee. "Merry Christmas."

Renee shook the box. It rattled. Carefully she removed the ribbon and wrapping paper and opened the present. Inside the box was a key. Puzzled, she held it up. "I don't understand."

"It's a gift from several of us," Ruth said with a smile. "Hunter and Ray wish they could be here, but they have their own families to be with tonight. It's a key to your new home in Martin's Glen. It's a gift from many grateful people."

"We can't accept this, Grams," Will said. "It's too much."

"You've become very good at giving, Will, but you have a lot to learn about accepting a gift graciously."

David smiled at Ruth. "Perhaps Louise and I should make an announcement, too. It may seem too soon after Creigh's death, but I've been a widower for nearly four years, and Louise and I are planning to be married next spring."

"Ah," Ruth Martin said, "I get all of my Christmas wishes." She looked at Justin. "It's getting late, young man. If you want to see that new house before you go to bed, you'd better hurry."

The snow had stopped and a full moon had risen over the eastern mountains as Will eased the Jaguar into the driveway of the home in Martin's Glen. The key fit the lock and they entered their new home. It smelled of new paint and carpet, and Hunter Hoggard had placed a Christmas tree in the great room. It had no decorations on it, except for a huge red bow with Merry Christmas written in gold glitter.

Renee's eyes were dancing, and she snuggled up against Will. "Merry Christmas, sweetheart."

Will kissed her and said, "Merry Christmas to you." He kneeled down next to Justin, who had tugged off his shoes and was feeling the carpet with his bare feet.

He felt tears forming in his eyes as he said, "Merry Christmas . . . son."

Justin threw his arms around Will, "Merry Christmas, Dad."